STACY HENRIE

The Outlaw's Secret

D0011828

HARLEQUIN® LOVE INSPIRED® HISTORICAL

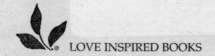

LOVE INSPIRED BOOKS

Recycling programs
for this product may
not exist in your area.

ISBN-13: 978-0-373-42511-2

The Outlaw's Secret

www.Harlequin.com

Printed in U.S.A.

Tate Beckett's jaw was clenched so tight he thought it might snap.

If he wasn't careful, this woman, with all her probing questions, would figure out he wasn't the Texas Titan after all. Then his covert work, posing as his outlaw twin brother, would be finished.

No. He wouldn't let her ruin his plans. Not when he was on the most important case of his career.

"If she comes," Tate announced, "she rides with me."

Fletcher shrugged. "Fine. The three of you will head northwest. Silas and Clem know the way to the camp."

"Where are they going?" Essie asked, her eyes following the other two men.

"We're splitting up. No one will suspect two or three men riding together, when they're looking for five."

"Ah. Very clever."

He reached a hand down to help her up, frustration churning in his gut. His focus would have to be divided between paying attention to the trail to the gang's hideout and playing nursemaid.

"Thank you," she said brightly as he pulled her onto the horse. As she situated herself behind him, she managed to jab him with the handle of her valise— twice.

It was going to be a long ride.

Stacy Henrie has always had a love for history, fiction and chocolate. She earned her BA in public relations before turning her attentions to raising a family and writing inspirational historical romances. The wife of an entrepreneur husband and a mother to three, Stacy loves to live out history through her fictional characters. In addition to author, she is also a reader, a road trip enthusiast and a novice interior decorator.

Books by Stacy Henrie

Love Inspired Historical

Lady Outlaw
The Express Rider's Lady
The Outlaw's Secret

Visit the Author Profile page at Harlequin.com.

God giveth power to the faint; and to them that
have no might he increaseth strength...
—*Isaiah* 40:29

For M.
I hope you know, as Essie comes to, that your optimistic, bright nature is a beautiful gift.

Chapter One

Near Medicine Bow, Wyoming, 1892

The squeal of the train wheels jerked Essie Vander-fair's attention from the doodles and half-formed thoughts scribbled inside her notebook to the window beside her. Nothing but hills of sagebrush and late-morning sunshine met her curious gaze. They shouldn't be stopping yet. But even as the thought entered her mind, the locomotive shuddered to a halt.

Impatience brought a frown to her lips. She still had hours to go before she reached her room at the boardinghouse in Evanston, where she planned to stay sequestered until her next brilliant dime-novel idea presented itself. Most of what she had in her notebook wouldn't create the successful novel her publisher wanted.

"I wonder why we've stopped," her seatmate remarked, bouncing her drooling baby on her lap.

The little boy was every bit as handsome as his mother was beautiful. Her lovely chestnut hair and sky-colored eyes reminded Essie of her three older sisters. She looked nothing like them with her blond hair and muddy-green eyes.

A twinge of envy wound its way around her heart at the lovely picture the mother and babe made. That might have been her, if Harrison hadn't decided she wasn't serious enough or committed enough to make a suitable wife.

Not serious enough about life. How many times had she heard those words? Not just from Harrison but from her own family, too. But Essie had gotten revenge as far as her old beau was concerned. The villain in her last dime novel had sported the name Harris and the same pointy nose and mustache as the man she'd once fancied herself in love with.

Movement out the window caught her eye and she leaned closer to the glass. Five riders with bandannas over their mouths and noses rode toward the stalled train.

Her heart galloped as she realized who they must be. "It appears…" She wet her dry lips. "That we are being accosted by train robbers."

She hadn't spoken loudly, but the man in front of them clearly heard her anyway. "Train robbers," he bellowed. Panicked murmurs swept through the passenger car.

"Oh, my," the babe's mother cried, her face draining of color. She clutched her child to her bosom. "Whatever do they want?"

"Money, most likely." Essie stuffed her notebook into her valise, anxious to be ready for whatever lay ahead. "Although they might wish to take a few women along as hostages, as well."

Like in *The Train Robber's Bride*, the latest dime novel from her professional nemesis Victor Daley. It seemed whatever story line Essie pursued, Mr. Daley came up with a similar one but achieved much greater success. If only she could think of an idea that would scoop his...

The woman's face had grown even paler. "At least I have a child," she murmured. "They won't take a woman with a baby."

"Either way—" Essie snapped her valise shut "—I won't let them hurt you or your child." Lowering her voice, she explained. "I have a derringer in my boot." She wiggled her shoe for emphasis. Not that one gun would be a match against five, but at least it was something.

Her seatmate looked askance. "Whatever do you own a gun for? Do you know how to use it?"

Essie couldn't help laughing, in spite of the tense situation. "Ma'am, I was raised on a ranch and now live on my own in a city. I know my way around a great many weapons. Now switch me seats."

Speechless, the woman rose and sank into the vacated spot as Essie slid toward the aisle. *Please watch over us, Lord, in this most unorthodox situation.* Or could this be the Lord's working in her life already? Maybe this was an answer to her prayer to help her write a more exciting tale than Mr. Daley. But would it be good enough to erase the troubled frown she'd seen on her publisher's face during her recent visit to Ohio?

"Look, Miss Vanderfair," he'd said, peering over the top of his glasses at her. "You have talent, more so than any other female whose work I've read. But we can't afford to publish more of your stories. Not unless your next one can outsell the likes of Mr. Daley."

The remembrance of those ominous words set her pulse kicking faster with dread than seeing the train robbers. She needed a new story that would be a guaranteed success—and soon. Otherwise she'd have to go back to the ranch and admit defeat. Wouldn't her siblings crow over that one?

Just one little idea, Lord. That's all I ask.

A train robbery wasn't a bad place to start. *The door to the passenger car opened with a clatter*, she mused, composing in her head. She'd pen it down in her notebook later. *The devastatingly handsome train robber stepped inside, his black gaze keen as it swept the passengers, finally alighting on the beautiful, demure heroine. Her heart beat wildly in her throat as their eyes locked. What did he—*

Someone screamed, jerking Essie's thoughts back to reality. A man stood in the doorway at the front of the car. But instead of the tall, handsome hero of her imagination, the man blocking the doorway stood at five feet tall and sported what must be a bulbous nose beneath his bandanna. Essie smirked. Real life was never as interesting as fiction.

"Sorry to keep ya, folks," the man said in a tone that implied anything but regret. "We'll get you movin' on in a short lick. But for now, just sit tight while we work."

"What does that mean?" an older woman across the aisle whispered loudly to her husband.

He glared at the robber. "It means they're likely going to blow up the train's safe."

Several gasps followed the man's pronouncement,

but Essie let out a sigh of relief. If their focus was the safe then the robbers would probably leave the passengers alone. Essie patted the sleeve of her seatmate in reassurance. "We'll be on our way soon." If the conductor wasn't harmed.

"Has any injury come to the train conductor?" she bravely asked the robber.

He chuckled. "The conductor and that guard'll be right as rain once they come to. The Texas Titan don't like roughin' people up too much."

The Texas Titan was *here*? On her train? Essie had read plenty of newspaper articles about the man and his legendary outlaw career. He usually worked alone, though. Why had he joined this gang? She wished she could ask him. An interview with a real-live outlaw, or five, would provide any novelist with a gold mine of research.

And give her a leg up on the competition.

Essie's eyes widened at her own bold idea. The men weren't likely to talk to her on the train, where she'd be slowing down their getaway. Would she be able to convince them to take her with them? More important, did she dare attempt such a harebrained scheme?

Her publisher's dire prediction ran through her head again: "We can't afford to publish more of your stories…"

But her next story was sure to be a success if she included firsthand accounts from these men.

"I'm going to do it," she whispered to herself. She had her gun and the Texas Titan was known for his benevolent treatment of women and children. She'd be safe with him.

"I'm going to get off here," she told the woman beside her. "But you and your baby will be fine."

"You're going to what?" The woman's eyes bulged with shock.

Essie didn't bother answering, afraid her seatmate would try to talk her out of her plan. Instead she shot to her feet and walked toward the robber manning the door.

"Excuse me, might I have a word?"

He blinked in confusion then scowled. "Get back to your seat, ma'am."

"First, I have a request."

"We ain't gonna take no hostages, if that's what you're frettin' about. So sit back down." His hand rose to touch the Colt revolver sticking out of the holster at his waist. Essie fought a smile. A little distraction and his gun would be in her hand before he'd even noticed she'd moved. She'd learned that trick from a lawman while writing *The Deputy's Destiny*. But she would only attempt it if necessary. She would try reasoning and friendliness first.

"Very kind about the hostages, but I'm in need of a different act of generosity."

His bushy eyebrows rose. "I don't know what you're playin' at…"

"I'm not playacting." Essie sniffed. "I'm a writer."

The man choked on a laugh. "A writer? What's a woman doing writin'?"

She ignored the insult, though it echoed the question she'd been asked over and over again by well-meaning friends and family for the last three years. "I've decided I would like to go with you and your gang. For research purposes."

"Research?" He scratched at his forehead beneath his cowboy hat. "What're ya gonna research?"

"Your lives, your motivations, your goals." She smiled fully, the last of her hesitation melting away. "I want to know why you do what you do and how you do it."

He shook his head, his eyes clouding with confusion. "I gotta talk to Fletcher first. He's the bo—"

A thunderous boom shook the car. Essie gripped the nearest seatback to stay upright as cries of horror split the air. Clearly, the robbers had blasted open the safe. The robbery was almost over. If she didn't finish convincing one of these men to let her come along, they'd leave without her. And her chance to keep publishing would surely disappear with them.

"Nothin' to fret about, folks," the robber said, yelling over the chaos erupting inside the train car. "We're nearly done."

Hoping she might have more success speaking with a different robber, Essie took advantage of the man's diverted attention and dashed through the door behind him. She hadn't gotten more than a foot, though, when she crashed into a solid body exiting the opposite car.

"What are you doing out of your seat?" a deep voice growled in her ear.

"I'm sorry." She clung to the railing to steady herself. "I'm trying to…"

Her voice faded into silence as she lifted her chin and found herself peering into piercing blue eyes. She'd always been rather tall for a girl, and yet her head only came to this man's nose. He wore a hat like his companion, but his bandanna had slipped off his face, allowing her a clear view of his chiseled features. Features she knew at once. This was the Texas Titan.

She was already imagining the handsome train robber she would pattern after him for her new story, the one who would sweep the heroine into his arms and carry her away...

Except he didn't seem intent on carrying anyone away, let alone sweeping a woman into his arms. Instead he gripped Essie's elbow, hard, and spun her back toward the door she'd burst through. "You need to return to your seat. Now!"

Essie dug her heels in. "I'm afraid you don't understand. I'm coming with you."

"What?" he choked out, his dark eyebrows arching.

"Yes. I explained everything to your companion there..."

"Clem," he supplied, his firm expression unwavering.

"Yes, Clem. And he said—"

Clem hurried to join them, pulling his own bandanna away from his mouth. "Sorry, Tex. She wanted to talk to Fletcher."

"So you really are the Texas Titan?" Her cheeks heated when she heard the breathless awe in her voice.

The Texan dropped her arm and gave a curt nod. "One and the same."

"Have you given up working alone?" No time like the present to get her first few questions in.

His eyes narrowed as he scowled. "For the time being. Now, let's get you back to your seat." He resumed his clasp on her elbow.

"But I'm not going back to my seat. As I said, I'm going with you."

"And I say you aren't." He maneuvered her past his troubled-looking partner. "This isn't some parlor game, young lady," he hissed. "All of these men are armed and dangerous."

She furrowed her brow, annoyed. As if she didn't know who or what she was dealing with. "Including yourself?"

"I beg your pardon?"

"You are also armed and dangerous, are you not? You said 'these men' as if you aren't a part of them."

The Texan shook his head, annoyance rippling off him like heat waves. "I can't waste any more of my time arguing with you. Will you please—"

His entreaty disappeared beneath the commotion of approaching horses. The other three robbers rode up to the train, leading two riderless mounts behind them. "What's the holdup?" one of them hollered. "We gotta go before that guard recovers."

Essie seized the opportunity. "Which of you gentlemen is called Fletcher?"

"Who's askin'?" The tallest of the three stared hard at her, his gray-blue eyes cold and calculating. She'd have to keep an extra watch on him.

"I'm a writer," she answered, drawing herself up to full height and maintaining her own level gaze. "I would like to interview you. All of you. I would like to immortalize your lives in fiction."

Fletcher gave a smirk. "Very flattering, lady, but we're on a schedule." He wheeled his horse around. "Clem? Tex? You comin' or not?"

"Wait." She moved to the railing, her valise clutched tightly against her chest. "My name is Essie. Essie Vanderfair."

The name stopped the gang leader at once, as she'd known it would. "Vanderfair?" He looked her over with blatant interest. "You related to Henry Vanderfair? The railway tycoon?"

Essie dipped a nod. "He's my great-grandfather." It was the truth, though she hadn't ever met the man or spoken with him.

"Fletcher," the Texan interjected from behind, "let's go. Leave her be."

The man pushed up the brim of his hat. "Hold on a minute there, cowboy. We might be lookin' at a real nice ransom if we bring her along. I heard the Vanderfairs have more money than Rockefeller. And I'm sure they'd pay handsomely for the safe return of one of their own." He turned to Essie as he added, "But only after you get your interviews."

"So you'd kidnap her?" The Texan crossed his arms and glared at their leader.

Fletcher glowered right back. "What are you, *the law*? Besides, it ain't kidnapping. Not if she comes of her own volition."

"And I do." Essie traversed the train steps with purpose, her chin high. "I assure you, gentlemen, I will not be a burden."

She heard a snort above her, but she ignored the Texan. Her appeals were best directed toward the group's true leader.

"I will make your robberies famous, Mr. Fletcher. I'll share your tales of danger and riches to the world. Without using your actual names, of course."

He tipped his hat in acquiescence. "Of course," he echoed, his smile more sly than affable. He thought he had the upper hand, but he'd underestimated the skills she'd picked up over the years, both on the ranch and as a novelist. Which was fine by her—she preferred to be underestimated by everyone except her publisher.

"Does that mean I may come along?"

"Don't see why not."

"Fletcher," the Texan said, the name a warning.

But the robber leader waved Essie toward the horses. "We need to meet up at camp by dark."

She pushed out the breath she'd been holding and hugged her valise. She'd done it—she'd convinced them, and now she would be the victor instead of Victor Daley. An astonished laugh bubbled out of her. "What is our final destination, Mr. Fletcher?"

"Our hideout. And that's where you can interview me, Miss Vanderfair."

Tate Beckett's jaw was clenched so tight he thought it might snap. Of all the rotten misfortune. He had to run into a nosy busybody like Miss Essie Vanderfair on his first job with Fletcher's gang. If he wasn't careful, this woman, with all her probing questions, would figure out he wasn't the Texas Titan after all. Then his covert work, posing as his outlaw twin brother, would be finished.

No, he thought, his teeth grinding in resolve. He wouldn't let her ruin his plans. Not when he was on the most important case of his career as a Pinkerton detective.

"If she comes," Tate announced, stalking down the steps, "she rides with me."

Fletcher shrugged. "Fine. Jude and I will head east, then cut back west to the campsite. The three of you will head in the opposite direction and then veer east. Silas and Clem know the way to the camp."

Without a backward glance, Fletcher and Jude charged off at a gallop.

"Why are you splitting up?" Essie asked him, her gaze following the other two men.

Releasing a soft grunt of impatience, Tate climbed into the saddle of his horse. "Because no one will suspect two or three men riding together, when they're looking for five."

"Ah. Very clever."

He reached a hand down to help her up. The wide-eyed look she gave him as she placed her palm in his resurrected the churning frustration in his gut. Now his focus would have to be divided between paying attention to the trail on the way to the gang's hideout and playing nursemaid to this young lady so she didn't get hurt.

"Thank you," she said brightly as he pulled her onto the horse. As if he were taking her for a Sunday buggy ride instead of bringing her to the hideout of a gang of wanted outlaws.

Tate rolled his eyes. As she situated herself behind him, she managed to jab him in the back with the handle of her valise—twice. It was going to be a long ride.

Urging his horse forward, he allowed Silas and Clem to take the lead as the three of them rode across the Wyoming plain. Low hills were visible in the distance.

"Do you know what you're doing?" The question escaped Tate's mouth before he'd even finished thinking it.

"Riding a horse? Yes." She joined her hands around

his waist as if to prove her point. "I've done this count-less times."

He shook his head. Not just at her words but to dis-miss how nice it felt to ride with a woman again—something he hadn't done in years. *Not since Ravena.* Tate pushed thoughts of the dark-haired girl back to the deepest recesses of his mind, a place where they'd stayed put for the last eight years. Right beside the re-gret and guilt he still harbored for Tex, his twin brother.

"I mean coming with us, Miss Vanderfair." He didn't bother disguising the irritation in his voice.

"As I said earlier, I want to interview you." She shifted her weight, poking him with her valise again. He ground his teeth over a growl.

"Why?" he countered, eager to riddle out her true motives. After all, that was his job as a detective.

"Because I'm an authoress of dime novels. I pen stories of romance and adventure." Her tone held a touch of pride.

"A fine occupation but—"

An amused sniff sounded at his back and inter-rupted his interrogation. "I'm perfectly aware of what others, especially men, think of my profession, Mr. Tex. You don't have to feign interest. I can assure you I've heard every ill sentiment there is regarding dime novels and their creators. Nothing you can say would surprise me."

A bit of a smile worked at his mouth at her chal-lenge. He was never one to back down from a chal-lenge. "I'm not feigning anything, Miss Vanderfair. I think writing novels would be hard, whether you're a man or a woman." He cleared his throat before add-ing, though he wasn't sure why, "My mother wrote poetry up until she died, and I would've been honored to see her work published."

The ensuing silence proved that he'd been right about surprising her. Tate's smile rose to a grin.

"Still," he continued, "what does writing dime novels have to do with you accompanying us?"

Her answer came swiftly. "I'd like to write a novel about train robbers, and naturally the best research is firsthand." He could easily imagine her chin tipped high as she spoke, her pert little nose in the air. "I saw an opportunity and I took it. I suspect that's something you and I have in common."

He couldn't argue with that. But who courted trouble in the name of "research"? If nothing else, his job of the last eight years had shown him what happened when seemingly good people went looking for trouble. They always found it.

Removing his hat, he wiped his sweaty forehead with his sleeve. Though it was mid-September, temperatures the last few days had been overly warm. That, or it was his irritation toward the woman seated behind him.

"There's a scar behind your ear." A featherlight touch skated his marred skin. "How come the Wanted posters don't mention it?"

Icy panic drove any thoughts of heat from Tate's mind. Clapping his hat back on, he gripped the reins tighter as he answered matter-of-factly, "Don't know. Maybe whoever made up the poster didn't know about it—I don't usually have someone right behind me when my hat's off."

Inside, though, he was reeling. Essie Vanderfair, with her doe-eyed determination, had just identified the most prominent visible difference between him and his identical twin brother.

Thankfully, Essie didn't seem to notice his now-rigid posture or tense shoulders. She began prattling about some of the more famous crimes of his brother's. Tate tried to ignore her, concentrating instead on the hilly landscape. But with each tale she shared, her voice full of near admiration, his alarm grew. She wasn't just overly curious; she apparently knew a great deal about Tex's life of crime.

What if she caught on to more discrepancies between him and his brother? That could ruin everything.

At that moment, Silas called from up ahead, "We gotta keep this pace for another thirty minutes. Then we'll be to the spot where we stowed those horses this morning."

"That's ingenious," Essie murmured. "I'll have to write that down in my notebook tonight."

Tate swallowed a groan. If only Fletcher hadn't agreed to let her come along. This assignment could not go wrong. Fletcher was merciless—if he caught on to Tate's true identity too soon, Tate doubted he'd be able to get out of it alive.

It would be much easier, for him and his job, if Essie Vanderfair could wait to interview these men until he had them behind bars.

Now, there's an idea.

A new plan began to take root inside him and he clung to it with all his might. If he could somehow give Essie the slip when they changed horses, both of them would be better off for it. She wouldn't get hurt riding across the country with a notorious outlaw gang and he wouldn't have to watch his carefully orchestrated mission fail.

It wasn't like he'd be leaving her stranded, either. With one of three tired but workable mounts to choose from, she'd eventually encounter a train or a town on her ride back to civilization. Of course, with her keen perceptiveness, he'd have to be smart in how he managed to leave her behind. But it shouldn't be too hard a task. After all, he was one of the best Pinkerton agents out there. And no one was going to take away his chance to see justice served.

Chapter Two

Essie slid from the horse to the ground with help from the Texan. Three fresh mounts clustered in the shade of the narrow canyon formed between two hills. Gripping her valise, she walked a few paces away from the men to stretch her legs.

It had been some time since she'd ridden a horse. Her own two feet could get her everywhere in Evanston, which meant she didn't require an animal or a carriage. But she did miss the thrill of riding, something she'd done nearly every day back on the ranch.

Thoughts of home, and her family, pinched at her excitement until she pushed them away. She'd just been handed the greatest opportunity of her writing career and that was what mattered today. She was really and truly here, with an outlaw gang. Wherever here was.

She moved toward the group. They were swapping the saddles to the fresh horses.

"Thirsty?" the Texan asked.

Before she could answer, he tossed her a canteen. Essie dropped her valise and easily caught the water container between her hands. A flicker of surprise passed through his blue eyes—he clearly hadn't expected her to catch the canteen—but he shuttered his expression once again.

"Thank you," she said, giving him a smile. She took a long drink and then stepped forward to hand him the canteen.

"Keep it. There's still plenty of riding ahead."

Essie cocked her head to study him as he saddled his new horse. He was different in person than he sounded in the newspapers. More serious, less charismatic. A gentleman, though. The reports had been correct there. Unlike him, the other two outlaws were doing their best to ignore her. Not that she minded. She was grateful the Texan had insisted she ride with him, so she wasn't off somewhere with Fletcher and his companion, by herself, at this precise moment. She wanted to interview the gang's leader…but she didn't want to be alone with him.

"We'll be a few more minutes." The Texan threw the words over his shoulder at her. "Might want to wait in the shade."

Turning, she located a patch of shadow to one side that wasn't currently occupied by the six horses. She picked up her valise and went to sit. A stiff breeze fanned her face. Essie pushed out a contented sigh as she shut her eyes.

"There's no need to be afraid," the train robber intoned in a deep voice, crouching beside the heroine. "You'll come under no harm, as long as you're with me."

She swallowed back the bite of fear in her dry throat. "Truly?"

He nodded and his blue eyes peered deeply into hers. "Here, have a drink." His fingers lingered against her own as he passed her his canteen. "We still have a long way to—"

The whinny of a horse followed by a cry from one of the men shattered the peace of the moment. Essie opened her eyes. They widened in shock when she realized all three outlaws were galloping away from the canyon, and from her.

"Wait!" She scrambled to her feet. "Come back!"

Her voice was drowned out by the thud of the horses' hooves. Had they forgotten her, quiet as she had been the last few moments? No, surely the Texan wouldn't leave her. Only minutes had passed since he'd tossed her his canteen. The one now lying in the dirt beside her valise.

She reached for the derringer in her boot, hoping to attract their attention with a shot in the sky. Before she could extricate it, though, she saw the Texan glance over his shoulder. Their eyes met, bringing Essie instant relief. She laughed off her earlier concern of being left behind and released her gun. Of course he wouldn't forget her.

Only, instead of coming back, he whipped his face forward once more and appeared to urge his animal to move faster.

The merriment drained from Essie's lips as she watched the three men move farther away. The Texan had seen her—she felt certain of it. So why hadn't he returned for her?

Reality doused her with a coldness that made her shiver. *He meant to leave you here. That's why he was so generous with his canteen.* She balled her hands into fists and glared at the man's form in the distance. How could she have fallen for such a trick? He hadn't wanted her to come along from the beginning, so he'd cleverly worked out a way to leave her behind.

"Ooo," she muttered, kicking at a clump of sagebrush. Handsome or not, the man certainly wasn't a gentleman, as the newspapers claimed. Unless his benevolent treatment meant leaving women and children to fend for themselves. But, like his boss, Fletcher, the Texan had underestimated her. Landing himself in the same unsavory category as Victor Daley. "And I will best you both," she hollered to the quiet prairie.

The horses shifted at her impassioned cry, drawing her attention. While none of them sported a saddle, they'd been left with their bridles on, and Essie had no qualms about riding bareback. How many times as a young girl had she taken off without a saddle on her horse, Brownie?

Gathering her valise and the Texan's canteen, she approached the tired-looking horses. She would have to take the ride slow, at least at first. A dappled gray gelding studied her in turn as she scrutinized each horse. The star on its forehead reminded her of Brownie.

"I think we'll give you a try."

She led the horse away from his companions to a sizable rock. Gripping the handle of her valise between her teeth, she held the horse's reins in hand and climbed onto the rock. From there she easily slipped onto the horse's back.

Bending down, she scooped up the canteen from off the rock and settled her things in her lap. "All right, boy. Let's go." She nudged the horse in the flanks, pointing him in the direction the robbers had taken minutes before.

Once they'd broken free of the chain of hills, Essie studied the ground for tracks. She'd done extensive research for her book *The Bounty Hunter Betrayed* and now it was about to pay off in real life. The Texan had messed with the wrong dime novelist if he thought her incapable of doing something as simple as follow after them.

Sure enough, she spotted the impression of horse hooves in the dirt and a partially trampled sagebrush farther on. If she kept heading in that same direction, she would eventually stumble into the trio.

She bent forward over the horse and coaxed it to go faster. There were interviews to conduct. And no one, not even a handsome, sly, backstabbing Texan, was going to stop her.

"The camp is next to those hills," Silas said, pointing. The sun had already begun dipping toward the horizon.

Tate noted the spot absently. It was hard to focus on much of anything except the guilt that had been dogging him since he'd left Miss Vanderfair behind.

For the hundredth time he reassured himself that she'd likely be fine. She had his canteen and her pick of a horse. But he couldn't drive away the image in his mind of her standing there, waving at them to come back, her hazel eyes wide with shock.

Running his bandanna over his dusty face, he followed the other two men toward the base of one of the hills. Eventually he spotted Fletcher and Jude up ahead. They appeared to be starting a fire.

Tate stopped his horse and climbed out of the saddle. He needed a good night's sleep. A chance to put the train robbery—his first and only—and Essie Vanderfair safely in the past, where they belonged, so he could focus all of his energy on what lay ahead.

He handed his horse's reins to Silas, the horse master, and headed off to look for more wood for the fire. Clem wouldn't start cooking until the flames were blazing, and Tate's belly was already rumbling for food.

A hard hand wrenched his shoulder before he'd gone far, jerking him backward. Tate fought the instinct to drive a fist into the offender's stomach. He could easily handle himself in a fistfight, but he had to maintain the easygoing demeanor associated with his brother.

"Where's the girl?" Spittle flew from Fletcher's mouth as he snarled the words. "Silas and Clem said they didn't know."

Tate shook off the outlaw's hold as he wiped the back of his hand across his jaw. Should he pretend he didn't understand what Fletcher meant? Or would it be better to come clean with the truth?

Opting for honesty, at least where it concerned Miss Vanderfair, he took a wide stance with his feet and casually folded his arms. "I left her back when we changed horses."

"You what?" Fletcher narrowed his gaze. "You left her behind without talkin' to me?"

"She was trouble, Fletch, and you know it." Tate maintained a level look. "We don't need some overly curious female poking her nose in our business."

The robber leader reached out and fisted Tate's collar, his dark eyes menacing. "You don't tell me how to run my operation, cowboy. I'm still the leader here." His foul breath cured Tate of wanting any supper, at least for the moment. "That girl means a hefty ransom, and it's easy money. We simply post a telegram and the money arrives in no time." He shoved Tate back. "Now, go get her."

Anger simmered hot inside Tate as he glared back at Fletcher. All of these outlaws were the same—greedy and remorseless when it came to ruining the lives of innocent people. *Just like your brother*, a voice chided inside his head. He tightened his jaw, willing his emotions to stay concealed, controlled.

"And if I don't?"

Fletcher's mouth curled up in a sneer. "Try me, Tex." He lifted his hands in a mock gesture of innocence. "But now your life is tied with hers." He walked away, adding over his shoulder, "I think you're smart enough to figure out what that means."

Clenching and unclenching his fingers, Tate forced a deep breath between his gritted teeth. He wanted to slam his fist into something, though it wouldn't change the situation. For better or worse, his fate—and his entire operation—now lay in the hands of Miss Essie Vanderfair. If he didn't return with her, he'd be expelled from the gang at the very least and his case would go up in smoke. At the very worst, he'd wind up dead.

Which meant he'd better go back and retrieve her.

He marched to the horses and saddled his mount again. The other men glanced between him and Fletcher in obvious confusion. "Better hope she's alive and well," the outlaw leader called out, shooting him a condescending grin as Tate swung up onto his horse.

The anger in his gut iced into anxiety as his mind filled once more with horrible visions of Miss Vanderfair injured, or worse. He shoved aside the nagging thoughts. She was fine, most likely.

Still, he couldn't help praying as he urged his horse back the direction he'd just come. *Please, Lord. Let me find her and let her be all right. For both our sakes.*

Essie eyed the darkening sky ahead and swallowed hard. In a short while she wouldn't be able to see much of anything, let alone the robbers' tracks, if the clouds dropped their rain. Sliding to the ground, she pressed her lips over a cry at the throbbing ache in her legs. Too many years had passed since she'd ridden bareback.

"Want some water, boy?" she said to the gelding. If she focused on something else, she could ignore the pain.

She set down her valise and cupped her hand to capture as much of the water from her canteen as she could. The liquid disappeared into the horse's mouth at once. The poor animal was thirsty, even though she'd kept him moving at a slow gait. She allowed him another mouthful and then she drank from the canteen herself.

When she'd finished, she sloshed the water against the sides of the container. There wasn't much left, judging by the sound. And she had nothing in the way of food for herself, either. But at least there was food for the horse.

"Why don't you sample the grass over here?" She led the gelding to a patch of yellowing grass among the dirt and sagebrush. "I'll see if I can't spot their trail again."

Looping the reins around a large sagebrush, Essie returned to the place where she'd dismounted. She walked slowly, searching the ground for tracks. A few yards away she found the imprints from the trio's horses.

A feeling of optimism bloomed inside her. Her tracking skills, though a bit novice, had proved to be more than adequate. She'd be back with the train-robbing gang in no time at—

The crack of thunder from above made her jump and caused the gelding to skitter to one side. She hurried to soothe the horse as fat drops of rain began to strike her head and shoulders. If the downpour washed away the tracks…

Essie swatted away the troubling thought. Surely she'd stumble onto the men's campsite before too long.

After tying up the canteen in the reins to free both her hands, she clutched the handle of her valise between her teeth once again and attempted to climb onto the gelding. But without the aid of a rock, she had to try three times before successfully hauling herself onto the horse's back. By then the rain had picked up, pounding the prairie as though it were as angry as she'd been earlier.

Essie could hardly see more than a few feet in any direction. Wiping strands of hair from her face, she untied the canteen and turned her mount toward the spot where she'd last seen the tracks. She kept her valise and the water container crushed to her chest with one hand while she grasped the reins with the other.

Cold droplets slid down her dress collar and pulled

her hair from its pins until it lay soaked against her back. There was nothing to do, though, but keep going. The horse plodded on, its head down. She wished she could lower hers, too, but she needed to make certain they were traveling in the right direction, drenched or not.

Thankfully, it wasn't long before the rain ceased its thunderous fury and dwindled to a light sprinkle. After another few minutes it stopped altogether.

"Look at that, boy—we made it through." Essie ventured a smile and shifted her grip on the reins to pat the gelding's neck.

But her relief ended abruptly when she leaned to the side to study the ground. Any tracks made by the three horses were no longer visible. A pinprick of alarm punctured her hope further as she realized the light was beginning to fade around them.

She moved the horse in one direction then back in another. It was no use. The outlaws' trail had disappeared and everywhere she looked the curve of the hills appeared the same. How was she to know where to go now?

Determination warred with her growing anxiety and she set her jaw. "We're not giving up. We have to find them." For more than just her interviews. The outlaws were her only ready source of food and fire and civilization. Unless, of course, she ran into other occupants of the plains...

She swallowed hard at the memory of the bloodcurdling tales she'd read, and those she had penned herself, of travelers beset by warring Indians. Although in her book *The Indian Warrior's Bride*, the heroine had not only survived an attack on the wagon train but had found love, too.

Still, a shiver, that had nothing to do with her drenched clothes, ran up Essie's spine. It was one thing to write such fanciful tales; it was another matter altogether to live them.

Which meant only one course of action remained open to her. She stopped the horse and bowed her chin. "As You can see, Lord, I'm in another predicament. Though I recognize, unlike earlier, this one is largely of my own making." *And the Texas Titan's*, she thought with a frown. "But if You wouldn't mind sending some help…"

The gelding lifted his head and whinnied. Someone, or something, was coming their way.

Essie swallowed hard and peered through the dimming light. "Please let it be the two-legged kind of something," she prayed, thinking of wolves and coyotes.

A rider crested a nearby rise. Essie's heart slowed its frantic hammering, but only for a moment. While not a wolf, she hoped the stranger was good and decent and kind.

"Let him be a friend, not a foe," she whispered. "A friend, not a foe." She couldn't see the man's face beneath his hat, but she felt a flicker of relief that at least he was dressed in the clothes of a horseman and not an Indian on the warpath.

Just as she was about to call out a greeting from her dry throat, the man lifted his head, revealing the face of the Texan. The man who'd left her behind— on purpose.

"Very funny," she muttered, lifting her eyes upward.

Sending her help in the form of *that* outlaw could only mean one thing—something she'd suspected for a while now. The Lord certainly had a sense of humor.

Chapter Three

Tate's mouth curved into a grin at the sight of Essie Vanderfair. He sent up a quick prayer of gratitude at finding her alive and well. And to think he'd stumbled onto her after riding just a little more than an hour. She'd wandered closer to Fletcher's camp than he would've thought possible. A blessing for both of them.

"You're a ways off from any kind of town," he called good-naturedly as he approached.

Instead of relief at seeing another human being way out here, she fixed him with a thorny glare. "I wasn't trying to find a town. I was tracking you." A bit of color flooded her cheeks. "At least until it started to rain."

Tate stopped his horse beside hers. He'd ridden through the rain, too, but his hat had helped keep his head and face mostly dry. Essie looked drenched, her hair hanging limp against her back.

"You remind me of a cat I once rescued who nearly

met his end in a swollen stream." He couldn't help a chuckle, which only narrowed her gaze even further.

"And you remind me of a…a…" She closed her lips.

"A what?" he prompted, more curious than offended. "Can't think of a good rejoinder, Miss Vanderfair?"

The corners of her mouth quirked upward. "I'm full of good rejoinders, Mr. Tex. But I prefer to give my comeuppance in fiction."

That wiped the smile from his face. He didn't need her writing about him—or rather, his outlaw brother—in some sensationalized story. "My apologies. Your hair—" he motioned to the long wet mane "—looks…nice like that."

One eyebrow rose in silent question. His neck felt warm, despite riding through the cool rain earlier. It wasn't a lie, though. He liked it when a woman left her hair long instead of pinning it up. Ravena had always worn it long and flowing.

He couldn't help comparing her to Essie, even as he fought memories from his youth. Ravena and Tex wove through nearly every one, and thinking back on the happiness they'd once shared left a bitter taste in his mouth. While not as stunning a beauty as Ravena had been, Miss Vanderfair had nice hazel eyes. Ones that apparently turned more green than brown when she was either determined or amused. With her hair down and her cheeks still pink, she made a rather lovely picture. Not that he'd noticed.

Clearing his throat, he turned his horse around. "Let's get going." He nudged the animal forward, but they hadn't gone more than a couple of feet when he realized she wasn't following.

Tate twisted in the saddle. "What's the problem now?"

Her eyes maintained their emerald color. "I'm not going anywhere with *you*. The man who deliberately left me out here—alone."

"You had some water," he offered lamely, "and a horse." But the paltry excuse only brought her chin up in a greater show of annoyance. So much for hoping she hadn't realized he'd left her behind on purpose.

She prodded her horse forward. "Good day, Mr. Tex."

He'd underestimated her pluck, and her anger; that was for sure. She wasn't weeping all over him in gratitude at finding her, either. Instead she was going to stubbornly wander around Wyoming until she happened onto Fletcher and his gang. Or so she thought.

"Where are you going?" he called after her, leaning on the saddle horn as if he had all the time in the world.

Essie turned. "To find Mr. Fletcher and conduct my interviews." Her chin hadn't lowered one inch. "And I'll do it without your help, thank you very much."

"You might be able to follow my trail for a few minutes, but the rain washed most of it away."

As he'd suspected, his words brought her and her horse to a full stop.

"You need me," he added.

And he needed her, too, though he wasn't about to reveal that information. It might make her overconfident, and that could mean serious trouble for him.

Tate blew out a sigh, hating that his covert mission was now squarely tied to the woman glaring at him.

She didn't bother to hide her emotions, which meant he could easily read the thoughts on her face. Frustration, dejection and, finally, acceptance. He had her and she knew it.

"Shall we continue, Miss Vanderfair?" He guided his horse alongside hers. "I don't know about you, but I'm famished, and even Clem's cooking is better than no cooking at all."

But she didn't humbly nod in acquiescence or make a move to follow him. No. She smiled at him instead. A smile that set fresh uneasiness churning in his stomach.

"I'll come with you, Mr. Tex, if you allow me to interview you first."

He sat back, feeling as if he'd been punched. The little imp had overthrown his plan with a cleverer one of her own.

The last thing he wanted, or needed, was to answer her nosy questions while still pretending to be his brother. He'd foolishly hoped they'd already be at Fletcher's hideout before Essie could attempt to corner him into talking about the past. But that door had closed. He was caught, and he suspected she knew it, too.

"Fine. Just know I may not answer every question."

A tiny furrow creased the space between her brows. "How am I to get the information I need—"

He shook his head. "Don't know, but that's my offer. Take it or leave it, Miss Vanderfair."

She sized him up in a way that made him wonder what she saw. For one tiny moment he had the strangest wish to tell her that he wasn't really an outlaw and she was riding straight into possible peril. But he couldn't say a thing that might persuade her to turn around and ride hard in the opposite direction.

A small seed of protectiveness, one born out of something deeper than simply keeping the innocent safe, sprouted in him as he regarded her, too. Tate tried to eradicate it. After all, he hadn't been able to protect Tex or the people his brother had wronged as part of his illustrious outlaw career. But something about Essie tugged at the locked handle of his heart, even before she gave him her answer.

"Very well, Mr. Tex." Her eyes shone dark green again. "I accept your terms."

"Were you born and raised in Texas?" Essie asked, a thrill pulsing through her at interviewing her very first outlaw. "Is that how you came by your name?"

The Texan shook his head. "I was born in Idaho. Lived there until eight years ago." He paused before adding, "My mother and her family were from Texas."

Essie kept her horse in pace with his, so she wouldn't miss hearing his answers. Though her hands weren't free to write down his responses, she wouldn't soon forget them. Like the stories she penned in her head, her interview would be stored in her memory for a few hours and easily retrieved once she was able to write it in her notebook.

"You mentioned your mother passed away." She gentled her tone so he wouldn't feel as if she were prying. "When was that?"

"Ten years ago." His shoulders stiffened, a clear indication he didn't like the topic.

"And your father?" she prodded.

"He up and left us when I was nine. Next question."

His abrupt manner did a poor job of hiding his pain. Essie swallowed a twinge of unease. Things with her parents and siblings might be strained, but at least she had a family. "Any brothers or sisters?"

"A brother."

"Older or younger?"

Another long pause preceded his answer. "Younger."

So much for delving deep into the life of an outlaw. She needed to think up better questions if she wanted to draw out more of his story. "When did you first become an outlaw?"

He cleared his throat, his face still rigidly pointed forward. "It was right after I left Idaho."

"Were you desperate for money?"

"No."

His response surprised her. She'd long believed money was the driving reason for most outlaws' choices. Cocking her head, she studied his tense expression. Was he being truthful? It was hard to know after so short an acquaintance. "What drove you to such a life, then?"

"Anger, mostly."

"At whom?" she prompted. She sensed she was on the brink of learning something critical, if the Texan would only comply.

He adjusted his weight in the saddle. "My parents. God. My girl…" His Adam's apple bobbed up and down. "My brother."

A tremor of victory rocked through Essie at his words. This was exactly what she'd been hoping to achieve. To excavate from these outlaws' pasts those events and people who'd influenced who they'd become. Their stories were going to make her novel successful.

She could envision the newspaper article touting her praise now, though she might forgo having her photograph taken. No need to highlight her plainness.

Female authoress Essie Vanderfair, who shares no acknowledged connection to the railway magnate Henry Vanderfair...

She opened her eyes at the disturbing intrusion into her daydream. These men didn't need to know this piece from her family's past. At least, not yet. Once she'd conducted her interviews, she would calmly explain why a ransom from Henry Vanderfair would not be forthcoming, and then she would ride back to civilization. Or make a well-executed escape. Then she would write her novel. Her wildly successful novel.

Satisfied, she continued with her reverie. *Female authoress Essie Vanderfair pens the greatest dime novel of all time. Fans of Victor Daley have abandoned the pedantic musings of their former literary hero to snatch up Miss Vanderfair's clever and engaging story of five train robbers who—*

"Is the interview over?"

The Texan's voice jerked her back to the present. She straightened, her muscles still aching from riding bareback, as she cast a sidelong glance at the man's saddle. He might have offered it to her.

"I was just thinking." She schooled her thoughts back to their conversation. He'd mentioned his parents and a brother. "Were you and your brother close?"

"Used to be."

She resisted the desire to roll her eyes at another

short response from him. "When was the last time you saw him?"

"This interview is supposed to be about me, not him," he countered in a voice seeping with irritation. She'd clearly touched upon another sore topic.

"True, but I believe our past and current relationships can shape our decisions." In her case, they'd driven her to do what others deemed improper or undoable. Perhaps it was the same with the man riding beside her. "If you won't discuss your brother, then tell me about this girl you left behind," she tried next, hoping a change in the conversation's direction would elicit a longer answer.

But she was disappointed in that, too.

"There's nothing to say about her. I haven't seen her in eight years."

Another tender subject. She exhaled a sigh through her nose. Would it be this difficult to interview the other outlaws? She hoped not.

"Do you still harbor feelings for her?" The question fled her lips before she could swallow it back. He wasn't going to give her an answer. And why should she care if he had loved, or still loved, this other woman? She didn't.

Instead of shooting back an angry retort, though, some of the starch left him. "Not in that way. But there's some…regret…there." He shot her a glance, his mouth turned down. "Next question."

"All right." She didn't bother to hide her growing annoyance. "What was your most exciting robbery?" Perhaps focusing on the more daring aspects of his chosen profession would result in the replies she really wanted. Men enjoyed bragging, didn't they?

He barked with laughter, startling her and the horses. "There's nothing exciting about robbing innocent people."

"Then why do you keep doing it?" she countered, her gaze narrowing in on his face.

His attitude and actions didn't seem to match. He was an odd mix of contradictions and nothing like the newspapers portrayed him to be. Maybe none of the reporters had actually spoken to him in person. If they were going off the hearsay reports of witnesses for their articles, that would explain the added charisma and excitement allegedly surrounding this man. A man who was ungentlemanly and morose in real life.

Turning his head, he mumbled something that sounded very much to Essie like "I don't know" before he twisted to face her again. "That's enough interviewing for today." He pushed his horse to a gallop. "Let's pick up the pace," he called back to her. "I don't want to be riding all night."

Essie hurried to catch up, her earlier excitement all but evaporated. Her first interview hadn't gone at all as she'd expected. And now she only had a few tidbits to work with.

She glared at the man's back, only partially grateful to him for coming back for her. He was hiding something; she could sense it in every unyielding line of his form. But what could it be?

If he thought she'd be satisfied with their second-rate interview today, he was gravely mistaken. She would ferret out every last detail of his story. After all, her father used to tell her, with a mixture of exasperation and pride in his voice, "You'd worry a dog right out from under its bone, Essie."

And this time, that *dog* was a handsome outlaw with a secret.

Chapter Four

Tate slid from the saddle, casting a glance over his shoulder at Essie to see her doing the same. The smell of burned beans and smoke permeating the air around the camp wasn't exactly appetizing, but he didn't mind. He was starving and tired—and he couldn't shake the wariness in his gut regarding Miss Vanderfair.

She'd remained surprisingly silent during the last thirty minutes or so of their ride. But Tate had the sense he'd awakened a sleeping bear with his vague answers earlier. Essie wouldn't be thrown off easily, but then, neither would he.

"Welcome back, Miss Vanderfair," Fletcher said, rising from his choice spot by the fire. "My apologies for the earlier misfortune. You can be assured if you'd been with me that you wouldn't have been left behind."

Essie looked at Tate, but he couldn't read her expression. Was she still angry? He, for one, was glad she hadn't ridden with Fletcher. He didn't trust that man any further than he could throw him. And, anyway, it was easier to keep an eye on her when she was close by.

"As you can see," she said, "no harm was done."

She went to stand by the fire, her hands outstretched to the flames. While the day had been warm, the evening had brought a drop in temperature. He could see that she shivered beneath her dress jacket, but she still maintained a smile.

Annoyance rippled through him. Why couldn't she just ask for a blanket if she needed one? No one was going to cater to her needs out here. Stalking to the edge of the camp where the saddlebags had been stowed, he yanked out a blanket.

Returning to the fire, he plopped the blanket around her shoulders. Her gaze jumped to his, her eyes wide. They weren't dark green anymore, as they'd been at the end of her interview. Now they shone more brown. "Thank you."

He nodded once then turned to Clem. "Any supper left?"

The outlaw dropped a helping of beans onto two tin plates along with some biscuits that looked anything but light and fluffy. He passed the food to Essie and Tate.

Graciously accepting hers, Essie took a seat on the ground. Tate selected a spot nearby. Fletcher and Jude wandered over to where Silas was seeing to the two horses. The three outlaws appeared to be in deep conversation, though they kept their voices low enough that Tate couldn't discern their words. He'd have to learn at some point what they were discussing, but right now, he needed to satisfy his empty stomach.

The first mouthful of beans, with its scorched flavor, made him grimace, and yet he was too hungry to quit eating. Out of the corner of his eye, he watched

Essie take a bite. The moment the food hit her tongue a startled expression crossed her face, though, to her credit, she didn't gag or cough. Instead she visibly swallowed and scooped up another spoonful.

"This is my first time having camp fare, Clem. Is this your usual cuisine?"

Tate stuffed a piece of tough biscuit into his mouth to keep from laughing. Especially when Clem scratched his head and looked confused. "What do you mean by…cuisine, ma'am?"

"She means is this the food you usually eat on the run," Tate explained.

"Oh, that." Clem rubbed a hand over the salt and pepper hairs covering his chin. "We have beans and biscuits, like this here meal, a fair amount of time. But also small game. Once we reach the hideout, the eatin's better."

Essie murmured acknowledgment. "And where is your hideout?"

Tate tensed at the question, though he forced himself to appear as if he wasn't paying attention. So far Fletcher had dodged or outright refused to reveal the hideout's location to Tate. But if Clem talked…

"It's in Hole-in-the-Wall country, ma'am. But that's still a long ride from here. At least a week."

The desire to holler with victory nearly overpowered Tate. He'd suspected the gang of hiding out in northern Wyoming, somewhere quite remote. Now he knew the name. And over the next seven days he'd know exactly how to get there, too.

"What's this hideout like?" Essie asked as she broke her biscuit into two and dipped one half into her beans.

Tate held his breath. Any minute now Clem would surely stop talking or Fletcher would march over and demand he shut up. But the outlaw didn't even pause or look the least bit uncomfortable.

"It's real rough country, ma'am." He rested his arms on his knees and leaned slightly forward. "But there's plenty of grass for the horses and a creek for water. There's even some cabins for wintering over."

Tate's jaw went slack as he studied Essie and Clem in turn. What had made the man disclose so much to a complete stranger? He'd been trying to siphon information about their hideout ever since he'd joined up with Fletcher's gang a few weeks ago. And yet, in the matter of a few minutes, Essie had drawn out details he hadn't even come close to discovering for himself. Maybe having her along would actually prove helpful to his investigation.

The thought had barely registered in his head when she turned and smiled at him. Something in the smile obliterated his good mood. "Had you heard of the Texas Titan before you met him, Clem?" She posed the question to the other outlaw but kept her gaze locked on Tate.

"Well, sure, ma'am. I 'spect everybody has."

"Tell me, then…" She cocked her head to one side as if in deep thought. "Does he fit the picture you imagined of him?"

Tate shifted on the hard ground, the meal in his stomach turning as ashy as it tasted. What was she doing?

"Don't rightly know, ma'am. He looks like them Wanted posters all right."

Essie finally returned her attention to her plate.

Only then did Tate dare suck in a breath. "He does very much resemble his description in the posters and newspapers," she agreed. "But no one has yet mentioned—"

"Food's sure good tonight, Clem," Tate interrupted, smacking his lips in an exaggerated fashion. He cringed at the way his voice carried loudly across the camp. "I'll take another helping. What about you, Miss Vanderfair? Care for more food?" He leveled a hard look her way, though he didn't miss Clem's puzzled expression as the outlaw refilled his plate.

Essie pursed her mouth to the side, her eyes narrowed. If only he could decipher the thoughts inside that wily head of hers. "No, thank you. I find I'm quite done." Tate sensed she was talking about more than just the meal.

Sure enough, after setting aside her empty plate, she swiveled to face him. "Remind me, Mr. Tex. What was the first crime you committed?"

"It was a bank robbery in Texas." Tate shoved another spoonful of beans into his mouth, though he didn't taste a thing this time.

The memory of seeing that first mention of his brother's name and description in the newspaper still burned his gut with guilt every time he recalled it. He'd known Tex was angry and vengeful the last time they'd seen each other, but he hadn't thought his twin would turn to a life of crime in retaliation. That first robbery led to others, each more daring than the last—more banks, then trains. All performed single-handedly and pulled off without a hitch.

Sometime around the fourth robbery, Tate had had enough. He'd sold the family farm and applied for a job with the Pinkertons. If he couldn't help his brother, he could at least help others by bringing down other criminals.

"What was your last solo job?" Essie's question cut into his thoughts.

He glanced at her and found that hard, emerald look in her eyes. Did she suspect something? "That would be a train robbery in Utah Territory."

She nodded, though she didn't drop the shrewd look. "How much did you take?"

"Six thousand dollars," Tate said with a forced note of pride. In reality, disgust filled him at the thought of Tex taking even a dollar that didn't belong to him.

Thankfully he'd kept abreast of Tex's activities through the years. Not only did it afford him with the correct details to share with Essie, but it had also alerted him to the past four months of silence when it came to his brother's criminal activities.

Tex had seemingly disappeared. Of course, Tate hoped the stop in robberies meant his brother had decided to change his ways. But, whatever the truth, he'd recognized a golden opportunity to bring in the Fletcher gang. With Tex out of the criminal scene, Tate could impersonate him as the notorious outlaw. It wouldn't be too far-fetched for the Texas Titan to have wandered as far north as Wyoming, either. Medicine Bow, the closest town to where they'd stopped the train, was well-known for falling victim to train robberies.

So far Tate's cover had worked, getting him closer to taking down Fletcher than any other detective had ever come. And it would continue to work as long as he kept his wits about him, especially around Essie Vanderfair.

A flash of surprise—or was it disappointment?—crossed Essie's face. Had she been trying to trap him with his own words? Then the emotion fled, replaced by a smile. "Thank you again for the supper, Clem. May I help with cleaning up?"

Clem's face flushed, but he shook his head. "Ain't much to clean. I'll do it."

"Very well. I believe I shall work some before turning in."

"Work?" Tate echoed, setting aside his plate. He still had a lot left of his second helping, but he no longer felt hungry.

"Writing, Mr. Tex," she said. She gathered her valise, while still holding the blanket around her shoulders, and retreated to a spot a little ways from the fire.

Clem looked toward Tate and chuckled. "She's an interestin' little thing, huh?"

"Something like that." Tate eyed Essie as she began scribbling in a notebook. Satisfied she wasn't going to engage Clem in any more conversation tonight, he stood and moved toward the others who were still in heated discussion. "Sounds serious over here," he said as he joined the small group.

Fletcher shot him a glare and crossed his arms in a defensive stance, the saddlebag of cash from the train draped over his shoulder. "It is, but I don't know that it's any of your business."

"Come on, Fletch," Jude said. "Let's see what Tex has to say."

The outlaw leader studied Tate and then sniffed.

"All right. We've been debating the merits of taking one more job before heading to the hideout."

Tate struck a casual stance and kept a deadpan expression, trying to hide the alarm Fletcher's words inspired. He'd been hoping the train robbery today would be his only criminal activity. "What's the reason?"

"A little more cash and supplies to see us through the winter," Jude volunteered when Fletcher didn't jump in with an answer. "Once the snow hits around here and the temperature dips real low, we don't do much traveling, especially not in a hurry."

"So you're wintering over now?" Again the news blindsided him. He'd hoped they'd leave for another job *after* they reached the hideout. Then he'd make up some excuse for staying behind before riding to the nearest town and rounding up the law. When Fletcher and the gang returned, it would be to a sheriff and his posse, all waiting eagerly for the outlaws' arrest. But a decision to winter over now could jeopardize that plan.

"Got a problem with that, cowboy?" Fletcher watched him closely. "You don't have to join us for the winter."

And miss his chance at seeing them brought to justice? Not happening. Tate fought the urge to clench his jaw in determination; he had to appear affable. But he wasn't going to waste this opportunity or leave Essie to fend for herself, either.

He chose his next words carefully. "I told you in the beginning I'm done with doing things on my own. Too many close calls. If you're wintering over, then I aim to, as well. If you have another job planned, I'm in on that, too."

For once Fletcher offered a smile that almost bordered on genuine. "That's what I wanted to hear."

"I still think that we ought to keep moving," Silas said with surprising force. Tate had dubbed him "Silent Silas" in his head on account of the man's quiet, non-talkative nature. "Today went well, but there's nothing between here and Casper worth taking on. Besides, we got that girl's ransom coming."

Uncrossing his arms, Fletcher gazed across the campsite toward Essie. A feeling of unease crept over Tate. Did Fletcher plan to keep Essie around until the spring? There was no telling what the outlaw would do—he was as fickle as a woman with two beaus. But Tate would do all in his power to get Essie back on her merry way sooner than later. At least the forthcoming ransom seemed to be holding Fletcher in check as far as mistreating her.

"I get to say if we do another job or not," Fletcher finally growled. "But since I ain't made up my mind, we'll continue on to the hideout as planned. Tex, you're on guard duty tonight. Wake Jude up at two o'clock to switch places." With that, he marched toward the fire.

Jude and Silas threw tight looks at one another then followed after their leader. Tate remained by the horses another minute, doing his best to rein in the annoyance rippling through him. He didn't like having Fletcher order him around, but it was a necessary part of infiltrating the gang and getting the man to trust him.

Breathing out a heavy sigh, Tate collected his rifle from his saddle and returned to the campfire. The other four men had laid out their bedrolls. Fletcher was using the bag with the stolen money as a pillow. Essie, on the other hand, still sat with her blanket wrapped around her shoulders, writing.

Tate grabbed the remaining blanket and sat beside her. She didn't glance up. While guard duty meant little sleep, at least this way he could keep an eye on her during her first night with them. "Don't you think you ought to get some rest?" he asked as he set his gun next to him on the ground. He left his revolver in the holster at his waist.

"A Winchester Model 1886," she murmured.

"What?"

She lifted her chin and pointed with her pencil at his gun. "Your rifle is a Winchester, the 1886 model, correct?"

Tate nodded in disbelief. "How did you know that?"

A small but lovely smile lifted her lips. "As the authoress of dime novels set in the West," she said, her gaze returning to her notebook, "I would be remiss in my research if I didn't know a Winchester from a Sharps."

He didn't bother to swallow his startled laughter. There was clearly more to Miss Essie Vanderfair than he'd suspected. "Do you know how to shoot it?"

She shot him an arch look. "I was raised on a ranch. I can shoot anything with a trigger."

Leaning back on his hands, Tate regarded her appreciatively. "Are you writing a story right now?"

The glint of steel fell from her face as she shook her head. "Unfortunately, no. I'm merely getting down your answers from our interview earlier."

The recollection of her nosy questions and keen discernment made his stomach twist with apprehension. "It's been a while since your interview. How do I know you're remembering my answers correctly?"

Essie shoved the notebook into his chest, making him wince. "Have a look yourself."

He studied the page before him and the two columns of neat, looping writing penned there. Above one column, Essie had written "Questions." The other column she'd labeled "Answers." Tate read through several of her questions. *Were you desperate for money? What drove you to such a life?* Then he glanced at the second column for the answers. *No. Anger, mostly. My parents. God. My girl... My brother.*

Though he didn't have a perfect memory, he remembered enough of his responses to know she'd penned them—word for word. "How did you remember these?" He handed her back the notebook but kept hold of his end when she reached for it. "You weren't taking notes."

"No, I wasn't," she said, ducking her chin. The firelight revealed the blush on her cheeks. "But when I come up with things to write down for my stories, I can keep it all there in my mind until I can get to paper and a pencil. Then I just note it down, like reading a page out of a book."

"Can you recall everything you hear?" Having her on this job was proving more and more useful. If she happened to overhear anything or if the outlaws kept babbling to her as Clem had done earlier...

But his hopefulness died when Essie shook her head. "I can't recall everything. Usually it's easiest with information relating to my work. Though even that, after a few hours, half a day at the most, gets blurred."

Tate relinquished his hold on her notebook. Resting his arms on his knees, he threw a sideways glance at her as she began writing again. What was it Clem had said about her? *She's an interestin' little thing.* Tate had to agree.

Miss Essie Vanderfair surprised him and it had been some time since he'd been truly, and pleasantly, surprised. It hadn't been an entire day since they'd met, and yet he found himself more and more intrigued by her as the hours passed. If only he weren't on assignment, and a dangerous one at that, he might have invited her to dinner at a hotel restaurant and plied *her* with questions instead of the other way around.

But he *was* on an assignment, he reminded himself as he stared into the flames of the fire. And the fascinating woman seated beside him unknowingly held the key that could expose him for the detective he was and the renegade he wasn't.

Frowning at the thought, he picked up his rifle and placed it across his knees. He'd have to keep his distance from her, while also doing his best to smooth over any more of her suspicion. He couldn't guarantee the safety of either of them if his secret was revealed.

All done. Essie stuck her pencil in the center of her notebook and smiled tiredly at the filled page. She'd penned every question and cryptic answer of the Texas Titan's as well as the novel scenes she'd composed in her head earlier. Stretching, she tried to release the kink in her neck from bending over.

You'll be stooped and wearing spectacles if you keep up all that foolish writing. The remembered words erased the smile from her mouth. What would her family think of her being here, with these armed men?

She glanced at the Texan seated silently nearby, his rifle across his knees. He hadn't said another word since discovering her unusual talent for remembering things she heard or wrote inside her head. What could he be thinking just now?

Lowering her gaze, she read the last few sentences she'd written. *The outlaw stared morosely into the fire as if seeing the tortured memories of his past. Or was it the possibility of a bleak and lonely future that pilfered his smile? The heroine met his gaze across the flames and a jolt of tenderness ran through her as his haunted blue eyes beckoned to her. His masculine mouth held her attention next and she pondered for a moment what it might be like...*

"You ready?"

Essie slammed her notebook shut, her cheeks burning. Had he seen what she'd written? Good thing she hadn't begun penning any of her scene ideas when she'd shown him her notebook earlier. "What do you mean?"

The Texan regarded her with a glint of amusement in those *haunted blue eyes* of his. They certainly were beckoning when they watched her that way. Blinking, Essie glanced in the opposite direction. She wasn't writing about him; she was writing about her own fictional hero. Though perhaps she ought to change the hero's eye color...and hair color...and build. *Oh, bother.*

"Are you ready to turn in? If so, I'll put out the fire."

Glancing at the flames, she suddenly realized this was the reason she'd been able to write so long—the Texan had kept the fire burning so she could see. Her gaze jumped to his. This wasn't the only chivalrous gesture he'd performed tonight. He'd given her the blanket that was keeping her warm, too. Perhaps she'd misjudged him earlier, thinking he wasn't as much of a gentleman as the newspapers touted.

"Yes, I'm finished," she answered quietly, not wishing to disturb the four outlaws who were sleeping. One of them more loudly than the others. "Thank you," she added, waving a hand at the fire, "for not banking it sooner."

He dipped his chin in response and set aside his gun to kneel by the fire. Essie slipped her notebook inside her valise and then positioned it to act as a pillow. Lying down, she shut her eyes and tried to relax. But the hard ground poked through her blanket and into her side. Sleep was likely to be a distant friend for a while longer.

At least her present discomfort wasn't exacerbated by feelings of fear. She still had her small gun stowed in her boot, so she wasn't afraid to fall asleep in her present company. Especially with the Texan nearby. Something more than the newspaper compliments made her feel safe in his presence.

And yet even his solid frame watching over everything and everyone couldn't chase away the doubts that suddenly assailed her—now that the thrill of joining the outlaw group had faded.

What am I doing here? she asked herself for the first time since stepping off the train. Her family would be horrified if they could see her now. Though their shock would likely be followed by exclamations of self-satisfaction. Of course she'd ended up here—a lone woman among wanted thieves, so desperate to cling to her dream of publishing that she'd risk her reputation and her career on a chance. If her other interviews went anything like the one with the Texan had, her life as an author would truly be over.

Tears blurred her eyes as she watched him finish banking the fire. She couldn't give up—not yet. Clem had been quite forthcoming at supper. Surely the rest of the outlaws weren't as cryptic as the Texas Titan. Although she suspected Fletcher might be worse. Still, three good interviews and the opportunity to share in a real retreat to a hideout would provide her with more information than she'd ever dreamed of.

Certainly more than Victor Daley ever had.

"Can't sleep?" The Texan returned to his spot, but instead of taking up his gun again, he pulled a pocket watch from his vest. After checking the time, he rested his elbows on his bent knees.

"Not yet," Essie replied honestly. She dragged in a full breath of smoke-scented air and blew it out slowly. A few tears made their way down her cheeks, but she no longer felt the urge to give way to sobbing. Her family might not believe her to be strong—and maybe she wasn't—but God had given her a talent for seeing the good. And that was what she would think about. The not-too-cold evening, a blanket to keep her warm, the brush she'd thrown into her valise that would come in handy tomorrow morning...

"You ever sleep out under the stars?"

She twisted her head to look up at him. "All the time in the summer. I was usually the first one out there, but eventually my brothers and sisters would pile outside to join me."

He smiled, though even in the dying light, it appeared more sad than nostalgic. "My brother and I slept outside a lot, too." He shifted his position, the heel of his boot digging into the ground. "How many siblings do you have?"

"Eight."

His eyebrows shot upward. "Eight, huh? Are you close with any of them?"

Pain lodged inside her chest at the question. "My brother Nils. He's a year older."

"Where is he now?"

She turned her gaze to the stars overhead as bitter-sweet memories filled her thoughts. "He, um, died. Four years ago. He was thrown from his horse." Her father had wanted to shoot the skittish animal, but Essie had pleaded with him not to exact revenge on the innocent creature. Even while her heart had ripped in two at the loss of her brother.

"I'm very sorry, Miss Vanderfair."

"Thank you." She glanced at him, but with his chin lowered, his face was shadowed by his hat. "You lost your mother. I can't imagine what that must have been like."

While her parents and the rest of her siblings hadn't championed her dreams of writing as Nils always had, they were still alive and seemed concerned about her welfare. Letters came from the ranch nearly once a week, asking how she fared and when she might return home.

The Texan cleared his throat, though he didn't lift his head. "It was a great loss. But we pulled through it. At least, one of us did."

"Your brother didn't feel her passing as keenly?"

"He did." His chin rose and he leveled her with a look both intense and regretful. "But he felt like he had to…to…overcompensate. To be father and mother, even if there wasn't much difference in our ages."

Essie rose onto her elbow and rested her head in her palm. "I suppose most families have someone like that. Wanting so desperately to protect and care for the others, even if it stifles those they love."

He frowned. "How does wanting to protect and care for someone stifle them?"

"It does so in many ways." She sat up and faced him, eager to help him understand what she'd come to see the last three years on her own. "If one is never allowed to stumble about or tread down uncertain paths, that person will likely never reach his or her true potential. They'll be perpetually stuck in a web of safekeeping that offers no growth because there is no opportunity to learn from trial and error."

Her impassioned speech was met with stony silence. Essie fiddled with the edge of the blanket, embarrassed. Not for what she'd said but because she'd spoken it to a man she hardly knew.

"You are rather wise for someone so young."

At that, she laughed outright, then clapped a hand to her mouth, afraid she'd wake the others. She was enjoying their open conversation and suspected it would come to an abrupt end if anyone stirred. "My sisters would be the first to point out that I am far from young. I turned twenty-three this summer."

Even in the dim light, she caught sight of the full smile he threw her way. And it left her a bit breathless. "Twenty-three sounds young to someone who's twenty-nine."

She chuckled. "I'll remember that." A breeze swept

over the camp, swirling the ash around the fire and shooting a chill up Essie's spine. Pulling the blanket tighter around her, she lay back down on her make-shift pillow.

"Cold?"

"A little. But it'll pass soon enough."

A jacket dropped onto her shoulders and back, bringing welcome warmth. "How are you going to keep out the cold?" she asked, peering up at him.

He settled on the ground once more and hoisted his blanket for her to see. "I've got this, when I need it."

"Thank you." Essie burrowed into the thick material. No longer as chilled or as uncomfortable as before, sleepiness began to creep over her, but she hoped to keep it at bay. At least for another minute or two. "Can I ask you one more question?"

"Just one?" The teasing note in his deep voice made her smile. "For the rest of the trip?"

"No," she said emphatically. "One more *tonight*."

He pushed out a sigh, though he didn't sound nearly as irritated as she'd expected. "All right, Miss Vander-fair. One more."

"This is purely out of curiosity. Your answer won't go into my book."

She thought she heard him mutter, "That's a relief."

"They call you the Texas Titan, but what's your real name?"

Tension, heavy and silent, radiated from him, eras-ing the companionship of moments ago. Essie gripped the edge of the blanket tighter, waiting. Would he an-swer her or not? She didn't need the information, but for some inexplicable reason, she very much wanted to know.

The scraping of his heel against the dirt preceded his soft answer. "You can call me Tate."

"Tate," she whispered.

"But only out of earshot of the others. Understand?"

"Yes," she said with a nod. "Good night, then… Tate."

"Good night, Miss Vanderfair."

Her heart beat faster as she opened her mouth and said, "Call me Essie. It's only fair."

A low chuckle sounded in her ears. "Try to get some sleep, Essie. We've got another long ride tomorrow."

Smiling in triumph, she closed her eyes, but it was still some time later before she could turn her thoughts from the silent figure guarding the camp. And from the memory of her name on those nice, masculine lips.

Chapter Five

According to his pocket watch, a gift from his mother years ago, Tate had been awake off and on the past four hours. Jude had taken over guard duty at the appointed time, but Tate had kept his spot near Essie. Though he felt sure no harm would come to her while he slept, the possibility had him waking every hour and unable to get back to sleep the last thirty minutes. It was going to be another long day.

When Clem rose, Tate sloughed off his blanket and got up, too. Essie appeared to still be sleeping, judging by her even breathing and occasional soft snores. He found himself smiling as he went in search of wood for a fire.

His thoughts soon returned to what Essie had said about the danger of overprotecting one's family. Was that what he'd done with Tex after their mother had died? Or when he'd tried to intervene between his brother and Ravena?

A frown replaced his earlier smile. He'd done and said what he had out of love and concern—for both

Tex and Ravena. And yet had he unknowingly stifled his brother's potential instead of letting consequences play out naturally?

The question drudged up memories and emotions he preferred to keep buried. Chief among them was guilt, even though he wasn't the brother living on the wrong side of the law. Maybe when this was all over, he would track Tex down. Find out why his brother had disappeared four months ago. Despite the mile-wide canyon of disagreement and bruised pride between them, Tate hated to think of his twin hurt, or worse.

After finding a few decent-size sticks, he headed back to camp. Essie was awake, wearing the jacket he'd loaned her last night. The thing dwarfed her, but she'd rolled the cuffs back so she could brush her hair. Unlike yesterday, after the rainstorm, the unbound blond waves looked smooth and glossy this morning. Tate had the strangest urge to run the ends through his fingers.

"Thank you again for your jacket, Ta—Mr. Tex," she quickly amended, her eyes widening at her mistake. But Clem didn't seem to be paying attention, and Jude, now relieved of guard duty, was dozing on one side of the camp. Fletcher and Silas were off by the horses.

Not for the first time, Tate questioned what had possessed him to give Essie his real name last night. He was certain no one knew the Texas Titan had a brother, let alone a twin. Disclosing such a personal detail, though, had the potential to get him in loads of trouble. Especially if Essie slipped up in front of Fletcher. But, after hearing her talk about her own brother before she'd fallen asleep, Tate had felt compelled to share something real in return.

"Here's your jacket."

Tate belatedly realized she'd been sitting there, holding the jacket out for him. "Keep it. At least until the day warms up." He rather liked how she looked in the oversize garment, her hair flowing around her shoulders and her small but capable hands peeking out from the cuffs.

He tried to push aside the thought as he dumped the wood next to the cold ashes. But he couldn't deny the fact that Essie was far more attractive than he'd given her credit for on the train yesterday. Not that it mattered. He was on a mission and she believed him to be an outlaw—and that was the way he needed it.

"What's for breakfast, Clem?" Essie asked in a cheery tone as she put away her brush and folded her blanket up neat and tidy.

Clem exchanged a look with Tate. "Uh…that'd be beans and biscuits again, ma'am."

A slight frown appeared between her brows, but it vanished the next moment. Tate was beginning to realize her smiles and optimism weren't a show or a cover for fear—her cheerful disposition was apparently as real as her knowledge of guns and tracking and family relationships.

"That sounds good and hearty." She smiled at Clem. "May I help? It's been some time since I cooked, but I used to make decent biscuits at home."

The outlaw cook glanced around as if fearing her help might cause him trouble. "All right," he finally said with a shrug. "I 'spose you can do the biscuits."

A full smile curved her mouth, reminding Tate

once again that she was as pretty as she was intriguing. "I'll try not to disappoint."

Tate coughed to cover a laugh—anything would be an improvement over Clem's clumsy cooking. Essie shot him a disapproving look, as if she could somehow read his thoughts and didn't want him wounding Clem's feelings. With nothing more to do, he excused himself, calling over his shoulder, "I'll go see what the plan is for today."

Silas was saddling the horses while Fletcher watched. "Hear anything suspicious last night, cowboy?"

Tate shook his head. "Not a peep."

"Good." Fletcher situated the saddlebag of money onto one of the horses. "No lawmen will likely catch up to us, then."

"What's the plan?"

"We'll split up again, just in case. You, Silas and Clem can ride together. And me, Jude and the girl."

Uneasiness churned inside Tate's empty stomach at Fletcher's words, though he hid it behind a thoughtful look as he casually crossed his arms. No way was he letting Essie out of his sight. Not yet, and maybe not at all. Though she wasn't completely helpless, she was still a bit naive, viewing their flight to the hideout as a grand adventure.

"We can do that," he said with nonchalance. "Though I thought the girl was my responsibility."

"She is, but I don't trust you, Tex." The outlaw leader threw him a level look. "You left her behind yesterday. What's to say you aren't gonna try another move like that today?"

Tate's jaw tightened. "Because I now understand that if something happens to her, I'm to blame."

Fletcher nodded, a sneer on his mouth. "You got that right, cowboy."

"Besides." Tate pressed on. "She'll likely slow you down today." Though he doubted it. Essie could ride better than any woman he'd encountered. "And if you do run across the law, you'll have far less explaining to do if you aren't riding pell-mell over the hills with a woman in tow." He let that reason settle in before he finished with, "As the leader of this gang, you've got to keep yourself far from the most risk."

Scowling, Fletcher rubbed a hand over his whiskered jaw. "You may have a point, cowboy." He pushed up his hat and stared in the direction of the camp. Tate could see Essie working over a pan at the fire. "You take the girl with you. Clem will come with us. Now let's eat."

Tate hid his smile, in spite of the relief coursing through him, as he trailed Fletcher and Silas to the fire. The smell of freshly cooked dough filled his nose and made his mouth water.

"Your breakfast, gentlemen," Essie announced when they approached. "Courtesy of Clem and myself."

"I only done the beans," Clem muttered, scooping portions of them onto the tin plates. But his brown eyes glowed with obvious appreciation at Essie for including him.

Tate thanked her as she passed him a full plate. The biscuits looked as light and airy as clouds. Maybe Essie could be cajoled into taking over all the cooking for the duration of her stay.

Lifting a biscuit to his mouth, anticipating the flakiness melting on his tongue, he paused when he caught sight of Essie's dipped chin and shut eyes. She was giving thanks for the food. He lowered his arm, feeling a twist of regret at not praying himself. He hadn't known Essie was religious, but he found he wasn't surprised. And while he couldn't outwardly show his own faith, not if he wanted to maintain his brother's identity, no one would hear his Heaven-sent thoughts.

Pushing his beans around his plate, he offered his own silent prayer of gratitude. *Lord, thank Thee for this food. Thank Thee for keeping me...and Essie... safe. Guide my actions and bless my efforts. Amen.*

He lifted his gaze and found Essie watching him, a puzzled frown on her mouth. Did she suspect he'd also been praying? Clearing his throat, he bit into the biscuit with relish, hoping to throw off her perceptiveness, then grinned at her. "Best biscuits I've ever tasted," he said after swallowing the delicious morsel.

"Amen to that," Jude and Fletcher admitted at the same time. Even Silas was silently nodding approval.

Essie lowered her gaze from his, her cheeks flushing a pretty shade of pink, and ducked her head. Was it all the compliments that made her blush? Or his in particular? Tate couldn't help hoping his words had affected her the most.

Once the fire was out and their belongings stowed, it was time to saddle up. "Who am I riding with today?" Essie asked. Still sporting his jacket, she held the handle of her bag between her hands and watched him and the others expectantly.

"You'll ride with Tex and Silas, on your own horse," Fletcher said as he swung into the saddle. "We'll split up one more day and meet up again at the camp tonight."

"Oh...wonderful."

Tate thought he detected a note of disappointment in her voice, but he wasn't certain of its source. Was she wishing she could ride with Fletcher and Jude? Or was she regretting the fact that she wouldn't be sharing a horse with him this time? He had to admit he wouldn't mind having her ride with him once more, even at the risk of being badgered by her bag handle and her questions.

Raking his hand over the bristles of his jaw, he reined in his bizarre thoughts. "I'll help you up, Miss Vanderfair." Somehow the idea of calling her *Essie* in front of the others felt too personal.

He helped her onto the horse she'd ridden yesterday and then climbed onto the back of his own mount. Shifting his weight, he flexed his hands around the reins, preparing himself for another long day of riding—this time bareback, since he'd opted to give his saddle to Essie. But to see Fletcher and his gang eventually apprehended, he'd ride twice as far and twice as long.

After picking their way through a short range of hills, Fletcher, Clem and Jude headed northwest, while Tate and Essie followed Silas northeast. Both groups would double back at some point to meet up at the next camp. Looking over his shoulder, Tate saw Essie coming steadily behind him. She rode well, especially with a saddle.

"I can ride bareback," she said, catching up with him. "I did it yesterday."

"And I can do it today."

She arched her eyebrows at him. He was beginning to recognize it as her telltale sign of skepticism. "When was the last time you rode without a saddle?"

Tate glanced at the sky, trying to remember. "I might have been ten."

"I was fifteen, which means it's been fewer years for me."

"Then that's all the more reason for you to enjoy having a saddle today." He urged his horse a little faster. Couldn't she just be grateful at his attempt at being a gentleman? He'd already fended a curious look from Fletcher after moving the saddle to her horse earlier.

To his consternation, she kept her horse in pace with his. "I don't want to be a burden. I'm a lot stronger than I look."

Tate shot her a glance. "I wouldn't say you've been a burden so far. Especially not after that breakfast this morning." He couldn't help a smile when he thought of her biscuits. It was the first decent food he'd eaten since joining Fletcher's gang. "I don't doubt your strength, either."

Instead of smiling, though, she turned in the saddle, facing away from him. He hadn't seen her this agitated since he'd found her wandering over the prairie the day before, angry at him for leaving her behind. There was more underlying her words than stubbornness or pride.

Sudden understanding filled his mind. "Who's told you that you aren't strong?"

"A great many people," she murmured, loud enough to be heard over the horses' hooves but soft enough to convey the hurt behind the words. "Everyone I know, really."

He opened his mouth to contradict her, to remind her that God knew her strength and He was the only

One who mattered. But he forced himself to swallow the truth. Talking about faith with her would only raise her already-heightened suspicion about him.

A cloud of uneasiness settled over them before she twisted to look at him again. "It doesn't matter." She offered him a smile, but it didn't strike Tate as quite as genuine as some of the others he'd seen since yesterday. "And thank you for the use of your saddle."

He nodded in acknowledgment though he couldn't shake his regret over not being able to talk more openly with her. Silas maintained the lead position, which suited Tate just fine. He didn't know the geography like the outlaw did and, this way, he could observe their surroundings without drawing scrutiny from Fletcher's man.

"It's a glorious day for a ride, isn't it?" Essie declared, the gloom of moments ago apparently forgotten. "Beautiful sunshine, beautiful countryside."

Tate resisted the urge to roll his eyes. The landscape consisted of nothing but undulating stretches of grass and sagebrush with white, rocky bluffs rising in the near distance. It struck him as rather bleak.

He scrutinized the terrain again in an attempt to see what Essie found fascinating. He supposed the countryside did hold a certain wild beauty to it. And if it wasn't for the potential dangers ahead, Tate had to admit he might actually be able to enjoy himself. He couldn't recall the last time he'd gone for a ride simply for the pleasure of it and not because it was part of a job. Maybe there was something to be said for Essie's skill to see the bright side of things.

That had been Tex's personality. Always looking for the next fun adventure, always trying to make others laugh and enjoy themselves. It wasn't a bad way to live, but Tate had eventually come to resent his brother's wide-eyed optimism. Someone had to be responsible, and as the older twin by five minutes, he'd felt compelled to take up that burden after their father left.

Some responsibility you showed, Tate's head argued back. *Not only does your brother up and leave, but he becomes an outlaw, too.*

Tate frowned. He was doing all he could to right the situation, wasn't he? Steeling himself against further thoughts of Tex, he focused on taking mental notes of the scenery they rode through.

According to his watch, they stopped at noon beside a tiny creek to water the horses and fill their canteens. Silas handed around some jerky and some of Essie's biscuits that Clem had insisted they save for later, despite protests from the others about finishing all of them at breakfast.

Tate had just taken a bite when the sound of rapid horse hooves reached his ears. "Did you hear that?" he asked, swallowing hard.

Silas cocked his head. "Someone's coming."

"I believe it's more than one someone," Essie said.

Sure enough, two riders crested a nearby hill, heading straight for them. Tate squinted against the sun to get a better look. "Who is it?" Was it Fletcher and one of the other outlaws? If so, something must have happened.

"They ain't with us," Silas murmured, his grim expression mirroring the wariness twisting Tate's gut.

"Then who…?" The question died on his tongue as the sunlight reflected off a shiny silver star on the taller stranger's jacket. Tate's uneasiness spiked to alarm. He glanced at Essie and Silas, lunch entirely forgotten. "We've got ourselves a problem."

"What do you mean? Who are they?" When Tate didn't answer, Essie studied the approaching riders more carefully. They weren't dressed like fugitives. In fact, they almost looked like... Something glinted in the sun, momentarily blinding her and making her look away. But she'd caught enough of a glimpse to know one of them wore a sheriff's star.

Fear rolled through her at the realization. The two lawmen were nearly upon them and here she stood with two wanted outlaws. Would she be considered an accomplice? Should she turn Tate and Silas over to them to save herself?

"This isn't going to look good to them," Tate said, glancing at the horses. "If we try to run or split up, they'll just chase after us. But if we wait for them to come to us, what reason can we give for being out here, so far from any town or ranch?"

A flash of memory had Essie peeling off Tate's jacket from around her shoulders and spreading it on the ground. It was a similar trick to one she'd used with her hero in her book *The Lawmen's Legacy*.

"What are you doing?" Tate's voice held exasperated panic.

"Sit," she commanded them both. "We're having a picnic."

Tate stared at her as if she'd grown a second head. "A what?"

"A picnic." She took a seat on the edge of his jacket and motioned for the two men to do the same.

Throwing another look at the lawmen, Silas frowned and sat.

"Mr. Tex? Please join us." She forced herself to take a bite of her jerky, though every sense was attuned to the men on horses less than a hundred yards away. "Now," she snapped.

He pushed out a sigh, his expression full of doubt and dread, but he finally lowered himself onto the ground.

"Eat." She lifted her biscuit to demonstrate, hoping they'd keep playing along. They wouldn't be very convincing if both men kept scowling at her when the lawmen reached them. Then again, most men probably didn't fancy a picnic, especially out here.

"Hello there," one of the riders called out.

Essie swallowed the bite in her mouth, which barely made it down her dry throat. "Hello," she called back. She could feel the tension rolling off the two men next to her.

The lawmen jerked their horses to a stop, though the creatures danced a bit at the sudden drop in speed. "Whatcha folks doing way out here?" the sheriff asked. His dark eyes lingered on each of them in turn. Essie had to remind herself to remain the picture of perfect calm.

"We are having a picnic, Sheriff." She smiled at the two strangers. "Care to join us?"

Tate reached out and squeezed the toe of her shoe, hard, as he nonchalantly bit off a piece of jerky. She furrowed her brow at him, trying to wordlessly communicate the importance of acting as if they were doing the most ordinary thing in the world. And that meant extending an invitation to these two strangers to join them.

Releasing her foot, he seemed to get her message. He lifted his piece of jerky in the air. "We don't have much, but you're welcome to share it."

Essie allowed herself a breath of relief.

The sheriff and his partner, who Essie guessed must be a deputy, eyed their food and shook their heads. "No, thanks," the sheriff said with a chuckle. "Our womenfolk sure know how to fancy up a plain meal, don't they?"

"That they do," Tate agreed, shooting her a brief look. Essie couldn't decipher if he thought her crazy or downright brilliant. Possibly both.

She maintained her smile while silently pleading her plan would work and the men would leave them alone. She couldn't turn Tate and Silas in, not yet. Not when she'd only had one interview—and not the most thorough or helpful one at that. She peered in Tate's direction. If she had to turn him over to the law, would she have the courage to do it? She hoped so, and yet she didn't want that moment of testing to be now.

"What brings you out here?" Tate questioned. She noticed he and Silas kept their hats tugged low, but she had no such way of covering her face. Still, there was no reason why the law would be looking for her. *She* wasn't featured on any Wanted posters.

"We're looking for some train robbers," the deputy said. "Five of them, though we have reason to believe they may have kidnapped a young woman and taken her along with them."

Essie's pulse thrashed harder in her veins. "How horrifying. I hope the young woman is safe."

The sheriff appeared to be studying her carefully, so she kept her chin upturned, her expression as terrified as she felt inside. "So do we, ma'am." He swung out of his saddle and led his horse to the creek. "You folks see anything suspicious?"

"While you've been out here *picnicking*?" The deputy's tone conveyed a good dose of sarcasm. Climbing off his mount, he and the animal joined the sheriff at the water.

Irritation prickled Essie's skin. She might be picnicking with outlaws, but they were picnicking nonetheless. "This is a lovely spot, isn't it? Not many more weeks and long outings such as these will be on hold until spring."

The sheriff removed his hat and ran his sleeve across his forehead. "I reckon you're right, ma'am. These warm autumn days will soon be a thing of the past." He replaced his hat. "You folks from somewhere nearby?"

"I'm not," Essie said before Tate and Silas could speak. She wouldn't lie, and if she could keep the sheriff focused on her, then those with her wouldn't have to lie, either. "I'm here on business."

"Business?" The deputy made a show of looking around them at the nearby hills. "What sort of business brings you way out here?"

She sat straighter. "Writing business. I'm a novelist."

The deputy started to smirk but a glance from his boss silenced him. "What sort of books do you write, ma'am?" the sheriff asked.

"Dime novels. Tales of adventure, woe and romance." She motioned to Tate and Silas. "My friends here have been educating me on life in Wyoming."

"Is that right?" The sheriff looked Tate and Silas over. "They treating you well?"

Another question she could answer honestly, at least at this point. "Yes, sir. Very well."

A long pause followed her answer—one ripe with unspoken questions and searching glances from the sheriff and his deputy.

Uncomfortable strain emanated from Tate and Silas, but Essie hoped the lawmen would blame it on the forced picnic. Just when she thought she might scream from the tension, the sheriff blew out a sigh and gathered the reins of his horse.

"Thank you for your help, folks. I hope your writing goes well, ma'am." He tipped the edge of his hat to her. "If you do run across anything or anyone you find suspicious, you let someone know."

"Will do, sir. And I hope you liberate that young woman soon."

The sheriff and the deputy climbed onto their horses. "Good day, folks," the sheriff called to them. Then they were off, galloping east again.

Essie remained frozen, along with Tate and Silas, her hands clasped in her lap, until the pounding of the hooves grew faint. When she could no longer hear anything but the beating of her own pulse in her ears, she blew out a long breath. Her palms still felt clammy with icy sweat and her lips hurt from smiling in the face of her fear. Never again would she draw a blank when trying to describe her characters' emotions after an encounter with the law.

The hero's heart drummed with alarm at the sight of the sheriff's star. Despite the warm day, a shiver crept over him. His only thought was saving the hero-

ine from any culpability. But how? His fingers itched
for the gun in his holster, but drawing his weapon
would surely—

"Miss Vanderfair?" Tate's voice cracked through
her thoughts like a gunshot. "Essie! You all right?"
His hand settled over hers.

She regarded his strong-looking fingers, the warmth
of his touch sweeping away the cold alarm she'd felt
earlier. "I…I'm fine. Just writing in my head."

"You can still write after that?" he quipped, chuckling as he released her hand. "That was close."

"Too close," Silas added, his face looking more
gray than tan. "Wonder if they ran across Fletch and
the others."

Tate shook his head. "I doubt it, from the direction
they were headed. But that doesn't mean they haven't
got other men on the search."

Silas stood, with less confidence in the movement
than normal. "Good thing we split up, then."

Climbing to his feet, Tate reached out to help Essie
stand. "That stunt you pulled just now…"

She allowed him to help her up then turned away
from him in the direction the lawmen had gone. "I
know. It was risky, but it worked, didn't it?" She crossed
her arms over the bite of disappointment that he didn't
appreciate that she'd saved him—all three of them—
with her quick thinking.

Instead of walking away or continuing to air his
grievances at her harebrained idea, he stepped in front
of her so he was looking her in the eye. "It worked bril-
liantly, Miss Vanderfair." His awed tone sent a cascade
of happiness spilling through her. No one had ever
called anything she'd done brilliant before, except for

maybe Nils. "Where in the world did you come up with that idea?"

"I put it in one of my books." She shot him a smile, a genuine one, not the stiff ones she'd offered the sheriff and his deputy. "Or something similar. In my story, the hero was the lawman and he tricked the villains into thinking he and his deputy were simply having a picnic while passing through. It wasn't until the bad men sat to join them that the hero pulled out his gun—and his badge."

"Guess it works both ways." He matched her smile. "You know, you are something else, Miss Vanderfair," he said, shaking his head as he scooped up his jacket. "Who knew you had such a bag of tricks inside that pretty little head of yours?"

Essie gaped at him. Had he just called her pretty? Her? Heat filled her cheeks. "I guess looks can be deceiving."

"More than you know," he murmured, though she wasn't sure she'd heard him right. Especially when he frowned and fell back a step. "We'd better get going." Silas had already remounted.

"Right." She exhaled to clear away any lingering emotions from their tense encounter with the law. And those stirred by this handsome outlaw before her.

She moved to her horse, but before she could get a shoe in the stirrup, Tate came over to assist her. "Thank you," she whispered, trying to ignore the feel of his grip at her waist.

As she swung up into the saddle, he bent close. "I appreciate what you did. But why didn't you take the chance to save yourself by turning us in? Why did you play along?" His blue eyes were troubled, his brow creased.

Essie fingered the reins. "I need these interviews."

"Fine. But at what risk?"

"Let's go, Tex," Silas said, frowning from atop his horse several yards away. "We need some distance between us and those lawmen."

"Coming." Tate shot her another look and started to turn away.

"My publisher has threatened to stop publishing my books." The words were out before Essie could pull them back. "I've got to write something far better than anything I've written before or I'm sunk. These interviews could mean the difference between success and failure. That's why I played along."

He studied her a long moment, making her squirm a little in the saddle. Did he approve or not? She tipped her chin up, reminding herself that whatever he thought, she wasn't going anywhere. Especially after her less-than-stellar interview with him.

"I suppose that makes sense." He glanced down at his hands. "But I hate to think that was your one chance to…to stay safe."

A shiver of dread ran up Essie's back. Did he somehow suspect that no ransom would be paid for her safe return? No, he couldn't know that. But if Tate was concerned about her safety, should she be more so? She clutched the reins tighter, causing her horse to dance to the side.

"Whoa, boy." She patted the animal's neck to soothe him and take a moment to calm herself. "I'll be fine," she said to Tate. "Haven't I been so far?"

Amusement lit his gaze. "Yes, you have. And quite

ingeniously so." But before he turned away to mount his horse, Essie caught sight of his tense expression.

Perhaps she'd best get her interviews done sooner than later. And there was no time like the present to get to work. "Mr. Silas," she called out as she rode past Tate.

The other outlaw twisted and glanced back at her. "Yes, ma'am?"

"Will you allow me to interview you? While we ride?"

He appeared to think it over, his mouth turned down a bit at the sides. Would he refuse? She hadn't exactly received verbal consent from any of them but Fletcher to answer her questions. Then he dipped his head in a decisive nod. "After what you done back there, ma'am, I'd be mighty ungrateful if I didn't let you interview me."

Triumph whooshed through Essie's veins and out her lips in the form of a laugh. She'd thrown off the lawmen, for the time being, and Silas would submit to her questioning. Things were going well and it was only her second day. It was all too easy to brush aside Tate's earlier concern. She was going to be just fine.

Chapter Six

Feminine laughter floated back to Tate, jerking him from his half-dazed state. His less-than-restorative sleep the night before was finally catching up to him. Sitting straighter in the saddle, he eyed Essie and Silas up ahead. He'd dropped back to give them a little privacy when he realized Essie intended to interview the outlaw.

Another laugh reached his ears, but it didn't come from Essie this time. It was Silas who was laughing. How in the world had Essie coaxed anything more than silence from the man?

Tate watched them another moment as they conversed. And then it wasn't Silas and Essie riding in front of him anymore. It was Tex and Ravena. He could see their faces so clearly, open and trusting and happy, that he had to blink to make sure they weren't real.

Frowning, he averted his gaze and scowled at the surrounding hills. His twin brother and the pretty dime novelist had at least one thing in common—neither took life seriously. How many times had Tex joshed him for being too serious, too solemn? Even Ravena, who was far more like him than she was Tex, had urged Tate to find more joy in the world and the people around him.

Joy, he scoffed to himself. Where was joy found in a war-injured father who gambled away their money faster than the farm could bring it in, then up and left them in the dead of winter? Where was joy when his mother lost her fight against illness and a broken heart? Where was joy when his own brother left him unconscious and bleeding in the dirt to run off and embrace a life of crime?

His jaw tightened at the painful march of memories through his mind. He'd learned early on that someone had to gravely face the world and its ills—and that someone had been him.

"You are older than your years," his mother used to say with a note of love and regret. On the other hand, Tex was always known as "the spark of joy" in her life. The one who could nimbly laugh at the world, who needed sheltering from its cruelties. Until those cruelties caught up to him.

Tate wondered again where Tex had ended up. Was his twin still alive? He swallowed hard at the possibility he might be the only Beckett still living. Though he hadn't seen Tex in eight years, at least he'd known his brother was out there, mostly from the Texas Titan's exploits he'd read about in the paper. And while everything in him abhorred his brother's decisions, there'd been comfort there, too, knowing a part of his family, a part of himself, still existed out in the world.

He tried loosening the viselike muscles of his jaw,

but tension still rippled off him. What was it about this trip that had his thoughts turning to the past, to Tex, again and again? Even after taking on his brother's name and persona, he'd managed to keep most of his memories buried, but not these last two days.

Up ahead Silas and Essie had slowed. It was probably time to rest the horses again. But the thought of standing around, talking, didn't suit Tate's black mood. Back in his teenage years, he'd have grabbed his gun and gone hunting. Sometimes he shot something; sometimes he didn't. It didn't really matter—it was the chance to be alone, with God and nature, that restored his spirits. Perhaps he needed the same thing today.

"I'm going to see if I can find something more for Clem to cook than beans," he announced, climbing off his horse. Silas and Essie had already dismounted.

"Sounds good to me." Silas actually shot him a half smile as he gathered the horses' reins. The man appeared more relaxed than Tate had ever seen him.

Tate shouldered his rifle. "I won't be long." He checked his pocket watch. "Thirty minutes at the most."

"May I come along?" Essie asked.

He wanted to refuse, to insist he have a moment's peace, alone. But the open, expectant look on her face made him bite back the words.

"If you keep up," he conceded as he started walking.

Not that he had any doubts she wouldn't. Once again, Essie Vanderfair was proving herself exceptionally adept. She'd saved him earlier from ruining his disguise—and his entire mission—with her fast thinking.

He heard Essie's soft steps behind him, but she didn't speak for a few minutes. Searching the surrounding countryside, Tate hoped to find a rabbit or a grouse. Why, even a gopher or two would bring some welcome meat to their nightly fare of beans and biscuits.

"How well do you know Silas?"

"I only met him when I joined up with Fletcher."

"Hmm," Essie murmured. "He's an interesting man."

"He warmed up to talking to you."

She gave a soft smirk. "Really? What's he normally like?"

He stopped walking to let her catch up. "The man is as silent as the grave most of the time. Have you heard him say more than ten words since you joined us?"

Essie looked thoughtful. "Well, I've only been with you for a day, but I suppose you're right." She strolled past him, a small smile on her lips. "Though he had plenty to say during our ride."

Her remark hung in the air, begging for him to question it further. Tate puffed out a sigh. So much for the peace and quiet of hunting alone. "What did he have to say?"

"Far more than you did," she said, but her tone conveyed only amusement. "Do you know he used to be a groomsman at a mansion in Boston?"

Tate glanced back over his shoulder at Silas in the distance, surprised to hear this detail about the other man's past. Then again, where Fletcher and his comrades had come from or what they'd done before robbing trains and banks was also a mystery to him. "No, I didn't know that."

"What's more, he fell ardently in love with his employer's youngest daughter," Essie continued eagerly. "And the daughter fell equally in love with him. For two years they kept their mutual understanding a secret. But, of course, they came from two completely different stations in life and that was bound to cause trouble sooner or later."

"So what happened?" Tate asked almost without thought. The way her voice and words wove the story left him eager for more and made him wonder what her dime novels were like.

She sighed, her gaze distant. "They decided to elope and head west together. A night for their escape was set, and Silas, who'd been setting aside a little money every month, was ready and impatient to make her his bride." Essie shot Tate a pained smile. "But it wasn't meant to be. Another servant, who also admired this daughter, discovered the plot and told the girl's father. When Silas went to meet his beloved at the appointed place, his employer was waiting there instead."

Tate felt a familiar jab of pain in his chest. He'd seen how loving the same girl could make waves. "What did the father do?"

"He fired Silas on the spot and forbade him from ever seeing his daughter again. Heartbroken, Silas managed to get a note to her, informing her that he was still heading west as they'd planned. She wrote back that she was determined to join him, if he would only send a ticket." Essie slowed to a stop and folded her arms. Tate stopped, as well.

"So, did she join him?"

With a shake of her head, she continued the story. "He sent the ticket but she mailed it back, claiming she no longer loved him and was marrying someone else."

Essie began walking again, prompting Tate to move forward, too. He sensed the story wasn't completely over. "Silas still doesn't know what really happened to her—if she did change her mind about loving him and married another or not. Perhaps her father intercepted their letters and it was him who penned those lines to discourage Silas. It happened fifteen years ago, but the pain on Silas's face as he told me the story was as raw as if it was only yesterday she turned him down."

Tate whistled softly in disbelief. At least he'd known with certainty where he stood with Ravena. He'd made peace with that. He couldn't imagine the anguish of never knowing.

"He said after that he stopped caring about everything and everyone. After drifting across the country, he wound up in a card game with Fletcher. Silas lost all of his money but Fletcher liked him and, after one too many drinks, Silas spilled everything about his past, including his way with horses. Fletcher recruited him, and Silas wasn't in a position to say no. He was the last member to join Fletcher's gang."

"And he told you all of that?" Tate couldn't believe such a story had poured from a man who rarely strung more than a few words together at a time.

Essie laughed. "Yes, he shared the entire story himself. No supposition on my part."

Her happy peal of laughter reminded Tate of earlier, but this time he felt no irritation. "What had the two of you laughing before we stopped? I've never even seen Silas crack a smile, let alone a chuckle."

"Oh, he was telling me how scared he was the first time they robbed a train. He dropped his gun and nearly shot his own toe in the process. I asked if I ought to make my outlaw characters more afraid." She threw him a smile. "And he said, 'well, maybe just a little.'"

At that moment, Tate realized how far they'd walked, but he hadn't been paying attention to the ground or any potential catches for their supper. He'd been completely caught up in Essie's storytelling. And her ability to get the silent outlaw to share the whole thing.

He was starting to see he'd been mistaken in thinking her nosy the day before. Essie wasn't being meddlesome in asking her questions—she had genuine interest in people's answers and stories. And that interest had changed Silas from a man of stoicism to one of half smiles and laughter this afternoon. She had a gift, though Tate suspected she didn't know it.

"Tate, look," Essie whispered, placing her hand on his arm to stop him.

For a moment he was more fascinated in studying the petite fingers seeping warmth through his sleeve than he was over what she'd discovered.

"Do you see it?"

He pulled his attention from her hand and looked in the direction she was pointing. There, beside a squatty sagebrush, stood a grouse as still as a rock, poised to scurry at any second.

He'd have to add hunting to Essie's list of skills.

"Well done," he murmured with a chuckle as he brought the gun to his shoulder and aimed. His mood had taken a definite upturn in the last thirty minutes—and not just from the promise of a real meal. Essie's company had proved to be more of a boon than a burden. And for that he'd be doubly grateful.

With a belly full of more than biscuits and burned beans, Essie happily scribbled her interview with Silas into her notebook. Tate had insisted on cooking the grouse and had done a fine job. The meat had tasted wonderful.

"You don't think those lawmen suspected a thing?" Fletcher asked. It was the same question he'd posed before dinner when he and the others had rejoined her, Tate and Silas.

Tate shook his head. "Nope. They're long gone by now."

"What'd you say?"

Pausing in the middle of penning a sentence, Essie held her breath, wondering how much Tate would tell of her quick thinking. She felt more than saw Tate's gaze settle on her, and then he cleared his throat.

"I...uh...pretended we were passing through, having a jolly ol' picnic."

The breath left her mouth in a squeak. Silas cut her a quick look before lowering his head and staring into the fire. Why had Tate taken the credit for her actions? She gripped her pencil harder, marking the page with a thick, dark dot.

Fletcher hooted. "A picnic? Now, that's funny. Did the sheriff buy it?"

"Completely," Tate said, though his tone sounded a bit strained. "You sure you didn't see anything suspicious on your ride?"

"I told you already, cowboy. The only person we ran across today was some drifter. But he proved a boon to cross paths with. Am I right, boys?" he called to Clem and Jude. The two men murmured agreement. There was a shuffling noise as Fletcher pulled something from his saddlebag. Essie looked up to see it was a shiny flask. "Paid a pretty penny for this but figured it was worth it." He sloshed the thin bottle. It sounded half full.

Tate's face darkened. "You used some of the train money to buy that?"

"Sure did." Fletcher scowled. "You gotta problem with that, cowboy? I'm thinkin' maybe you just forfeited your chance to join us in a round."

"I wasn't going to drink anyway," Tate grumbled.

"Good. More for us." Fletcher tipped the flask back and guzzled several swallows. When he'd finished, he smeared the back of his hand across his mouth. "Your turn, Clem."

Would they all get drunk? It didn't sound as if Tate was joining them. But still… Uneasiness drove Essie to her feet, her notebook and blanket hugged tightly to her chest.

"Where are you going, Miss Vanderfair?" Fletcher said, his brow furrowed.

She swallowed her dry throat. "Just over there." She indicated a spot ten feet from the campfire. It would be cooler and harder to write without the fire's bright light, but she didn't want to remain in the middle of their company as they became inebriated.

"Fine." The outlaw leader shooed her away. "Another teetotaler," he muttered with a shake of his head.

Keeping her chin up, Essie found a level spot of ground and took a seat. She swept her blanket around her shoulders then patted her boot, where her gun was still stowed, to reassure herself she wasn't completely defenseless.

Now back to work. She opened her notebook and picked up her pencil, but before she could resume writing, Tate approached her.

Essie squinted at the page in front of her. She wouldn't look at or acknowledge him. Maybe then he'd get the hint she didn't want to talk to him. Not after he'd claimed her idea as his own.

To her dismay, he settled next to her. "You're angry."

It wasn't a question but she stated flatly, "Yes, I am."

"At me?"

"Naturally."

He lifted his knees and rested his elbows on them. "I had a reason for telling Fletcher what I did."

"I'm sure you did," she shot back, vainly trying to remember the last thing she'd been writing before walking away.

A deep chuckle washed over her. "Do you want to know the reason?"

Pushing out an irritated sigh, she tossed down her pencil and lifted her head. "Do I have a choice?"

He offered her an amused smile. One that made her traitorous heart leap a bit in response. But the smile fell a moment later as he stared in the direction of the men seated around the fire. "Don't underestimate Fletcher. He's ruthless and conniving. That makes for a dangerous combination." He shifted his gaze to hers. "I thought it might be safer for you to let him think I came up with the plan today."

Essie fiddled with the corner of her notebook, her anger deflating beneath the concern she saw in his blue eyes. "Safer how?"

"I don't want him knowing how skilled you are. He might take advantage of that."

His warning unsettled her, reminding her of his words earlier about keeping her safe, but she was also grateful for his good sense and fast thinking. She studied the men on the other side of the camp. They were talking loudly and laughing more freely as they passed the flask around. And yet here sat Tate—looking out for her, talking to her, choosing not to participate in the jovial drinking.

She glanced over at him, at the serious expression furrowing his handsome face. When had she begun to trust him, to think of him as a friend? A spike of panic drove its way through her heart at the realization. How could she trust an outlaw? Because that was what he was, in spite of his help and protection the last two days. Once she had her interviews and was on her way back to Evanston, he would still be an outlaw, living a life of crime and forever dodging the law.

"Am I forgiven?" he asked, scattering her thoughts. His tone held a mixture of gravity and teasing.

Essie blew out a sigh. While he might be an outlaw, he was still a person, with feelings and experiences. A person beloved by his Father in Heaven. Just as she was.

"Yes." She picked up her pencil again and tapped it against the page. "Can I ask you a question?"

"I expected no less when I came over here."

She smiled. It was impossible to stay annoyed with a man who was doing his best to protect her and keep her spirits up. "How come you chose not to drink? Was that for my benefit?"

Picking up a small stick, he rotated it around his

knuckles, back and forth, back and forth. "I don't drink," he finally said, his voice low. "Never have—never will."

"An admirable quality, though a bit unconventional in an outlaw." She might have to give that trait to her train-robber hero.

He shrugged, not missing a beat in twirling the stick. "I guess you could say I'm an unconventional outlaw."

Essie laughed. "I won't disagree with you there."

"You writing down your interview with Silas?"

She nodded. "His story was a far cry from what I'd imagined it might be."

"What did you imagine?" Tate switched the stick to his other hand and began rotating it again.

"I'm not sure, exactly. Certainly less cultured than his upbringing sounded, less heartache, maybe. More adventure and revenge."

"I'm guessing Fletcher's story might have more of the latter."

She sniffed in agreement, her attention riveted on his trick. "How do you do that?"

He looked startled. "Do what?"

"Twist the stick like that."

Tate looked down as if he'd forgotten all about the stick spinning over and under his knuckles. "Oh, it's easy. Something my father taught me, actually…"

The father who'd up and left his family when Tate was nine. Sadness choked the air between them. Another reminder that these men weren't what she'd expected. Had it only been two days since she'd insisted she ride along with them? It felt more like two weeks.

The stick had stopped moving. Essie reached out and plucked it from him. "Will you teach me how?"

She did want to learn, but she also wanted to see him relax again.

She couldn't read the emotion in his blue eyes when he looked at her. But his shoulders rose in another shrug. "All right, though I can't guarantee you'll get it."

"You just said it was easy," she protested, though she was laughing.

He grinned. "Only because I've been doing it for years." He scooted closer to her, his solid presence chasing away the cold. "To start, you grip the stick between your thumb and finger."

Essie followed his instructions.

"Then you place your next finger under the stick and rotate it."

She tried but ended up dropping the stick in the process.

"It's okay. Hold it again." This time his fingers slid over hers, capturing them and the stick. Essie's pulse jumped at his touch. His hand felt wonderful and natural clasped over her own. "I'll help you."

"I can't," she whispered, bringing her gaze to his.

Was it her imagination or had his eyes darkened?

"Why not?" Tate asked, but his voice didn't sound any steadier than hers. His thumb began tracing circles on the back of her hand.

Only inches separated them, she thought, unable to resist composing in her mind a similar moment for her story. *All the hero had to do was lean forward to cross the trifling distance. The heroine's heart galloped as she waited in breathless anticipation for the kiss she knew would...*

Shaking herself back to reality, which surely did

not include being kissed by Tate, Essie forced a light laugh. It sounded more like a strangled cough. "Your hand is covering mine."

He glanced down. "Ah…right." To her disappointment, he pulled his hand away. "Sorry. It's probably easier to just try it on your own."

Essie frowned, hoping Tate would think it was in concentration. But inside she felt befuddled and annoyed. She couldn't let herself enjoy this man's company.

He's an outlaw. Try to remember that, Essie.

Channeling her determination into the trick, she began rotating the stick, slowly at first and then with more speed. "I got it." She performed the act for Tate.

"Look at that." He shot her a crooked smile. "It took me longer than one lesson. You sure you've never done this before?"

Nudging his firm shoulder with her own felt like the most natural thing in the world for her to do. But the inherent familiarity in such a gesture also made her blush. Thankfully he probably wouldn't notice in the dim light. "No, I've never done it before."

He tipped up the brim of his hat and leaned back on his hands. "Another skill you've mastered quicker than I would have expected."

"What did you expect?" she countered, hiding a smile at his veiled compliment. She twirled the stick around her fingers again and then switched to try it with her left hand.

Tate laughed. "I expected trouble." He shrugged. "Maybe some helplessness. A little crying."

Clasping the stick to her palm, she pivoted to face him directly. "I hardly ever cry and I rarely find myself in completely helpless situations." She cocked her head. "However, I, too, expected some trouble. From you." He threw her another pulse-skipping smile that only confirmed Essie's words. If she fell for this man, there would be trouble indeed.

"I ought to let you get back to your writing."

"Oh...yes."

She set aside the stick to pick up her pencil, though she wished he would stay nearby. His company was more welcome than that of the others drinking around the campfire. *But it's more than that*, her heart argued. She liked talking with Tate, liked teasing him, liked earning his respect and feeling his equal.

Tate didn't make a move to stand. He didn't seem to want to leave her any more than she wanted him to go. Essie's heart pumped faster with wild hope, even as she tried to squelch it. The man probably only wanted to avoid the drunken revelry on the other side of the camp.

"You're welcome to stay here," she found herself offering, though she didn't look at him, "if you want. I can write just fine alone or with company."

He hesitated a moment. "All right. If you're sure."

"Quite sure." Essie began writing again, but she found herself more distracted than she'd been before. Her focus kept straying to Tate seated silently beside her, a faraway look on his face. What was he thinking? Could it possibly be about her?

Cheeks flushing, she forced her mind to return to Silas's story as she wrote down every detail. Sometime later she realized the camp no longer rang with loud exclamations and uproarious laughter. She lifted her chin to find the other four outlaws sprawled out and sleeping around the dying campfire.

"They're all passed out," Tate said with a sniff. "Good thing Fletcher didn't assign any of them guard duty tonight."

Essie shut her notebook. "Do you think that's wise? Not to have anyone guarding the camp?" While she was grateful the ruckus had died down and she wouldn't have a drunken guard keeping watch as she slept, she still worried a little about the lawmen finding them again.

"I'll wait up another hour or so," he said, as if reading her thoughts. "Though we ought to move closer to the fire."

The urge to kiss his cheek in gratitude all but overwhelmed her. But Essie fought it back with stern reminders of the futility of such a gesture. Before he could help her stand and resurrect her frantic heartbeat with his touch, she climbed to her feet. "Thank you, Tate."

He stood, his gaze alighting on her face. "You're welcome, Essie."

She didn't think she'd ever tire of hearing him say her name.

She followed him back to where the others noisily slept. After stowing away her notebook, she wrapped herself tightly in her blanket. She selected a spot slightly apart from the inebriated outlaws and lay down. Tate fed more wood to the flames then settled a foot or two away from Essie.

Though he said nothing more to her, she felt comfort at knowing he was nearby. She shut her eyes and, unlike the night before, found sleep within easy reach.

* * *

The next morning Fletcher informed all of them that they would be traveling as a group for the first time since leaving the train. Essie wasn't sure whether she welcomed the new arrangement or not. It was easier to converse with Tate when it was only two or three of them riding together. But perhaps some distance between her and the handsome outlaw would be good.

That didn't mean she wanted him riding bareback, however. It was her turn to do without the saddle. While the others were busy finishing off a fresh batch of her biscuits, she slipped away to put the saddle on Tate's horse.

Before she could finish cinching the straps, though, a deep voice demanded, "What do you think you're doing?"

Essie squeaked in surprise and whirled around to find Tate watching her sternly, his arms crossed over his chest. "Giving you the saddle," she said as she turned back to the horse.

"I didn't ask for it."

"I know." Her fingers fumbled a bit under his scrutiny, but she was determined.

"Essie." He reached out and placed his hand over hers, stilling her frenzied movements. "I appreciate the thought, but I'm perfectly capable of going without a saddle for less than a full day's ride."

She seized upon his words to keep from drowning in his warmth and nearness. "What do you mean less than a full day?" she asked as she gently removed her hand from beneath his.

A flicker of something filled his blue eyes before

he shuttered it. Could it be disappointment? Inwardly she shook her head.

"Fletcher says we're to stay the night at a ranch about twenty miles south of Casper. Which means we'll be riding between fifteen and twenty miles total today."

"Who owns the ranch? Is it safe to stay there?" Images tromped through her mind of a lawmen's ambush when they arrived. Perhaps she ought to write that into her book, too.

Tate pulled the saddle off his horse. "I don't know who owns it. I've never been there. Some family who's partial to outlaws and not the law, according to Fletcher. I think we'll be fine."

"*We'll* be fine," Essie said, grabbing the other end of the saddle, "if you'll stop being stubborn and let me put this back on your horse."

"Me, stubborn?" A half grin lit his whiskered face. Most facial hair reminded Essie of Harrison, but Tate's beard had grown on her. She rather liked the rugged look on him. "And what if I don't agree to take the saddle today?"

She lifted her chin. "Then I won't be riding with you," she said before motioning to the others. "Any of you."

"I think I can live with that." He fully grinned as he jerked the saddle from her hands and placed it on her mount. "Can you?" he quipped. "You still have three more interviews to conduct, don't you?"

"You know full well I do." She crossed her arms and scowled at him, hating that he'd outmaneuvered her and they both knew it. "Can't let a girl be kind, can you?" she snapped.

He leaned close, his breath fingering her cheek. "Can't let a man be a gentleman, can you?"

Essie met his level look head-on, but after a long moment of peering into those sky blue eyes, her frustration began to fizzle away. "All right, you win."

When he started to smile, she pressed a finger to his mouth to stop the self-satisfied gesture. The arch of his masculine mouth against her fingertip felt wonderfully nice. "But…" She gave him a firm look. "You either procure a saddle at this ranch we're going to or we switch off who rides bareback from here to your hideout. Deal?"

Freeing her finger and taking her hand in his, Tate pressed a brief kiss to the back of her palm, his gaze never leaving hers. "Deal."

For the second time in so many minutes Essie slid her fingers out from under his, though her heart continued to race as if he were still holding her hand. She gathered her horse's reins and pulled in a full breath of the cool morning air.

"Thanks for the saddle. I believe I'll ride by Clem today and interview him." With that, she led her horse away from Tate and the mess of feelings and thoughts he was beginning to inspire.

Chapter Seven

Swallowing a groan of annoyance at himself, Tate watched Essie lead her horse to where the others had just finished breaking camp. It was time to go. He swung onto the back of his horse, wincing slightly at the ache from the long ride yesterday. But he felt no regret over letting Essie use the saddle again.

It was the least he owed her after kissing the back of her hand. He might have enjoyed the feel of her hand against his lips, but he didn't have the right to pursue this attraction he felt for her. So what had compelled him to do what he'd done? It didn't take him long to reason out the answer.

He'd been surprised but delighted by her determination to let him have the saddle. After being on his own for so long, without family around, he'd forgotten how nice it felt to have someone do something out of genuine kindness.

And maybe something more?

Tate drove the thought from his mind as he nudged his horse to fall in line behind the others. Essie had also looked downright adorable with that determined glint in her greenish-brown eyes, thinking she'd gained the upper hand by brokering a deal with him. One look at her pretty face and he couldn't resist the desire to steal some of her thunder with an innocent kiss.

But it wasn't completely innocent. He'd thought about kissing her ever since last night when she'd figured out that silly trick with the stick in no time at all. The more time he spent with her, the more his admiration for her grew. And yet there was nothing he could do about it. Pursuing Essie, while on an assignment, could prove dangerous for both of them. Which brought him right back to the annoyance he felt at himself for falling under her spell in the first place.

Tate pried his gaze from his horse's ears and realized he was falling behind. Urging the animal to go faster, he kept the horse at a trot to match the speed of the others. Apparently, Fletcher hoped to reach the ranch sooner than later.

He reminded himself he needed to pay more attention to the landscape and to these outlaws and less to a certain pretty dime novelist. At least Essie's interviews had already provided him with helpful information about Fletcher's gang.

You're trying to do everything on your own, Tate. The memory of his mother's gentle voice entered his mind. *You need God and He needs you. Never forget that.* Her tender entreaty felt like a balm to his current troubled thoughts. He hadn't done much to include God in his plans the last few weeks or so.

Glancing around to make sure no one was paying him heed, he lowered his chin and shut his eyes, grateful he was at the back of the group. "Bless my efforts," he prayed aloud, though he kept the words to a whisper. "Let this mission be successful, Lord. Amen."

The stranglehold of doubt and discouragement released its grip on him as he raised his head and blew out a cleansing breath. Of its own volition, his gaze went directly to Essie riding up ahead, next to Clem. The sun shone down on her smile, making her appear as if she were lit from the inside. As Tate stared at her, something inside him shifted, something he thought he'd locked behind an iron door.

Even if he couldn't do anything more than be her friend and protector, he would do both to the best of his ability. "Watch over her, too," he added with a look toward the blue sky. Then, with renewed purpose, he spurred his horse forward to face whatever the day brought their way.

"Tell me about your family growing up, Clem."

The outlaw cook squinted at the white clouds overhead. "Nothing much to tell, ma'am. Had me a ma and a pa and a whole passel of brothers and sisters."

Essie smiled. "I have a whole passel of siblings, too." She nudged her horse closer to his so she wouldn't miss any of his answers. "Did you feel like you fit in with your family?"

"Suppose so. Though I ain't ever had a place at school. Too stupid." He shrugged his shoulders as if his words were truth.

Maybe to him they were.

She felt a keen sadness at the possibility. While the man might not be scholarly, he did possess an innate openness and kindness. "Did you finish school?"

"No, ma'am," Clem said with a laugh. "I done quit

after the fourth grade. Though it didn't matter none. The cholera come through a few years later and took out the whole family, 'cept me and my older brother Pete."

Her sorrow transformed into immediate horror as Essie gaped at him. "You lost your entire family to illness?"

"Yep. So my brother and me, we walked for a few days till we come to this ranch. We worked as cowhands there." Clem adjusted his hat, his face thoughtful. "It wasn't a bad life."

Essie swallowed and forced a nod. She couldn't imagine losing her whole family and having to fend for herself. "What led you from there to here?" She waved her arm to include the other outlaws.

"Pete used to go to the saloon, though he never let me come along. He didn't much care for the cards or dance-hall girls. Just liked a good stiff drink now and then." His voice held a trace of grief and somberness as he recalled the long-ago memories. "He came onto this big fellow roughin' up a saloon girl. Pete stepped in to help her and the man pulled out a gun. My brother was a crack shot and he had his gun drawn and fired before the other fella knew what happened."

Clem rubbed a hand over his whiskered chin. A few white hairs attested to his aging, but he still rode and moved with the agility of a twenty-year-old. "When Pete realized the man was dead, he got spooked. He hurried back to the ranch and said we had to steal two horses and leave. The girl had been knocked clean out and hadn't seen any of it. So with no proof the other man drew first, Pete thought he'd be wanted for murder."

"Is that what you did? Stole two horses and left?" Essie prompted when silence followed his words.

Clem seemed to shake himself then straighten in the saddle. "That we did, ma'am. Stole two of the ranch's fastest horses and we hightailed it outta there. We hid out for a few months before Pete up and decides we gotta steal us a horse that we can sell so we don't go starving. We did and that kept us fed for a time, until…"

Essie sensed another awful turn in Clem's past. "Until?"

"Pete got shot and killed when we tried stealing us another horse. I couldn't even stick around to bury him." He brushed at his eyes with his thumb before his face hardened. Essie hadn't seen such a harsh expression on him before. "I swore I'd get back at the man who killed Pete. So I asked around to see who else hated him and found Fletcher. We lay low for two weeks, then went back and started taking his livestock. Over the next year, we stole every one of his horses and cattle. Finally he tucked tail and went back east."

Though greatly relieved Clem hadn't killed the other man to avenge Pete's death, Essie felt sorry for both Clem and the man who'd been robbed of his livelihood just for trying to defend his property. A frown pulled at her mouth as she compared Clem's story with that of Silas's and what she knew of Tate's.

"I'm so sorry, Clem." She hoped he knew how much she meant it. "About your brother and everything. That must have been incredibly difficult."

The man shrugged. "It's all in the past, ma'am.

And while this ain't always the best life, it's what I know and it's mine."

"Where did you learn to cook?" Essie asked, hoping to ease the shroud of pain still surrounding him.

Sure enough, Clem cracked a smile. "I picked up a few things watchin' my ma all those years ago. And good thing, too. Pete's beans were a thousand times worse than mine."

So he knew his cooking wasn't first-rate, but he tried anyway. The thought made Essie want to weep as well as smile. "I'm grateful for your abilities, Clem. I'm sure the others are, too."

"Can't say they don't prefer your biscuits."

"But man cannot live on biscuits alone."

They shared a laugh. "Anything else you need to know, ma'am?"

"I would love to know which outlaw heist you feel was the most exciting and which was the most dangerous."

For the next while, Clem regaled her with stories from his outlawing career. Once their conversation and her questions wore out, Essie smiled at him with genuine gratitude. "Thank you for telling me your story, Clem."

Tipping his hat to her, he moved on ahead to join Fletcher at the front of the group. Essie glanced behind her to see Tate taking up the rear. He seemed content to stay there today, and while she could see the wisdom in it, she longed to talk to him. Maybe he could help her sort out her jumbled thoughts at the moment.

These men's lives, past and present, weren't what she'd expected. They'd seen and experienced hard, painful things. Losing loved ones, losing homes, losing livelihoods. Outlawing wasn't the adventurous, carefree career she'd imagined or unknowingly penned into her novels. These men weren't characters from some book. They were people with feelings, regrets, hopes and fears. Just like her.

And if she'd been wrong about them, what else might she also be wrong about?

"The ranch is just up ahead," Fletcher announced, a rare grin brightening his face. "I can taste Winny's flapjacks and bacon now."

Tate's stomach grumbled at the mention of food. Their meager lunch of jerky and biscuits, several hours ago, had worn off too soon and now he was starving again. The thought of real food, a roof overhead and a chance to shave his beard spurred him forward behind the others. Even Essie had perked up at Fletcher's declaration.

She'd been more quiet than usual during their ride today. Of course, she still smiled and laughed and seemed generally pleased to have completed another interview. Tate noticed she appeared more somber, though, whenever she thought no one was watching. He'd asked her at lunch if she was all right. But Essie simply waved off his question, declaring herself to be fine.

Perhaps she was only fatigued. Three days in a saddle could do that to a person. She'd likely feel better after a full supper and a good night's sleep on something other than the hard ground.

After a few minutes the ranch came into view, nestled among the surrounding mountains beside a wide river. Tate blinked in surprise. Instead of the simple, one-room cabin he'd been expecting, a large, two-story house with a wide porch and several out-buildings stood before them.

Fletcher hadn't said much in answer to Essie's questions during lunch about the family who owned the ranch. The father had been killed years ago and his wife, two daughters and their ranch hands now looked after the place themselves. Clearly they were doing well, even though they occasionally harbored outlaws and provided them with fresh horses and room and board for a night or two. Tate had been stunned to learn there were seemingly decent people around here who didn't see anything wrong with aiding criminals.

Had there been a family similar to this one who'd helped his brother out on occasion? While Tate didn't condone such actions, he found himself almost hoping such a scenario might be true. Then Tex wouldn't have been completely on his own the last eight years. *Not like me.* Was his brother holed up even now with some outlaw-friendly folks somewhere?

The moment the group ground to a halt, the door swung open and two women stepped outside. "Mr. Fletcher!" The oldest, a woman with pepper-colored hair and graceful features, approached them with a smile as she dried her hands on a towel. "It's been a long time."

Fletcher swung out of his saddle. "That it has, ma'am." The outlaw removed his hat, but his eyes weren't on the matron of the family. They'd settled on the younger woman with chestnut hair who watched Fletcher with equal abandon. "Winny."

"Fletch." She gazed shyly at him, her red lips tipped upward.

Chuckling at the obvious interest between the outlaw leader and the young woman, Tate dismounted before helping Essie down, as well. Then he helped Silas gather up the horses' reins.

"You've brought a woman this time." The older woman walked forward toward Essie. "I'm Adelaide Paige. And this is my daughter Winnifred." Winnifred nodded in acknowledgment, but she was frowning. "Welcome to the BC Ranch."

"Thank you." Essie shook hands with Mrs. Paige. "My name is Essie."

"She's along to interview us," Fletcher explained, his eyes on Winnifred once more. The other girl visibly relaxed. "But she won't use any of our real names in her books."

Mrs. Paige looked surprised. "You're an author, then?"

"Yes. A dime novelist." Essie stood a little taller, her chin jutting out as if ready to do battle for her profession.

Tate swallowed another chuckle. She was more than just an author—she was smart, pretty, trail savvy, a good cook, kind… He tried to push the errant thoughts away.

"Well, if we let the likes of these men stay here, I suppose we can let a dime novelist, too." Mrs. Paige offered Essie a grin and then motioned for her to come into the house. "We'll let them take the horses to the barn, while we start laying out supper."

At that moment, another girl came out onto the porch. This one appeared to be a year or two younger than Winnifred and had dark, flowing hair. She was quite beautiful but Tate had no desire to stick around for any more of the introductions. He wasn't interested in getting to know any girls.

Except one, his heart argued before he wrestled the idea away.

Besides, he was hungry, and the sooner they saw to the horses, the sooner he could see to his own supper. Silas was already moving toward the barn, and Tate followed, leading two of the horses.

From behind, he heard Mrs. Paige introduce the other girl to Essie. "This is Isabelle. She's my youngest—"

A high-pitched squeal pierced the air, causing the horses to jerk their heads in surprise. Tate held on to keep them from bolting and turned to see the cause of the ruckus.

Isabelle came charging off the porch, heading straight for him. "Tex! I knew you'd come back. I just knew it."

Tate froze, panic filling his veins with ice. How in the world did she know his brother? When had Tex come so far north? Before he could recover from the shock, Isabelle cupped his face between her hands and pressed her mouth to his in a firm kiss.

Fighting alarm, Tate eased back. Hopefully his hat and the setting sun would hide the flush creeping up his neck. "Hello, Isabelle," he managed to croak out from his suddenly dry throat. "It's been…what…a few months?"

"Over four," she crooned, fingering the top button of his shirt. "And you promised not to forget me."

He swallowed hard. "Did I?"

"I thought you looked familiar," Mrs. Paige said. "Welcome back, Tex."

"Thank you, ma'am."

He caught Fletcher watching him, though it appeared to be with more curiosity than suspicion. "You've been here before, cowboy? How come you didn't say so?"

Tate removed Isabelle's hand from his shirt and gave her fingers a quick squeeze before releasing her. "Didn't want to spoil the surprise."

She smiled coyly up at him and he forced himself to match the happy gesture. "We can catch up at supper," she said, leaning in as if she planned to kiss him again.

"I can hardly wait." He tapped her on the nose to prevent another unwanted kiss. "Got to get these horses put away first."

After she sauntered away, he pushed out a breath. His acting skills could use a little work, but he'd at least convinced Isabelle that he was his brother. Now he just had to convince everyone he knew his way around a ranch he hadn't ever seen before.

Then he remembered.

He'd told Essie this morning that he had never been to the ranch. For the first time since Isabelle had accosted him, he looked at Essie. The others had gone inside, but she stood completely still on the bottom step of the porch, her eyes wide. They'd gone dark green in the last few minutes, and Tate could plainly see the shock and hurt reflected in their depths. When she realized he was watching her, she narrowed her gaze. The heat of her anger could be felt clear across the yard.

She believed he'd lied to her. And while everything inside screamed at him to walk over and tell her the truth, he couldn't. It would destroy the cover he'd worked so hard to maintain these last few weeks. And, what was worse, he would put Essie and himself in grave danger.

Throwing her a pained glance, he tugged the horses forward toward the barn. Silas would be halfway through getting the other animals settled by now. Although taking extra time, and skipping out on supper, didn't sound like a bad option anymore. He hated the thought of facing Essie's anger—not just the anger of a friend, either, but the anger from a woman he was beginning to care far too much for.

Chapter Eight

❧

Essie forced herself to eat the plentiful supper, though she didn't taste a thing. The flapjacks and bacon might as well have been sand and pieces of shoe leather for all she cared. Happy chatter bounced around the table, reminding her of her own family meals. But she felt wrapped in a cocoon of shock and anger that nothing could penetrate.

Her gaze shifted often to where Isabelle sat next to Tate at the far end of the table. The younger girl might as well have crawled into his lap with the way she kept latching on to his arm and leaning into him.

Admit it, Essie. You're jealous. She glared down at her half-empty plate as she dismissed the silly thought. She was not jealous of the other young woman, however doe-eyed and gorgeous she might be. It was only anger that she felt. Anger at Tate for lying to her this morning.

He'd tried to speak to her when he came in for supper, but she'd brushed past him and sat where he couldn't sit beside her. Essie didn't want to hear his excuses for why he hadn't been truthful. She'd come to trust him—more so than any of the others—but now she realized how silly she'd been to depend upon an outlaw.

Perhaps Tate recognized that she was starting to care for him and was embarrassed to tell her his affections lay elsewhere. Like on a ranch in the middle of nowhere. Her jaw tightened and she stabbed at another piece of flapjack before popping it into her mouth. She chewed and swallowed and, once again, tasted nothing.

The heroine's heart splintered further as she watched the loathsome, lying, despicable man at the other end of the table fawn over the young woman of questionable beauty. How long had they been working together? she wondered. For they only had eyes for each other. Her awful predicament was heightened when the hero announced...

"So you write novels?" Winnifred asked from her seat at Essie's right.

Essie cleared her throat. "Uh, yes."

The eldest of the two daughters gave her a shy smile. "What sort of stories do you tell?"

"Oh, romantic, adventurous ones. Full of trustworthy heroes, determined heroines and dastardly villains." Essie glared in Tate's direction as she loudly voiced the last two words. There was a dastardly villain if she'd ever seen one.

A pained look filled his brilliant blue eyes as he regarded her. She hoped it was contrition she saw there and not pity.

"Things aren't always so black-and-white," Tate said, his gaze falling away. "Some heroes fail and some villains prove far less dastardly than one might think."

Essie sniffed. "Not in my books."

"I love a good hero," Isabelle gushed, fluttering her eyelashes at Tate.

"Even if he turns out to be a villain?" he countered. The hint of bitterness in his tone surprised Essie, though Isabelle didn't seem to notice.

Instead the other girl smiled. "As long as it's true love…"

Essie resisted the urge to gag, the food in her stomach souring. There was no way she could eat another bite. Not while Isabelle kept making eyes at Tate and cooing about true love and heroes. That was all well and good in fiction, but Essie hated watching the scene play out in real life. Thankfully, Fletcher changed the topic of conversation when he asked how things on the ranch were faring. She wanted to hug him in gratitude.

Still, it was several laborious minutes before Mrs. Paige announced it was time to clear away supper. "We'll get started on the dishes, if you boys want to collect yourselves water for a bath and a shave out in the bunkhouse. Then and only then are you welcome to join us women in the parlor."

Most of the men fingered the growth on their chins with a laugh or a smile, but not Tate. He seemed to be trying to tell Essie something with his eyes, but she couldn't figure out what. Ignoring him, she stood and picked up her plate.

"You're welcome to wash up, as well, Essie." Mrs. Paige began gathering the dishes into a stack. "We can put the tub in your room. And I think Isabelle has a dress or two you may borrow."

The younger girl wrinkled her nose as she shoved

back her chair. "You can keep them. I'm not going to want them back."

Essie swallowed a retort to the other girl's baited comment about her appearance. Or the lack thereof. Her traveling dress and jacket were covered with three days' worth of trail dust. So was her hastily-braided hair that she felt sure still held a few tiny sticks from sleeping on the ground. But she wasn't here to dazzle anyone with her beauty. She was here to save her writing career.

Standing, Tate approached her from the other side of the table. "Essie, can I have a word?"

She grabbed up her plate and cup and shook her head. "I'm going to help clean up."

"You don't have to do that," Mrs. Paige said as she moved toward the kitchen door.

"No, I insist. I can wash up later."

"You can't avoid me forever," Tate murmured, his hand coming to rest for a moment on her elbow. The warmth of it seeped through her sleeve, but instead of calming her as his touch had before, this time it refueled her anger.

Pulling her arm away from his grip, she replied in a low voice, "I can certainly try. Besides, I don't need to hear any more. I've seen enough to know what's going on." She threw a pointed glance at Isabelle, who followed after her mother, her hips sashaying a little too much to be natural.

"It isn't what you think…"

"Why should it matter what I think?" she countered. "Good night, *Mr. Tex.*"

He let her go, much to her relief. But Essie still felt a painful hollow in her chest as she stayed in the kitchen, drying dishes. The ache was made worse by Isabelle's incessant prattling that centered on Tate. *How handsome he still looked. How nice it was to see him again. How he'd promised to come back someday and he had.*

By the time the last of the supper things had been dried and put away, Essie's head hurt and exhaustion overwhelmed her. But she didn't want to forgo a bath for sleep.

"Do you mind if I take that bath now?" she asked Mrs. Paige. Winnifred was in the dining room wiping the table, but Isabelle had, thankfully, disappeared outside. Probably to see Tate. Essie forced herself not to frown at the thought. It shouldn't—it didn't—matter how much time the other girl spent with him.

"Let me start heating some water and then we'll carry up the bathtub." Mrs. Paige filled two kettles from the pump inside and set them on to boil. Then she wrestled a large tub out from behind the stove. Essie grabbed one end and helped her lug it up the back stairs to the second floor.

"Men don't understand what trail life can do to a woman," Mrs. Paige said with a shake of her head. "How much she misses the niceties of a real home. Course, even they can't resist something other than camp food and the hard ground to sleep on." She chuckled as if she knew the great mysteries of the outlaw life. Maybe she did. Clearly she had some connection to outlaws, to allow them to use her home as a refuge.

Essie repositioned her hold on the heavy tub. "Have they ever brought a woman here before?"

"No." She backed into the open doorway of one of the bedrooms. "My girls were a bit surprised to see you ride up with them," she said with a light laugh. "I think they were worried you'd stolen the hearts of their men."

Winnifred had looked worried and surprised— Isabelle hadn't cared about anything or anyone but Tate. Essie's cheeks warmed at the unkind thought and Mrs. Paige's assumption. "I'm only here to interview them, I assure you. Once I'm finished, I'll be heading home."

They set the tub on the floor in the middle of the room. "Where's home?"

For a moment Essie's thoughts filled with images of the ranch and her family. But she pushed them aside. She'd made a new home, a good home, for herself. "Evanston."

"Had you met Tex before?"

Essie shook her head. "No, ma'am. Not until three days ago. How come?"

Mrs. Paige glanced out the window, her hands on her hips. Then she shrugged. "Just curious. The two of you act as if you've known each other longer than a few days."

Unsure how to respond, Essie kept quiet. That morning she would have said she felt as if she'd known Tate for weeks, but she'd been wrong about him.

"I can't put my finger on it, but he's different than he was the last time he rode through here."

"Different how?" Essie asked more out of politeness than interest. She didn't want to talk about Tate anymore. For all she cared, he and Isabelle could run off together and she wouldn't mind one bit.

The older woman gave a self-conscious laugh. "I

don't know, exactly. Last time he was more charismatic and certainly more attentive to Isabelle."

Essie refrained from stating her opinion of his attentiveness to Isabelle. After all, he hadn't looked too uncomfortable during their kiss in the yard. Just the thought of it resurrected her earlier anger. Still, she did find it interesting that Mrs. Paige's opinion of Tate coincided with her own and contrasted with what Essie had read in the newspapers.

"Perhaps he's more trail-weary this time," Mrs. Paige said, moving toward the door. "Winny and I will bring up the water and a clean dress for you."

"Thank you. May I help with the water?"

Mrs. Paige waved her away. "You already helped with the dishes. Just make yourself at home now." She disappeared into the hallway.

Moving to the window, Essie pushed aside the curtains to look down into the yard below. A few cowhands moved around, but there was no sign of Fletcher or his men or Tate. Not that she was looking for him.

She let the curtains fall back into place and turned around to study her room for the night. It was simply furnished but boasted pretty wallpaper and an iron bedstead. She fingered the beautifully sewn quilt, thinking of her mother. When Mrs. Vanderfair hadn't been cooking or cleaning, she'd had a needle and fabric in her hands. Essie could sew a decent-looking stitch, but she hadn't inherited her mother's remarkable sewing abilities as her older sisters had. Clearly sewing had been to her mother what words and stories were to Essie.

The realization brought a pang of sadness that they hadn't understood that about each other when Essie had been living at home. But she also felt a pinch of hope that perhaps someday they could find common ground in their shared love of creating.

A knock sounded at the partially open door. "Come in," Essie called.

Winnifred entered the room, a large kettle in hand. She shot Essie a smile and poured the steaming water into the tub. "Mother has another kettle-full she's bringing up. And I'll go get a dress for you."

Mrs. Paige came into the room as her daughter exited. "There's soap on the bureau there, and I'll pour some of this into that pitcher so you can wash your face."

"That sounds wonderful. Thank you ever so much."

"Truth be told, it's nice to have another woman around. We don't get much female company here. Not like when Jett and I were first married and living closer to town." A wistful expression settled on her pretty face.

Winnifred returned with a pile of clothes and placed them on the bed. The dress she'd chosen was simple in design, but Essie liked the cheery blue color and the sprigs of leaves covering the fabric.

"We'll leave you to it," Mrs. Paige said, motioning for Winnifred to follow her. "There's a brush in one of the drawers if you need one."

"I actually have my own, in my valise." In her shock and frustration over Tate, she'd completely forgotten to bring her bag inside. "It must still be with my horse, though."

Mrs. Paige led Winnifred into the hallway. "Winny will get your bag," her mother volunteered, "and leave it outside your door."

After thanking them again, Essie shut the door and went to test the water in the tub. It was the perfect temperature, though it wouldn't stay that way for long. Good thing growing up in a large family had taught her to wash and scrub quickly. And it was a habit Essie hadn't been able to shake, even after three years of living on her own.

In no time at all, she'd finished and was doing up the last button on her borrowed dress when she heard Winnifred outside the door. Essie crossed the room and opened the door to find the girl setting the valise against the wall. "Thank you for getting my bag."

Winnifred jerked to a standing position then laughed. "Did you even take a bath?"

"Yes," Essie said with a smile as she picked up her valise. "I'm one of nine children. I can wash in three minutes or less."

"One of nine? I can't imagine."

Essie moved back into the room and pulled her brush from her bag. The scent of soap floated off her hair as she began brushing through the wet tangles. How glorious it felt to have clean hair. "You can come in, if you like," she said to Winnifred when the girl hesitated in the hallway.

"If you're sure you don't mind." She took a seat on the bed. "You have pretty hair."

Spinning to face her, the brush motionless in her hand, Essie studied the girl's expression. Winnifred didn't appear to be teasing. "You really think so? It's not quite as lovely a color as my sisters', but it's what God gave me."

"Washed and brushed like that, it's a real nice shade of blond." Winnifred splayed her hands on the quilt and gave the bed a little bounce, likely unaware of how much her sincere compliment meant to Essie. "I think Isabelle is a little jealous of you."

"Of me?" Essie resumed brushing her hair. She certainly couldn't compete with the other girl in terms of beauty, though she had hoped Tate would appreciate a girl with more sense and propriety. "Why would she be jealous of me?"

Winnifred glanced up, an almost impish smile on her face. "She didn't like the way Tex kept looking at you."

Frowning, Essie turned to face the mirror. Had Tate been watching her through dinner? Every time she'd looked up, he'd seemed too consumed with Isabelle's attention to notice anyone else. But if he had been looking at her, what was the reason? Regret? Frustration that she refused to talk to him? Or was it something more?

A flutter of hope filled her heart, too strong to snuff out right away. But practicality eventually pushed it back down. She liked Tate—as a friend—and she hated the thought that he'd lied to her. Still, their relationship could never be anything more than respectful friendship.

As if thinking something similar herself, Winnifred asked, "What do you think of Fletcher?"

Essie pulled the brush through her hair several times, considering how to answer. "I don't know him… not very well," she responded truthfully. "What do *you* think of him?"

The girl rose to her feet and went to stand by the window. "He's different when he's here, or so I've heard. Less intense and angry. He can be downright sweet and helpful when he wants to be."

Fighting a look of disbelief, Essie simply nodded. She would have to take Winnifred's word when it came to Fletcher.

"But he's not the only one I like." She parted the curtains to stare down into the yard. "Our ranch foreman, Luke, would like to court me."

"What have you told him?"

Winnifred shrugged, her smile sad. "I told him I didn't know what I wanted. I love Fletcher, but there are times I'm certain I love Luke, too." She brushed at her eyes. "It's all so confusing."

Essie set down her brush and went to place a comforting hand on the other girl's shoulder. "What does your mother advise?"

"Oh, you know mothers." Winnifred gave an embittered laugh. "She doesn't want me to live a life as the wife of an outlaw. And I understand why." Essie could somewhat relate. Her mother and father hadn't wanted her to move so far away and live on her own. "If I marry Luke, we can stay here and he has a job for life on the ranch. I also wouldn't have to live every day wondering if Fletch will make it home or not."

"And yet?" Essie prompted gently.

Winnifred pushed out a sigh and turned from the window. "And yet I love them both and I can't decide."

She gave Winnifred's arm a soft squeeze, not envying the girl's decision. While she knew she could never marry an outlaw herself, the heart was a fickle master. Her feelings for Tate were evidence of that. "Keep thinking and praying about it. You'll know what to do."

"Thank you for listening." Her smile no longer drooped, to Essie's relief. At that moment, a tune floated through the open doorway. "Sounds like Mother's at the piano, which means the men must be back. We should go down to the parlor."

"You go ahead. I'm going to finish with my hair."

Nodding, Winnifred left the room.

Essie brushed through her hair once more then studied herself in the mirror. Should she braid it or pin it up? She liked how it felt, hanging long and clean down her back, so perhaps she would simply pull it away from her face. Remembering a ribbon she'd tucked into her valise weeks ago, she fished it out, tying back half of her hair and leaving the rest to fall past her shoulders.

The piano tunes, accompanied by gregarious singing, grew louder as she made her way downstairs to the parlor. Through the open door, she could see Mrs. Paige at the piano. Essie slipped into the room. Her gaze wandered over those assembled until it found Tate leaning against the window frame.

Gone were his beard and hat, giving Essie an unobstructed view of his clean-shaved jaw and piercing blue eyes. She swallowed in an attempt to bring moisture to her suddenly dry throat. The descriptions about his personality might have been exaggerated in the newspapers but not those about his handsome looks. That assessment was entirely correct. Little wonder, then, that he was attracted to dark-haired beauties like Isabelle.

At that moment, Isabelle rose from her seat beside the piano and went to slip her arm through Tate's. He threw her what looked to be a tight smile, but he didn't shrug her off, either. Essie glanced away from the lovely picture they made, pain pinching hard at her heart. It wasn't like she wanted to be on the arm of an outlaw.

Then why the sudden swimming of tears in her eyes?

She pressed her lips together and exited the room. Half-blind, she stepped quickly through the front door to the porch beyond. Sinking onto the top step, she allowed the stiff breeze to push the tears from her eyes.

She hadn't had a real cry since Harrison had accused her of not being serious enough about life and told her she'd end up an old maid if she didn't quit writing her "silly" novels. And she didn't plan to start weeping now. There was no use wasting tears on another man, especially an outlaw.

"I've got to take care of something," Tate murmured quietly to Isabelle, who clung to him like a bur he couldn't shake.

She pursed her lips in a pout. "You'll miss the singing. And, besides, you're leaving tomorrow. I was hoping to have more time together."

Tate stifled an audible groan. Exhaustion nagged at him—not from their ride earlier but from his efforts to keep up the charade of being his brother and Isabelle's outlaw beau. Without a clue what Tex had told this girl, he couldn't keep up the pretense of a future together. Even if he'd known what to say, the words probably would have stuck in his throat. *She* wasn't the girl he wanted to make promises to.

He couldn't tell Essie the whole truth, but he wanted her to know that he and Isabelle weren't a couple. The tortured look in Essie's green-brown eyes right before she'd fled the room had pierced him straight through his chest and propelled him to act. *Or at least try.* She'd been dodging his efforts ever since they'd arrived at the ranch.

Giving Isabelle a patient smile, he slipped her hand from his arm and gave it a friendly squeeze. It struck him then that this woman's touch and lovely porcelain face elicited none of the warmth and happiness that Essie's did.

"I'm sorry if I led you on tonight, Isabelle." He kept his gaze leveled on hers. "You caught me by surprise in the yard earlier." *Complete surprise.* "I can't reveal all that's happened since last time we met, but I think it's best if you forget me."

Her eyes widened in disbelief. "Forget you? How can you say that?"

"You're beautiful and lively, and will make some other man very happy. But you need to know that man isn't me."

"I see," she bit out, dragging her hand away from his. "Is it because you care for that other girl?"

Tate frowned in confusion. "What other girl?"

Isabelle waved away the question. "The one you brought with you. That Essie girl."

"No, I don't—"

"I told Winny I thought you liked her. Especially since you couldn't stop staring at her all through dinner."

He glared down at her, ready to argue that she was mistaken. Until he remembered Essie walking into the room minutes ago, her unfettered hair shining in the lamplight and her blue dress enhancing the green in her hazel eyes. She'd seemed surprised when he'd referred to her being beautiful the other day, but he'd meant it. And when she smiled...

A weight tugged at his heart at the realization he hadn't seen that smile in hours. He needed to talk to her—now. Even if he wasn't sure what to say. It didn't matter what Isabelle or anyone else thought of them; he and Essie could only be friends. But he feared they were no longer even that.

"Again, I'm sorry, Isabelle. I've got to go." He stepped past her, ignoring her angry expression and tightly crossed arms. Outside the parlor, he stopped, unsure which way Essie had gone. Was she back upstairs? Or had she gone somewhere else?

A glance at the front door revealed it was partially open. Tate headed out to the porch and found her sitting there, her arms wrapped around her knees. Closing the door softly behind him, he shored up his courage and determination, then approached her.

"Mind if I have a seat?" he asked, fully expecting her to bolt the instant she saw who'd come outside.

Instead she simply glanced up at him and then away. "It's not my porch, so you're welcome to sit where you want. Won't you be missed inside, though?"

"No." He knew she was referring to Isabelle. "We came to a mutual understanding that it's over."

Her lips parted as if she wanted to say something, but then they tightened as she lowered her gaze to the ground.

Tate took a seat next to her. Tension rippled off her hunched shoulders. He'd never seen her so despondent. "I'm sorry, Essie."

"For not telling me the truth or for..." Her voice

trembled and she coughed to clear it. And yet the tiny crack in her composure made him want to tell her everything. "Or for breaking my trust?"

Tate stared down at his hands. "Both." How had the simple job of impersonating his brother become so complicated? "I don't blame you one bit for not trusting me anymore. But I didn't lie to you this morning."

Her chin whipped up, her eyes smoldering with accusation. "What do you mean?" she countered, each word louder than the last. "You told me you'd never been here before."

Looking over his shoulder, Tate hoped the music inside would muffle their words. He didn't want to have to explain Essie's outburst to anyone. "Can we discuss this away from the house? Please?"

She pushed out a sigh and stood. "Fine."

Without thought, Tate took her elbow in hand to guide her to the corral across the yard, but Essie tugged her arm free of his hand. "I can walk. Where to?"

"Over by the corral is fine," he said, waving her forward toward the fence. He reached up to adjust his hat then remembered he wasn't wearing it. Without its brim to hide beneath, he felt unprotected and defenseless.

Essie stopped beside the fence, her arms wrapped across her middle. "Well?"

"I can't tell you the reason behind the discrepancy." She sniffed in annoyance as Tate glanced upward at the few glittering stars. "But you can still trust me, Essie. I need you to trust me."

"How?" she asked, but her bitter tone had softened.

Tate considered her entreaty. Telling her anything

that might cause her to doubt he was the Texas Titan was out of the question. But was there something else he could offer? Some part of his life that would allow him to maintain his disguise but also help her trust him again?

You're my brother, Tate. I trusted you to have my back.

The barbed words from eight years ago flashed through his memory. They were something he could share with Essie. Though the idea of talking of that fateful day sparked fresh pain inside him. He'd have to tell the events from Tex's viewpoint instead of his own, but it would still be something personal, something for her interview.

Facing her, Tate sucked in a full breath of the cool night air. "I want to tell you the story about the last time I saw my brother."

She straightened, her arms falling to her sides. "Really? Why?"

"You said it yourself—I didn't give you much to go on that first time you interviewed me. So I'm going to make it up to you now." He fisted his hands and then forced his fingers to relax. "I also hope it inspires you to trust me again."

"Are you sure?" She reached out as if to touch his arm, but stopped herself. "I don't understand why you said what you did, Tate, but I'm not as angry now. You don't have to prove anything to me."

Ignoring the out she'd just presented him with, he sat, his back against the fence rail. "You might want to sit, too. This is a potentially long story."

The glimpse of a smile lifted her lips as she settled next to him on the ground. "I love a potentially long story."

He chuckled, but he didn't feel any real mirth. "You might not like this one." She watched him silently, waiting.

Where should he start?

"The last time I saw my brother was eight years ago. We were still living in Idaho then." He rested his head on the rung behind him, thinking how Tex would tell this story. "Things between us had been strained ever since our mother died two years earlier. I didn't love the land like my brother did. The only reason I didn't up and leave earlier was because…well, because I was in love with this girl. Ravena."

He hadn't said her name aloud in ages, but it still had the power to conjure up a thousand memories. There had been a few years when he'd been as besotted with her as Tex had been. Tate had even attempted to win her affections. But she and Tex had had something, a bond as unbroken as the sky and as deep as a chasm. A bond she and Tate had never been able to form, despite their efforts. A bond Tex insisted Tate had helped destroy that night.

"What was she like?" Essie asked, her tone inquisitive but gentle.

Tate studied his hands. "She was very pretty and determined and kind. But also serious, more likely to see the clouds than the silver lining."

"Sounds a bit like you." She nudged his shoulder with her own and he attempted to return her teasing smile.

But Essie was right. He and Ravena were too alike, which was probably one of the reasons they hadn't

worked out. Tex had been the one to coax her into a
smile or to get her to laugh so hard tears leaked from
her dark brown eyes. She liked talking to Tate, but
Tex had brought the sunshine and lightheartedness
to her life.

"What happened?"

He cleared his throat, bracing for the next part of
the story. *Tell it from Tex's side*, he reminded himself.
"I decided I didn't want to stay in Idaho anymore.
Maybe I was just restless or maybe I was just tired of
my older brother always lecturing me about responsibility and the fruits of hard work and not being like
our father, who never did much but sleep and gamble."
The words were a perfect match to those he'd voiced
to Tex, and he inwardly winced as he imagined what
his brother must have felt hearing them over and over
again. "Whatever the reason, I made plans to leave,
but I wasn't going alone."

"Ravena was going with you," Essie murmured.

Tate nodded. "We made plans to secretly elope. No
one knew, not my brother or Ravena's grandfather. I
had everything ready." He swallowed the tightness
in his throat. "My brother had gone over to Ravena's
to return something to her grandfather. Ravena had
been packing, as well. When he found me in the barn,
saddlebags ready, he put our plan together right away.

"He was angry at me for leaving, or 'sneaking off,'
as he put it. How could we leave her grandfather behind? How did we plan to eat and live without a job
or money?" Tate shook his head, pain pooling in his
stomach as the angry assault of words from both him
and Tex filled his memory. "I was angry, too. I loved

Ravena and knew it would work out, even if we didn't have much but each other."

Essie shifted beside him but remained quiet, letting him purge the story from his heart.

"That's when my brother realized I was holding our mother's jewel earrings," Tate said. "They were the only nice things Ma ever owned—a gift from our father when they first married. Even when Pa would go on rampages, searching for anything in the house to gamble away, our mother never said where she'd hidden those earrings. It wasn't until a few years after he'd left us that she finally removed them from their hiding spot."

His lungs squeezed with hurt at the recollection of seeing those glittering jewels in Tex's fist. It had felt as if that same fist had lodged in his gut. "It was the one thing we had, besides memories, to remember her by. But I wanted to sell them, desperate for money for me and Ravena. My brother accused me of stealing and told me that Ravena deserved better than a thief." He licked his dry lips, thinking for the first time how much it must have pained Tex to hear those things. "My brother threatened to ride back to Ravena's farm and tell her grandfather everything."

Essie's warm fingers wrapped around his forearm and squeezed. Without real thought, Tate covered her hand with his, clinging to her touch as the only solid thing in this sea of pain.

"I don't know what I was thinking, exactly, with what happened next."

"Maybe you weren't thinking," she said softly.

Tate dipped his head in acknowledgment. Neither he nor his brother had been thinking straight. Where

Tate had seen only recklessness and deceit in his brother, Tex had likely seen only jealousy and blame in Tate. And Tate *had* been jealous—jealous that Tex could just up and leave whenever he felt like it, jealous that Ravena had ultimately chosen his twin, and jealous that he himself hadn't found a love like that.

"I knocked my brother out cold to stop him from ruining our plans." He couldn't describe the blow; otherwise Essie might remember the scar behind his ear. Tex's parting gift, courtesy of a smashed lantern. When Tate had finally come to an hour or so later, bloodied and his head aching, Tex was gone.

When Tate could stand without feeling like he might faint, he'd ridden over to Ravena's. She was still there, but Tex hadn't arrived, and even as the hour had grown later and later, he hadn't come. Tate had never seen him again. After a few months, he'd sold the farm, tried in vain to find his brother and then decided to become a Pinkerton detective after reading about Tex's robberies.

"I'm guessing you didn't meet Ravena?" Essie asked. He'd almost forgotten her presence, in spite of the feel of her comforting hand on his arm.

"No." Tate shook his head. What reason could he give? He wasn't sure what had motivated Tex to leave behind the woman he'd loved. Had his brother actually listened to the things Tate had said in anger about him not deserving Ravena? "I left Idaho after that."

Essie placed her hand back in her lap. "Do you regret not eloping with her?"

Did Tex regret his decision? Tate couldn't say. As for himself, he'd come to terms long ago over things with Ravena. By the time he'd sold the farm, they'd forgiven each other for that night. She'd even hinted at trying to make something work between them, but Tate couldn't. Whether it was because he'd realized they were too alike or out of loyalty for his brother, he couldn't say.

"I regret a lot of the things I said and did out of anger that night," he replied as himself this time and not as Tex. "But I don't regret not leaving with her."

Was it his imagination or did Essie sound as if she were letting out a held breath? "How sad and difficult that must have been for you. I can't say I fully understand your particular situation, Tate, but I know all too well the cost of people's judgment on your character."

Tate squirmed a little, guilt rising inside him over what he'd said about Tex's character. Was it little wonder his brother had been angry enough to smash him over the head and never look back? Telling the story from his brother's point of view had allowed him to put himself in Tex's shoes. Something he was ashamed he'd never tried to do before. While he still didn't condone Tex's actions over the last eight years, Tate could see where he could've been less quick to judge, more willing to understand. Perhaps things would have gone differently if he had.

"Thank you for telling me all of that." The breeze had picked up again and it tossed blond wisps across her face. Essie brushed them aside, but they promptly blew back into her eyes. Reaching out before he knew what he was doing, Tate swept the soft strands behind her ear. "N-now I understand much better why you chose this life," she added in a breathless voice.

He liked to think his touch affected her, even as her words jerked him back to reality. Tate regretfully lowered his hand from the softness of her cheek.

When she talked about "this life," she meant the

life of an outlaw. But Tate wasn't an outlaw. He was a detective, a good one, trying his best to rid this corner of the earth of injustice and greed. The truth barreled up his throat. It would be so easy to confess who he really was.

Tate opened his mouth to tell her, and then he closed it again. Maintaining his disguise for this job meant the difference between success and failure. His life depended on it—and so might Essie's if Fletcher ever learned Tate had entrusted her with his secret.

"I suppose we ought to get back," he said, climbing to his feet. He didn't know how long they'd been outside, but he didn't need Fletcher getting suspicious. Offering Essie his hand, he pulled her to a standing position. "They may still be singing."

Essie glanced at the house. "I think I'll forgo the singing. I want to write down your story in my notebook before bed."

Tate nodded. "I guess it'll provide you with a lot of material, huh?" He forced a chuckle.

She watched him a moment, her eyes almost black in the dying light. "I know that wasn't easy to relay, Tate. And I want you to know…" She pursed her lips as she looked away. Then suddenly she was standing on tiptoe and pressing a kiss to his cheek.

"I trust you again," she said, easing to the ground.

With the feel of her lips still tingling against his jaw, he fought the urge to tug her close and kiss her properly. "Why?"

"Because while you were talking, I was praying."

He lifted his eyebrows in surprise. "For what?"

Essie clasped her hands behind her back and offered him a smile, a real one this time. The sight of it filled his heart with as much joy as her simple kiss had. "For you and for me. And I feel like I should place my trust in you once more." She gazed up at him then with the most solemn expression he'd ever seen on her face. "So please don't break that trust again."

"I won't, Essie."

She gave a satisfied nod and started toward the house. As Tate trailed her, he sent his own prayer Heavenward. *Help me keep that promise, Lord.*

He couldn't tell her the truth or offer her any kind of relationship beyond friendship—not when his life was tracking one outlaw after another without the freedom to truly settle down. But Essie trusted him again, and tonight, that was all that mattered.

Chapter Nine

Essie waved a final goodbye to the three women standing on the porch. She'd stayed up later than she had planned last night, writing down every word of Tate's story. But in spite of the limited sleep, she felt rejuvenated and optimistic this morning. Perhaps that was what came from sleeping in an actual bed after two nights on the ground and having a stomach full of something other than burned beans and biscuits.

Or perhaps it's because Tate doesn't care for Isabelle like you thought.

Pressing her lips over a smile, she nudged her horse after the others. Breakfast had been a quiet affair, unlike the merriment last night. Fletcher and Winnifred had exchanged lingering, sad glances, and Isabelle had pouted, her seat as far away from Tate's as possible. Essie had chatted pleasantly with Mrs. Paige, while enjoying Tate's silent company from where he sat beside her.

As the group passed by the corral, she felt happiness bubbling inside her. That was where she'd kissed Tate on the jaw last night and where he'd gently brushed aside the hair from her face, stealing her breath and causing her heart to gallop. She hadn't planned to kiss him, but she'd wanted him to understand she fully trusted him again. And after hearing his tragic tale and sensing his burden of guilt and sorrow, she'd acted on the impulse to let him know she cared.

He hadn't said much this morning, but he had smiled at her when she'd entered the dining room. A smile that made her want to rush to the piano and plunk out a joyful tune, even if she couldn't play. Could that mean he might care for her, too?

She turned to watch him, riding slightly ahead of her and to the right. His hat shadowed his face once more, but she'd memorized every feature last night as he'd talked. He was more somber than her, which only made her want to make him laugh or smile all the more. And even if she didn't understand why he'd told her he'd never visited the ranch before when he clearly had, she did trust him. He was decent, kind, protective and didn't make her feel as if she were weak or a burden. In contrast to most everyone else in her life, save her brother Nils, Tate seemed to respect her career and believe her equal to the challenge of being a female dime novelist.

But he's also an outlaw, her head warned. The smile on her lips slipped to a frown as Essie looked away. Was she beginning to care too much? Her initial plan had seemed so simple—she'd interview these men, learn their pasts and discover information she might use in her next story. Her heart and feelings were to have no bearing on things at all. And yet the thought of not seeing Tate again, once she was finished interviewing everyone, brought a physical ache.

"What am I doing?" she whispered as much to herself as to the Lord. Now that she had more of Tate's story, she needed to focus on obtaining her last two interviews. And she would not lose her heart to an outlaw in the process.

She urged her horse faster, with the intent of passing by Tate in favor of riding next to Jude. She could get in her fourth interview while they rode. But Tate spoke before she could pull ahead of him.

"It's nice to have a saddle again." The Paiges had insisted he take one of their saddles, so neither he nor Essie had to ride bareback again.

"Yes, I'm sure it is." Essie licked her lips, doing her best not to remember how he'd kissed her hand when they'd bantered about riding bareback the day before.

Tate scrutinized the sky overhead. "Looks like another day of sunshine. Should be a nice ride to Casper."

Essie nodded. She needed to maintain her professionalism and not be sidetracked.

"You all right?" Tate asked after a moment, his expression changing to one of concern.

"Yes, of course." She pasted on a smile. "I, uh, think I'll interview Jude today. I mean this morning. Right now, actually."

He shot her a puzzled frown but Essie ignored it.

"All right," he said.

"I'll talk to you later, Tate."

With that, she pushed her horse into a trot to catch up with Jude, riding in the middle of the group. A prick of regret at not being friendlier to Tate pierced her determination. After all, he had been open and candid last night in talking about him and his brother. But the closer they became as friends, the more the lines in her head, and heart, blurred over what she felt for him.

She trusted him, but she didn't completely trust herself. At least when it came to giving her heart away. She refused to be like Winnifred or Isabelle, pining for a man who wasn't free or present to love completely. Such a thing might work in one of her stories but not in real life.

"I'll never be at liberty to truly follow my heart," the hero said, the heroine's face gently cupped between his large, strong hands.

Tears of sorrow and pain dripped over his fingers from her watering eyes. "Does this mean you're saying goodbye?"

He nodded, his gaze tortured with unspoken feelings. "I didn't intend for this to hap—"

"I know." She silenced his words with a hand to his lips. Those masculine lips she'd kissed only once but would never forget. "And yet..." she couldn't help whispering.

"And yet?" he repeated.

She was desperate to ease the ache in her heart and remain at his side. "If you give up your outlawing ways and turn your back on this life of crime, we can be together."

His gaze lifted to something over her head. "Can I live the life of an honest man? A free man?"

"Yes," she cried, clasping his wrist. "You can. And I will help you. We'll embrace this chance at a new life together, far from the influence of your partners."

A look of tranquillity shone from his handsome

face. *"Then so be it."* He drew her close. *"We will make it, together, my love."*

Essie blinked away the moisture in her eyes, but two or three tears escaped. Lifting her hand, she brushed the droplets away. Hopefully, Tate hadn't seen. She didn't want him thinking she was crying over him. But wasn't she? Wasn't she simply playing out her own wishes in her fictional story, imagining the happy ending they would never be able to have?

No. She straightened in the saddle, keeping her face pointed forward. Her story would be completely different from her experience with him. After all, it wasn't like she'd kissed him on the lips—nor had he given her any indication that he cared for her as more than a friend.

Still, it was a good scene and one she would write down tonight. She passed Silas and Clem, riding in the middle of the group. They both called out a greeting, which she returned. At the front of the pack, Fletcher and Jude were arguing. As Essie approached, the outlaw leader suddenly jerked his horse to a stop. Jude did the same.

"The answer's no." Fletcher glared at the other man. "So don't ask again, Jude, or I'll cut your amount. You hear me?"

Jude looked away, his face hardened with anger. "I hear you."

"What's going on?" Tate asked as he, Silas and Clem drew to a stop alongside Essie. He glanced at her, but she could only shake her head in response.

"Nothing. Everything's fine." Fletcher threw another dark look at Jude. "Let's keep riding." He kicked his horse in the flanks and started forward again.

Essie followed after the others, though she hung back when she saw Jude take up a position at the rear this time. Unlike everyone else in the group, he looked to be only a year or two older than her and he was the one she knew the least. But hopefully he'd be willing to talk, in spite of whatever altercation had just occurred between him and Fletcher.

Slowing her horse, she waited for Jude to ride up beside her, then let her mount fall into step with his. He flicked a glance at her, one eyebrow lifted, but he didn't speak. His mouth still formed a tight frown.

"That's a nice Colt 1851 Navy you've got there," she said, nodding at the gun she'd seen him toting around camp.

The next thing she knew, Jude had the gun in hand and pointed right at her. "You mean this Colt?"

Essie gave a startled laugh, as much at his skill as at the discomfort of having the barrel aimed in her direction. She'd never seen anyone draw a weapon that fast. "How long did it take you to learn to do that?"

Shrugging, he twisted around in his saddle to train the gun on Fletcher's back. "A couple years, but I was better than most by the time I was fifteen." He narrowed his gaze on the other outlaw. "I was a gunslinger before I joined up with Fletch."

Would he pull the trigger and shoot the gang leader in the back? Essie moistened her lips, thinking fast about how to distract him. "A gunslinger? Now, that sounds exciting. And since you're still alive, I'm guessing you're rather good."

A half smile replaced his scowl. "Never had a fight I didn't walk away from. Or at least crawl." He sniffed in amusement at his own joke and then holstered his gun, to Essie's immense relief.

"What can you tell me about your family?"

Jude tossed her a questioning look. "Is this my interview?"

"It can be," she said with a smile.

His shoulders visibly relaxed. "All right, then. My father was a preacher, so my eight siblings and me got religion morning, noon and night."

"I have eight siblings, too." She found it interesting that she, Clem and Jude all had large families in common, though she hoped Jude's hadn't come to the tragic end that Clem's had.

"Guess I don't have to elaborate on that score, then, huh?"

Essie chuckled and shook her head. "Where do you fall in the family?"

"I'm the oldest son," he said, but some of the amusement had fled his expression, "though I got me a bunch of older sisters. You?"

"Right in the middle." She adjusted the reins in her grip, wondering if she ought to say any more. "I had an older brother myself, whom I admired very much."

"Had?" Jude turned to study her.

A familiar ache filled her chest. "He died four years ago." She cleared her throat. "He had high hopes of being a fast draw, too, but he never quite got the hang of it." She laughed, thinking of a time when Nils accidentally shot a hole in the milk bucket and narrowly missed injuring their cow.

Knowing Jude would appreciate the story, she recounted it for him. He regaled her in return with several bullet mishaps of his own and a few stories about the antics he'd shared with his younger siblings.

Essie found herself laughing more than once as they exchanged stories. "I loved my brother very much," she said, interrupting the comfortable quiet that settled between them once the stories ran out. "And I don't think it was easy for him being the oldest son."

"Don't I know it? Nothing I ever did pleased my father." The lines around his mouth tightened again. "He talked all the time about me becomin' a preacher, too, but I wanted something more exciting out of life."

"Is that why you became an outlaw?" she asked, keeping her tone light.

Jude gave a bitter chuckle. "In a roundabout way."

She waited for him to continue, and after a few moments, her patience was rewarded.

"I left home at sixteen, doing different jobs here and there to get by. But I never stayed in one place for long. I had it in my head to see as much of this country as I could." He shifted on his horse, his gaze distant. "It wasn't long until I got a reputation for havin' a fast draw. So I did gunslingin' for a few years, earning money off of bets, but it never paid too well."

"Did you…?" She hesitated asking, but she needed to be thorough in her research. "Did you ever…kill anyone?"

His countenance turned instantly grave, making her throat go dry with apprehension. Then he grinned. "Nah. I may not be religious, but I always aimed to injure, not end a man's life."

Essie released the breath she'd been holding. "What made you switch from being a gunslinger to an outlaw?"

Instead of answering, though, Jude frowned and seemed to find sudden fascination in the ground. She sensed she was on the verge of another real story regarding these outlaws' past lives. But would Jude feel comfortable enough to share it?

After a full minute he blew out a loud sigh, appearing to make a decision. "I became an outlaw to make more money, so I could support…my little boy."

She couldn't help gaping at him. Jude had a child? "How old is he?" And where was the boy's mother?

"He's two years old," Jude said with obvious pride. "And I married his mama proper-like, Miss Vanderfair. But she…" His shoulders drooped and his gaze skittered away. "She only lived a couple months after his birth."

"I'm so sorry." Compassion flooded her at the thought of his pain. She'd know the grief of losing a brother, but losing a spouse… She shook her head, unable to comprehend the heartache of saying farewell to a sweetheart. Her attention went to Tate, riding up ahead. He wasn't even her sweetheart and yet she already knew that bidding him goodbye wouldn't be free of anguish.

"Where is your boy now?" she asked, pulling her thoughts back to Jude.

He straightened in the saddle as if casting off the sad memories of the past. "He lives with my sister and her husband, along with their five children. But my sister took sick this spring and she hasn't felt the same since. They don't have much money and the medicine she ought to have costs a fortune." When he turned to face her, she could see the worry and fear in his eyes. "If she dies, my brother-in-law will have to parcel out the children to other relatives, including my son. So you can see, Miss Vanderfair, why I need this money. I have to help keep her well, for her sake and for my boy's."

She might not agree with his choices, or with his sister accepting stolen money, but Essie's heart went out to the man. "That's a very difficult spot to be in."

"It is." The tight lines returned to his face as he looked at Fletcher again. "And Fletch says he won't divide up the money from the train until we reach the hideout. But I've got to get that money to Mary sooner than later."

"Have you told Fletcher about your son?"

Jude wheeled on her. "Yes, but he thinks I'm going soft because of him, that I oughta just let my sister handle things."

Not anxious to end up in the middle of the outlaws' feud, Essie pasted on a gentle smile. "I'll be praying for him, Mr. Jude. And for your sister."

He nodded, though his expression hadn't lost its stony appearance. "Thank you, but it's gonna take more than that to help them." His eyes narrowed. "It's gonna take action."

A feeling of discomfort crept up her back at the man's harsh look. "Thank you for letting me interview you."

Some of the anger left his face as Jude tipped his hat to her. "My pleasure, Miss Vanderfair. It's been some time since I had a woman to talk to and it's been downright pleasant."

"I enjoyed our conversation, too." And she meant it. She was grateful to have another full interview completed—and a good one at that.

But as Jude retreated into his thoughts, she couldn't

shake the growing wariness inside her. Something was brewing between him and Fletcher, and she could only hope that she, Tate and the others wouldn't be caught in the middle when things inevitably erupted.

Tate tugged his hat down tighter as the wind grew stronger. The nice blue sky and gentle breeze of the morning had morphed into fast-forming clouds and a stiff gust. He had a sinking suspicion their bout of good weather was about to end.

Turning in the saddle, he looked for Essie. She and Jude still rode at the back of the group, though it appeared their interview had ended. A glimmer of satisfaction ran through him before regret followed it. He shouldn't mind that Essie sought out the others for her interviews. That was the reason she'd come along in the first place and, after what she'd said the other day about her publisher, he knew she needed their stories to help her own.

But he couldn't deny a twinge of jealousy each time he heard her laughing and easily conversing with one of the other men in the group. It was he who was supposed to be protecting her, looking out for her. Although he didn't doubt Essie could probably handle herself just fine in about any situation. She'd make an excellent detective. A smile curved his mouth at the thought.

The smile deepened when he recalled—again— her kiss on his cheek the night before. He'd told her parts of his and Tex's story that he'd never told another person. And even though he'd greatly appreciated her compassion during the telling, he couldn't help wishing later that some of her empathy could have been directed at him. Not as his brother but as himself. As Tate.

The wind began to blow harder. Tate held tighter to the reins, hoping his horse wouldn't get spooked. He wasn't sure how much farther they had to go to reach Casper, but the sooner, the better. He didn't like the idea of being caught out in the open during a storm.

No sooner had the thought entered his mind than fat, cold raindrops started to fall, slicing sideways in the wind. Tate hunkered into his collar, one hand on his hat, the other clenching the reins. Within minutes he was half soaked and could hardly see where he was going. He nearly ran into Silas before he realized he and Fletcher had stopped. The group formed a tight huddle.

"We gotta get out of this," Fletcher hollered, trying to make himself heard above the buffeting wind and rain. "There's a burned-down cabin we passed half a mile back or so. We'll take shelter there."

Tate nodded silently along with the others and whirled his horse around to face the way they'd come. Now the rain slashed at his back, but he preferred that to the dousing in his face. He maneuvered his mount closer to Essie's. She glanced up long enough to throw him a grim smile before tucking her chin against the elements. Without a hat or a suitable jacket, she was taking the worst of the weather.

Nudging his horse even nearer, he removed his hat and reached out to plunk it onto her wet hair. She looked up in surprise, though she didn't protest his offer. "Thank you," she shouted.

Rain ran down Tate's face and into his collar, making him shiver. But he reminded himself that they'd have shelter soon enough. Wiping his eyes, he peered ahead, hoping to see the cabin Fletcher had mentioned, but the storm made it difficult to see much of anything.

At last, Tate spied the roofless building. Two of the walls were charred and had fallen in on themselves, but the other two stood relatively straight. Jumping from his saddle, he held on to his horse and did his best to assist Essie to the ground. Then he added her horse's reins to his. "Where do you want them?" he yelled to Silas.

The outlaw pointed at a half-ruined corral. "Tie them to the fence posts," he shouted back. "Then take off the saddles. We'll use the blankets."

Tate obeyed, leading his and Essie's horses to the fence and securing them before he removed the saddles, which he laid on the ground beside the fence posts. The rain and wind tore at his jacket and face, and by the time he'd finished and had the two blankets in his arms, he couldn't tell where everyone else had taken cover.

Moving in the direction of the cabin, he finally caught sight of Essie standing against the south wall. "Where are the others?" he asked as he drew closer.

"Along the east wall, I think," she said, pointing. She was visibly shivering, her arms folded tightly against her as she hopped from one foot to the other in a clear effort to keep warm.

Tate took a seat on the ground and motioned for her to do the same. When she sat, he spread one of the blankets across their knees. Essie took off his hat and offered it to him, but he declined. Using the other blanket, he formed a tent over their heads and then leaned back against the rough-hewn logs of the cabin, cocooning him and Essie inside. The smell of horses from the blankets mingled with the smell of wet earth beyond their makeshift shelter, but at least they weren't being battered by the storm.

After setting his hat on the ground, Essie glanced at him and laughed. The sound reminded him of the stream near his boyhood home. "You look like I must have that first day you found me after the rainstorm."

He chuckled. "Probably worse." They sat half a foot apart, the blanket arcing over them.

"Maybe." She lifted her hand, her eyes clouding with hesitation, before she brushed a clump of damp hair off his forehead. Her fingers felt warm where they skidded across his brow. "That's better." Lowering her hand, she trained her gaze on her lap.

The wish to kiss her, right then and there, held him momentarily captive. But then he reminded himself he'd be leading her on. He had no intention of getting involved with a woman—not while outlaws like Fletcher ran free.

Tate cleared his throat. "How long do you think the storm will last?"

"An hour, maybe longer," Essie said with a shrug. "You never know with these Wyoming storms." She shivered again.

"Are you still cold?" Without waiting for her reply, he scooted closer to her until their shoulders touched. "Better?"

She dipped her chin in a nod, a smile turning up her mouth. It struck him again how unruffled she could be when confronted with just about any situation. He hadn't met many women who would be as calm and cheerful in the face of a raging storm.

"How did your interview with Jude go?"

"Fairly well." She fiddled with the button at the cuff of her dress. The absence of her usual enthusiasm about her interviews alerted him that something was bothering her. He waited for her to voice it and, after a few moments, she whispered, "Did you know he has a little boy?"

Tate guffawed. "Who? Jude?"

"Shh," Essie said, putting a finger to her mouth. But he doubted anyone could hear them above the storm. "Fletcher knows, but I'm not sure if Jude has told the others."

"Where is this son of his?"

Essie studied her hands. "He lives with Jude's sister and her family. But his sister isn't well. He's worried if something happens to her that the boy will be farmed out to others. Jude's wife passed away shortly after the child's birth."

Letting out a low whistle, Tate shook his head and swallowed back the question he wanted to ask. Why would Jude choose the life of an outlaw when he had a motherless child to support? But such a query would likely sound suspicious coming from him, since he was supposed to be an outlaw himself. He guessed desperation was likely at the heart of the matter, and that brought a feeling of empathy for the other man. As Essie had pointed out the other night, each of these outlaws was running from a tragic past.

Was that what had motivated Tex to turn to robbery? More important, was running from the past what Tate had done when he had decided to become

a detective? He shifted on the hard ground, not liking
the direction of his thoughts. His profession was hon-
orable and just—not like these men or his brother's.
But wasn't he also fleeing from past tragedy, hoping
to drown it out with good deeds?

Wasn't I supposed to be a detective? he silently
prayed. *Wasn't that the right course, Lord, after everything that happened with Tex? After I helped drive
him to a life of crime?*

No definitive answer was forthcoming, other than
a sense of uneasiness he wasn't sure he was ready to
face. The only comfort came from the certainty that
God would be with him, whenever he figured out
the answer.

Once this mission was over, once he'd helped the
local law enforcement arrest Fletcher and his gang,
then he'd take some time to think things through. Perhaps he just needed a short leave of absence to get
his mind clear and focused again. After all, he'd been
tracking down outlaws week after week, without any
real reprieve, for years.

"Is it still raining?" Essie asked.

Her question tugged his thoughts to the present.
Tate peeled back a corner of the blanket and peered
out. The rain appeared to have lightened, at least
enough that he could see the horses huddled next to
each other by the fence. But the wind still roared
across the wet prairie.

Tucking the blanket back behind him, he nodded.
"I think the rain has eased up, though the storm hasn't
fully blown over yet."

Essie wrapped her arms around her knees, another

shiver making her tremble. "The temperature's still cold, too."

The blanket kept them decently warm, but they'd both been soaked before taking shelter. Tate didn't like the thought of her getting sick. Not minding the excuse to sit even closer, he lifted his arm and placed it around her shoulders. Essie burrowed into his side with a sigh.

"Better?" he asked.

"Yes," she whispered.

They sat in silence another minute or two, but it wasn't filled with strain. Tate discovered he rather liked holding her. Her hair smelled of whatever soap she'd washed it with at the ranch, and its softness felt nice against his clean-shaved chin.

"Shall I tell you a story?" Essie glanced up at him, her hazel eyes bright with anticipation. "To pass the time?"

Tate laughed, though he couldn't think of anything better. *Except maybe kissing the curve of those delightfully pink lips.* Clearing his throat, he settled more fully against the cabin wall. "All right. Tell away."

She rested her cheek against his shirt. Could she hear his heart thumping faster than normal? "Which one?"

Seeing as he hadn't read any of her stories, he wasn't partial. He suspected Essie could make the most boring of tales sound mesmerizing. "You pick."

Her nose wrinkled as she appeared to consider what to share. "Very well. I'll share the tale of *The Indian Warrior's Bride.*"

He smiled. "Sounds intriguing."

"Oh, it is," she said, her expression animated.

She began to tell the story about a young woman on her way to Oregon whose wagon train was waylaid by Indians. As he'd expected, Tate found himself caught up not only in the events and characters but also with the charm of Essie's storytelling. He liked the inflections of her voice and the way her face portrayed the emotions of the moment. After a while, he closed his eyes, allowing her story to take him far away from the soggy Wyoming prairie and the band of outlaws he still needed to apprehend.

It wasn't until he heard Essie yawning that he came back to reality. Tate opened his eyes to find her fighting sleep. Her words had longer pauses in between them. "And so… Deidra became… White Woman Dancing… and she and… Soaring Eagle—" She yawned again. "She and… Soaring Eagle…lived a long and happy…"

"Life," Tate murmured with a smile as she finally succumbed to her sleepiness. A short nap didn't sound too bad. Especially when he had little idea how much longer the storm would last.

Even as he tried to relax and sleep, though, he couldn't. He was too aware of Essie's quiet breathing against his chest and her dark brown lashes lying against her smooth cheeks. It seemed strange and bizarre that he hadn't known her four days ago. In many ways, he felt as if he'd known her for years.

Did she feel the same about him? he wondered. Or did she see him as only an outlaw, a man driven to this life out of selfishness and shame?

Tate squeezed his eyes shut and fisted his free hand against his leg. He wasn't that person; he wasn't even an outlaw—if he could just tell her.

He certainly couldn't have foreseen that his straightforward, albeit dangerous, mission would become so convoluted by the presence of one cheerful dime novelist. He was here to do a job, same as her. Anything more than that wasn't supposed to factor into his plans.

But it has, he thought with a rueful shake of his head as he relaxed his fingers. *And she has.*

What was it about Essie that had gotten under his skin? That had allowed her to take up residence inside his once-guarded heart? She was the subject of his thoughts before he fell asleep, when he woke in the morning and nearly every minute of their daily rides. It wasn't just because she was pretty, though she was that. She was also kind, intelligent and optimistic to a fault. She liberally gave of her compassion to these outlaws with no expectation in return, and she knew nearly as much as he did about guns and tracking and living by her wits.

If he didn't know better, he might have thought God had placed his ideal partner directly in his path, quite literally. Tate grinned as he remembered her running smack into him on the train. He'd been more than anxious about completing the train robbery without blowing his cover, and then he'd come face-to-face with Essie's determination and exuberance. He'd been no match against either.

But surely God hadn't orchestrated her entrance into his life to introduce him to his bride. Not when Tate felt duty-bound to continue as a Pinkerton detective. His mission wasn't settling down on a farm somewhere with a wife and family, while his brother and other outlaws continued to take from the innocent.

The smile slipped from his mouth as he gazed down at Essie once more. For the first time in his career, he wanted to quit. He huffed out a breath, feeling the futility of such a hope.

He couldn't give up his livelihood. He had to make restitution for the past, not look to the future. And yet that future seemed rather bleak and boring without Essie in it.

Tightening his hold around her shoulders, Tate rested his jaw lightly against her hair. He might not be free to ever follow his heart, but he would enjoy every minute he did have left basking in the warmth and brightness of Essie's sunshine.

Chapter Ten

Essie slowly came to consciousness, though she kept her eyes shut. She had little desire to move out from under Tate's arm. While she hadn't meant to doze off after telling him a story, she wouldn't complain about the needed sleep or the strength of his presence next to her. Of course, she was supposed to be keeping her distance, her head kept reminding her. Which she would do once this storm was over. But for now, she'd enjoy feeling safe and cozy at his side.

The sound of the wind had died down and her damp dress had dried considerably. Too soon it would be time to ride again. *Just a few more minutes*, she thought, listening again to the drumming of his heart beneath his jacket. From the steady rise and fall of his chest, she guessed he'd drifted off, too.

Before she could slip back into the serenity of sleep, someone jerked the blanket off their heads. Cold air smacked Essie's cheeks, eliciting a gasp from her. Bright light made her blink as she opened her eyes. Beside her, Tate sputtered awake, as well.

"Where is he?" Fletcher hissed at her, his face mottled with anger.

Fear crept over her—she'd never seen the outlaw so enraged. Essie cowed against Tate, grateful when he tensed with protection and gripped her hand in his. "Where is who?" she managed to squeak out.

"Jude! Who else?" Fletcher hollered back. Reaching out, he yanked her to her feet, breaking Tate's comforting hold. "What did you say to him?"

"N-nothing. I only interviewed him."

Tate leaped to his feet and tried to place himself between her and Fletcher, but the other man's fingers still bit into her skin beneath her sleeve. "Calm down, Fletch. What's going on? Essie and I were waiting out the storm right here, same as you. Same as Jude."

Fletcher stuck his face into Tate's, fury burning in his eyes. "Jude didn't wait out the storm. He up and left." At last he dropped Essie's arm and stalked a few yards in one direction, then circled back. "And you know what else? He took the saddlebag with the train money." His entire body shook with rage, his hands meaty fists at his sides.

"All of it?" Tate asked, glancing at Essie. Something in his gaze worried her as much as Fletcher's reaction.

The outlaw threw his hat on the ground. "Everything but the few hundred dollars I stowed in my boots."

Essie made a mental note to write that detail down later. At least Fletcher had been one step ahead of Jude.

"What I want to know," he said, his voice lower in volume but sounding every bit as ugly and dangerous, "is what you said to him during your little interview, Miss Vanderfair." Fletcher moved slowly toward her like a wildcat ready to pounce on its prey. "Did he tell you his plan? Did you help him escape?"

Tate edged in front of her again, but Essie put a hand on his arm to stop him this time. His eyebrows lifted in silent question, but she gave a quick shake of her head. She didn't want the two men coming to fisti-cuffs; she could handle Fletcher. Especially knowing Tate had her back.

"I asked him nothing but my typical questions, about his past, about his family," she replied honestly. "He did express concern about his little boy and his sister."

Silas and Clem exchanged confused glances, con-firming what Essie had already suspected. They hadn't known about Jude's son.

Fletcher glared at her as though trying to weasel out the lies from the truth. She tipped her chin upward and met his level gaze. There was nothing to hide. She hadn't been Jude's accomplice, only a willing listener to his worries. "Did he say if he was plannin' on see-ing them again soon?"

"If he was, he didn't say so to me." Essie rubbed her arm where Fletcher's grip had surely left a mark. "He did seem rather agitated when the interview con-cluded, but I had no idea that he would leave." And take the gang's money with him.

Fletcher scooped up his hat from off the ground and jammed it back on his head. His entire being ra-diated enraged tension. Essie couldn't help wondering if Winnifred had ever seen this side of her sweetheart. Or did the outlaw leader maintain a glib demeanor around the Paige family? She had half a mind to write Winnifred a letter, informing the other girl just how her beau acted when crossed.

"What are we gonna do?" Clem ventured to ask, his expression apprehensive. "About the money?"

"There's nothing to do. That money's as good as gone," Tate replied. "We don't know how long he's been gone or what direction he went. We'd just be wasting time trying to find him and that cash."

Fletcher didn't appear to be listening. Instead he stalked over to the corral fence and gave one of the posts a good kick. The weathered wood was no match for his boot and collapsed to the ground.

"Is that money so important?" Essie asked Tate, her gaze still on Fletcher.

Silas answered her. "We need it to purchase supplies for the winter in Buffalo before it snows. That way we don't have to leave the hideout again until spring."

She nodded in acknowledgment as a wave of sadness filled her at the thought of what situations these men frequently found themselves in. Hunted by the law, robbed by one of their own, reduced to live off what they were able to steal. The longer she rode with them, the more their adventurous way of life lost its sheen.

Glancing at Tate, she wondered what he thought of their reduced circumstances. If only he'd give up outlawing and find honest work. Then she wouldn't have to worry, once they parted ways, about how he'd survive the winter.

"We'll ride on to Casper," Fletcher announced, untying his horse. "Then camp north of there."

"What about our money?" Clem asked as the four of them moved toward the restless horses.

Fletcher scowled at Clem. "It's long gone, like Tex said. But I got an idea of how to get some more." Essie's stomach twisted with uneasiness at his tone and the feeling only grew worse when Fletcher threw her a calculated look. What was he planning?

Tate clearly saw the look, too. "Stick close by me," he murmured in her ear as he helped her into the saddle.

"I will."

As they resumed riding north, Essie kept her mount close to Tate's. She tried to take comfort, as she had earlier, from his presence and the sunshine that turned the rain droplets on the brush and grass into glittering jewels. But she couldn't shake or ignore the knot of anxiety in her middle. Fletcher was planning something and she felt certain she wasn't going to like it.

The mood among the group remained tense, though Essie tried to ease some by telling Tate a couple more stories. The two of them rode at the back, while Clem and Silas kept up with Fletcher at the front. Tate listened to her, and even smiled, but the mood wasn't the same as it had been while they'd waited out the storm. Every few minutes, a frown would replace his smile. Essie didn't need any further proof he was also concerned about Fletcher's plans.

After they'd navigated through the surrounding bluffs, and the buildings of Casper and the river came into view, a palpable excitement charged through the men. Essie's nervous tension drained away, too, at the signs of civilization. Horses, wagons and people picked their way up and down the muddy streets. And while not as large or populated as Evanston, the town appeared to offer travelers and residents a variety of stores and businesses. Essie spotted a hotel, a newspaper office and a drugstore.

Fletcher veered toward the hitching post beside one building and dismounted. The others followed suit. Essie did her best to keep her hem from dragging in the mud as Tate helped her climb down from her horse and make her way to the sidewalk.

Clem squinted at the storefront from beneath his hat. "What're we doing at the telegraph office?"

Essie froze in the middle of scraping dirt and horse droppings from her boots. Lifting her head, she locked eyes with Fletcher. The outlaw leader grinned and tipped the brim of his hat to her as if being cordial. "I believe Miss Vanderfair has a telegram to send, don't you, ma'am?"

Swallowing her suddenly dry throat, she smoothed the front of her dress, schooling her expression to hide her panic. This moment wasn't supposed to come now— if ever. She'd begun to believe Fletcher had forgotten all about the idea of demanding ransom for her—to her great relief. But she'd underestimated him. Whether he'd been planning such a move all along or this was a new idea spurred on by Jude's disappearance with their money, she couldn't say. Either way, she had to comply, especially after witnessing Fletcher's earlier rage.

If she chose to tell them now that they wouldn't be getting a single nickel from her great-grandfather, she would very likely put her life at risk. No, she'd have to play along a little longer and pray she was far enough away when Fetcher learned the truth about Henry Vanderfair.

"You all right, Essie?" Tate studied her face, which she felt certain had gone white.

She forced her lips to curve. "I'll be fine. Thank you." Perhaps she could pretend to send the message to her great-grandfather, but instead send a telegram to her parents, in the event word had reached them about the train robbery and her supposed "kidnapping."

Keeping her chin high, she swept past the men toward the door. "I'll only be a minute or two."

But Fletcher grabbed her elbow in his iron grip, causing her heart to jump and her hope to dwindle. "*We'll* be a minute or two. Wouldn't want you to feel like we'd abandoned you, Miss Vanderfair. We are gentlemen, after all."

So much for her alternate plan. With a stiff nod, she allowed Fletcher to steer her into the telegraph office as she tried to tamp down her fears. No one on the other end of her telegram would bat an eye at her message or feel any need to reply, which worried her the most. What if Fletcher insisted on remaining in town until she received an answer? Although escaping his wrath would likely be easier here in a town than out on the Wyoming plains.

"I'd like to post a telegram," she managed to say in a calm voice to the telegraph clerk. He handed her the customary slip of paper and a stubby pencil.

Taking the pencil into her clammy fingers, she found herself at a loss for what to write. What did one say in a ransom note? "Um…to Henry Vanderfair of New York, New York. From Essie Vanderfair."

"Had a slight mishap while traveling. Stop," Fletcher dictated. "Require funds in the amount of $1000.00 to proceed. Stop."

She stifled an audible gasp as she penned the words, unsure whether to be flattered by the amount he was demanding or appalled.

"Health and safety dependent on receipt of funds. Stop. Send directions for receiving funds to me care of the Grand Central Hotel, Casper, Wyoming. Stop."

Once she'd finished writing the message, Essie slid it across the counter to the clerk. "How much will that be?" she asked when Fletcher made no move to pay for the telegram. The clerk named the price and she fished several coins from her valise. What a shame she had to part with good money for something that would prove completely worthless.

"We'll book us rooms at the hotel while we wait," Fletcher said, taking her arm again and leading her toward the door. "They ought to get back to us by tomorrow or the next day at the latest."

Panic coated Essie's tongue. She couldn't stay ensconced in the hotel for two days, awaiting her fate. There wasn't likely to be a telegram in response, or if one did arrive, it would surely prove her great-grandfather's indifference to Essie. "But it isn't likely to come for some time…"

Fletcher stopped short of the door. "What do you mean?" he snarled, his gaze jumping to the telegraph clerk behind them.

"I mean…" She licked her dry lips, desperately trying to remember anything her grandmother had told the family about her father, Henry. "He, um, isn't likely to be in the country at present." Yes, that was it. She remembered hearing as a girl that Henry Vanderfair liked to travel to warmer climates for the winter. "Which means it could take some time, more than a few days, for a message to reach him and for him to reply to his secretary. Then that man would have to send the funds."

She allowed herself a sigh of relief, hoping she'd bought herself at least another week or two. They could continue on to the hideout and Fletcher could check back for a reply, long after Essie had fled the gang.

Cursing, the outlaw marched her out the door.

Tate threw her a concerned look, which she met with a tight smile. "The telegram's been posted," she said with false brightness.

"But a lot a good it's goin' to do us now," Fletcher barked.

Clem looked between her and Fletcher. "Why's that?"

"Because her great-granddaddy is likely out of the country, which means we aren't gonna get that money for some time." He removed his hat and slapped it against his leg. "We need those funds now."

Essie edged away from him to stand closer to Tate. His hand came to rest against the small of her back, bringing instant comfort. She trusted him—just as she'd said. Though she wasn't sure if he would be much help to her if Fletcher uncovered her deception while she was still in their company.

Fletcher began pacing the sidewalk. The taut cloud that had shrouded the group earlier returned. "Go back in there," he commanded after a minute, coming to a stop in front of her and Tate. "Have them change the last part of that message. I want the instructions about the funds sent to the Occidental Hotel in Buffalo instead. It's closer to the hideout, and we've got to go there anyway to get our supplies."

Glancing up at Tate, who nodded for her to go ahead, Essie stepped back inside the telegraph office. To her surprise, though, none of the men accompanied her this time, not even Fletcher. She was all alone. The realization soon gave way to a bold idea, one that made her heart hammer faster.

"Did you forget something, miss?" the clerk asked kindly from his post behind the counter.

"Sort of." She smiled, in spite of the sharp hope and fresh apprehension stirring inside her. "Did you happen to send that telegram of mine?" she asked as she approached him.

He shook his head. "Not yet. There were a few others ahead of yours." His tone conveyed apology.

"Not to worry." She glanced out the window to make sure the men were not paying attention to her. "I've changed my mind, actually," she said in a low voice as she leaned against the counter.

The clerk's brow furrowed with confusion. "So you don't want the telegram sent?"

Essie shook her head, trying her best to appear calm. "No, I don't."

He studied her a moment then shrugged. Moving to the nearby desk, he shifted through a stack of slips before extracting hers. "Here you go, then, miss." He passed the message across the counter to her. "I'd better return your money, too."

Taking the paper in hand, her gaze still on the figures outside the window, she tore the paper in two and then in two again. "Do you have a rubbish bin?"

The man nodded. Scooping up the incriminating pieces, he turned and dumped them into the waste bin. The sight made Essie want to sing or throw her arms around the stranger. Now she wouldn't have to worry about what Henry Vanderfair's reply might have been. By the time Fletcher made it to Buffalo to see about the ransom, she would be long gone.

She scooped up the coins the man placed on the counter and gave him a genuine smile. "Thank you for your help, sir."

Still looking a bit puzzled, the man smiled back. "I suppose you're welcome."

Chuckling, as much at his words as from the relief coursing through her, she walked to the door and stepped outside. "It's been taken care of," she said before Fletcher could ask.

He'd put his hat back on and stopped pacing, but he still looked displeased. She felt a prick of fear that his ire would be a thousand times worse if he knew what she'd just done. But what other choice had she had?

Clem cleared his throat, interrupting the tense silence. "What'll we do now, Fletch?"

"We probably shouldn't linger in town," Tate offered, glancing around at the people moving along the sidewalk. "Word about the train might not have reached here yet, but you never know."

"I agree," Silas replied as he moved to the horses. "It's best if we keep going, Fletch."

"Saddle up, then," their leader growled. He shot Essie a hard look that made her shiver, but she wouldn't be cowed. Fletcher had no way of knowing she hadn't sent the telegram. When there was no answer, he might just think her great-grandfather had refused to reply.

There was plenty of time to finish conducting her research, and she fully intended to use it.

Tate helped her climb into the saddle, and then she turned her horse around and followed the others out of town. Less than ten minutes later, they'd left the buildings and people behind. Only then did Essie realize her hands were shaking. Her time with the group had come so close to an abrupt, and possibly painful, end.

Thank You for the respite, Lord, and for the chance to stop that telegram.

Drawing in a full gulp of fresh air, she let it out slowly. Everything was going to be all right, she assured herself. Just a few more days and she'd be on her way back home, hopefully wiser and more than capable of writing the best book she'd ever penned.

The sun was still hours from setting when Fletcher stopped the group to make camp. Tate didn't complain. After waiting out the earlier storm, and the one brewing inside him as he and Essie had taken shelter, he felt more than ready to put this day behind him.

His gaze flicked to Essie—again. Something unpleasant had happened back at the telegraph office, though he couldn't guess what. She'd been fairly talkative and cheerful since riding away from Casper, but Tate had seen a glimmer of unmistakable fear in her eyes before and after she'd taken care of the telegram. Perhaps he could find out the reason after dinner, when they did their usual talking as she wrote in her notebook.

Essie, Clem and Silas dismounted, but before Tate could swing down from his own horse, Fletcher announced, "Hold up there, cowboy. We're going back."

Tate jerked around in the saddle to look at the out-law. "What do you mean?" Out of the corner of his eye, he saw Essie and the other men staring in shock at Fletcher, as well. "Going back where?"

Fletcher yanked his horse's reins, turning the animal in the direction they'd just come. "Back to Casper. We're going to rob the bank there."

Shock reared inside Tate and he frowned; he'd thought his involvement with robberies was over for this mission. "I don't think that's a good id—"

"I'm not askin' what you think." Fletcher glared at each of them in turn. "We can't get our hands on Henry Vanderfair's money for at least a week or so." Essie ducked her chin. "And that good-for-nothin' Jude ran off with the rest. So we're goin' back to re-coup our losses."

"You don't need me for a bank job," Tate said, try-ing to keep his voice nonchalant. "Why don't I stay here with Miss Vanderfair?" That would keep them both out of the fray.

"Now that I think about it, I'd like to join you," Essie countered, taking a step toward him and Fletcher. "It would be great research, seeing all of you in action again. I could watch from across the street—"

"No!" Tate and Fletcher barked at the same time. It was likely to be the only thing they ever agreed on.

She crossed her arms, her mouth a tight line. "That's why I'm here, gentlemen. To not only hear and record your stories, but to understand your op-eration, your way of doing things. I won't be in the way, I promise, and it would help me to witness such a scene in person—"

"You're here to interview us, nothing more."

Fletcher's steely tone made Essie visibly flinch. "Which means you're stayin' put."

To her credit, Essie offered no further argument.

Tate felt a wash of relief at having dodged a dicey situation. His desire to keep her safe and far away from any illegal activity had worked. "I'll stay with her," he volunteered again. Fletcher didn't need him on this job—three men would be plenty to rob the bank.

But Fletcher shook his head. "Clem will stay with her."

"And why is that?" Tate couldn't keep his voice free of tension.

"Because I still don't trust you, cowboy." He glanced at Clem and something unspoken passed between them.

"If I haven't earned your trust now, I don't know what will."

Fletcher threw him a snide grin, which only intensified the apprehension in Tate's gut. "Oh, I'm startin' to trust you on the jobs. Just not where Miss Vanderfair is concerned. I'm not convinced you won't let her run off while we're away." With a dip of his chin, he signaled Clem. The outlaw cook suddenly drew his gun and pointed it at Essie, though his face drained of color.

Tate tensed, making his horse dance beneath him. The urge to jump down and stand between Essie and that gun barrel was nearly overpowering. What if she was shot?

He clenched the reins and forced himself to remain in his saddle. The sight of Essie standing there with her wide-eyed, confused expression and white lips felt like a knife through his chest, but if he wasn't careful, he might anger Fletcher further or spook Clem into pulling the trigger. He had to protect her by staying calm and in control.

"Is a gun really necessary?" He pushed the question past his sand-filled throat.

After flicking an appreciative glance in his direction, Essie focused on Clem. "I promise I won't run away. Truly, Clem. I will stay right here." She held her hands out and slowly sank to the ground as proof of her words.

"If she does make a move to leave, you shoot," Fletcher ordered.

Clem had the decency to look miserable at the task before him, but it was evident to Tate where the man's true loyalties lay. And it wasn't with the kind, pretty lady seated on the ground, her knees now drawn up to her chest.

"Let's go." Fletcher kicked his horse in the flanks and started riding again without a backward look. And though he looked downright unhappy himself, Silas silently climbed back into the saddle and followed.

Tate hesitated, wanting to give Essie some reassurance to allay the worry he still saw on her face. "So help me, Clem, if I find even one scratch on her when I get back…"

Clem lowered the gun a few inches. "If she says she'll stay put, I ain't doubtin' that." Glancing in the direction Fletcher and Silas had gone, he frowned. "But you know I gotta do what Fletch says."

"I'll be all right," Essie said, her eyes locking with Tate's. It wasn't hard to read the trust, faith and determination glowing in their hazel depths. Even when she still thought he was an outlaw.

Not for the first time, he wanted to feel worthy of her trust. If only he could tell her the truth about himself and his reasons for being there.

"You'd better go," she added, "before he gets even angrier. Clem won't hurt me. Will you?"

The outlaw shook his head. "On my honor. As long as you don't run away, ma'am." He tucked his gun away, a clear sign he meant his promise, and moved to gather the other horses' reins.

"All right, then." Tate threw Essie one more look and then nudged his mount to get moving. If he didn't catch up to Fletcher and Silas soon, there was no telling what the gang leader might conspire to do next.

Chapter Eleven

When he spied the bank up ahead, Tate's heart sped as fast as a locomotive. How had he ended up here, about to be culpable in another robbery? The obvious answer was his need to maintain his cover, but that wasn't the only reason. Ever since Essie had stumbled into his life, nothing had gone the way he'd expected. But he was fast realizing that wasn't a bad thing. Far from it.

The terrible memory of Clem drawing his gun on her flashed through Tate's mind. For one awful moment he'd feared for her safety and also for the possibility of having her yanked from his life. And the latter thought had terrified him.

At some point in the very near future Essie would disappear from his life—for good. He wouldn't get to observe her adorable, tousled hair in the morning anymore. Wouldn't get to sit and talk with her at night. Wouldn't get to watch her face light up as she told him stories or to hear her sparkling laugh or to see her pretty smile. She'd simply be gone.

Tate swallowed hard against the pressure growing in his chest as he dismounted beside Fletcher and
Silas, down the street from the bank. There wasn't
any way to keep Essie around, and now that he knew
Fletcher had no qualms about holding her at gunpoint,
he knew she should leave, for her own safety. But he
hated the idea of never seeing her again.

*Is there another way, Lord? To stay my course and
still have her in my life?* He didn't like the idea of her
being a detective's wife—that came with its own dangers and challenges. But he was duty-bound to keep
ridding the world of injustice. Wasn't he?

"All right, here's the plan," Fletcher said, jerking
Tate's thoughts from the future to the present. "Silas,
you stay with the horses. Have 'em ready to go the
second we come out of the bank." Silas nodded agreement before Fletcher turned to Tate. "You'll guard the
outside of the buildin'. Make sure no one enters the
bank after I do."

"I can do that." The tension in Tate's neck and
shoulders eased a little at hearing his assignment. He
wouldn't have to participate in the actual robbery—
just keep other people from getting involved.

Fletcher fished a bandanna from his pocket and
tied it around his neck. "I want to make this quick."

Trailing Fletcher toward the bank, Tate tugged his
hat lower and tried to look like he belonged. The outlaw stopped outside the door, his fingers reaching
for his gun.

"No one comes in," he reminded Tate in a harsh
whisper. "Got it?"

Nodding, Tate blew out a full breath and leaned
casually against the bank's outer wall as Fletcher

disappeared inside. He steeled himself for screams or protests, but the only sounds were the ones coming from the street in front of him. A few seconds passed and an older woman exited the bank, which meant Fletcher hadn't made his move yet. What was he waiting for?

Tate avoided eye contact with the woman, feigning interest in the sidewalk. She started past him and then, to his surprise, spun back around.

"Do I know you, young man?"

Cold panic stole over him, but Tate fought it back with logic. Surely this tiny woman wouldn't recognize Tex—and Tate felt certain he had never met her before. Darting a quick look at her matronly face and gray bun, he shook his head. "I don't think so, ma'am. I'm just passing through."

She pursed her lips. "No, I'm sure I know you."

"I'm not from these parts," he said, maintaining a deadpan expression. Hopefully she'd lose interest and move on.

But she stayed put. "Let's see. Maybe you know my son Levi?"

Tate forced an apologetic smile. "No, ma'am. As I said, I'm not from here. I've only been here once." *And that was about an hour ago.*

"Maybe you courted my daughter Lizzy?"

Irritation began to snuff out his alarm. "I don't think so. Like I said—"

Before he could finish, he caught sight of a man heading for the bank. Tate stepped away from the wall to block the man's progress. "Sorry, sir. Bank's closed at the moment."

Frowning, the man glanced past him to the woman. "What do you mean? Closed?"

"Don't ask me," the woman replied. "It was open a minute ago."

The stranger sized up Tate and made another move toward the door. "If it was open for her, then it should be open for me."

Using his firmest detective voice, Tate repeated his announcement as he stepped in front of the man. "As I said, it's closed for a bit. I truly apologize for any inconvenience."

"Well, how do you like that," the man huffed, folding his arms and glaring at both Tate and the woman. "How long before we can go in?"

"I've already been in." The woman grinned at the man.

Tate resisted the desire to roll his eyes. The scene felt like something Essie might have written into one of her dime novels. "I don't think it'll be long now." At least, he hoped not. The woman was still eyeing him, clearly trying to remember why he looked familiar.

Sure enough, she turned to the other man. "Doesn't he look familiar to you?"

Belatedly Tate realized he should've used a bandanna, as well, though he'd hoped not wearing one would make him look less conspicuous. "Ma'am, I told you. I haven't been—"

The man began studying him intently. "Now that you mention it, yes, I think I've seen him before, too."

Tate glanced over his shoulder, willing the bank door to open and for Fletcher to appear and end this. Had Tex possibly come to Casper, this far north from his usual outlawing territory? Tate clenched his jaw in annoyance at the strangers and at his brother. "I'm telling you the truth."

"Wait a minute." The man snapped his fingers. "It's his picture I've seen. On a Wanted poster, maybe."

Dread clamped hard around Tate's heart. What was taking Fletcher so long? "Now, let's not jump to conclusions." He eased away from the bank door, hoping they'd follow. To his relief, they did.

"He's right," the woman declared, her eyes narrowing. "That's where I've seen you." She poked a knobby finger into his chest. "But which one are you?"

Another woman holding the hand of a young boy approached the bank. Tate inwardly groaned. Why were so many people seeing to banking needs at this time of day? He took a step toward the newcomers, but the older woman and the man both hollered, "Bank's closed."

The mother looked surprised, her gaze wandering over Tate and the others. "Closed? What for? Is something wrong?"

The man shrugged. "Don't know. But I think we've got ourselves a wanted man right here."

"Again, no need to jump to conclusions," Tate repeated in a rational voice. He held up his hands in a surrendering gesture, but the mother still gasped and pulled her child protectively toward her. To the boy's credit, he looked more in awe of Tate than afraid.

"Should we get the sheriff?" the mother whispered loudly.

The older woman dipped her double chin. "That's not a bad idea." She shooed her hands at the man. "Go see if the sheriff knows which criminal he is."

"Look," Tate argued, "I'm not a—"

"He's the Texas Titan," the boy announced with exuberance, his entire face lighting up.

"That's it." The woman snapped her fingers in triumph. "I knew I'd seen your face. You tried to rob this bank a few months back. But I thought you were shot up real bad." She scowled at him as if angry that he showed no sign of injury.

Tex had robbed this same bank and been seriously hurt? Pain squeezed at Tate's chest at the thought of his twin brother wounded and bleeding, but anger followed quickly on its heels. It was only a matter of time before Tex's choices reaped such inevitable consequences.

From the corner of his eye, Tate watched the other man stumble backward and then dash across the street. It didn't take detective skills to deduce the stranger was going for the sheriff. Tate whirled around and yanked open the door of the bank. "Time to go," he hollered inside. "We've got trouble."

Fletcher spun to face him, his gun in one hand and a bag in the other. On the other side of the counter, the bank clerk watched them with frightened eyes. "What's wrong?" Fletcher demanded through the bandanna covering his mouth.

"The sheriff's coming."

The outlaw cursed as he sprinted for the door. "Let's get out of here."

Tate needed no further prodding. Ignoring the cries from the two women and the boy, he rushed past them toward the spot where Silas and the horses waited. The rapid pounding of his heartbeat filled his ears. If they were caught, his mission would be over. He'd never know where the outlaws' hideout was located.

Clem would go free…and who knew what would happen to Essie. It was better to see his course through than to abandon it, and that meant getting away—now.

"Go, go, go," Fletcher yelled as they neared the horses. Silas scrambled up from where he'd been waiting.

"What happened?" he asked as he held Fletcher's horse. "Did you get the money?"

Tate hurried to mount. "He got it, but the sheriff's coming."

More commotion sounded from down the street, confirming his words. Above the melee, a male voice roared, "Pumping that Texan fellow with lead last time wasn't enough to keep him away, huh? Had to come back and try to rob our bank again."

Fletcher jerked around in his saddle and stared at Tate, his gaze dangerous and angry. Before the outlaw could demand an explanation, though, a shot rang out. Tate ducked his head right before the bullet struck the building beside him. Another shot followed and this time he didn't wait to see where it landed. He spurred his horse forward and started up the street.

A quick glance over his shoulder showed Fletcher and Silas were following, but so was the sheriff and a small crowd. While the three of them had the advantage of speed with their horses, the threat of the sheriff's gun from behind still had alarm spiking inside Tate.

The sheriff fired a third bullet and, this time, there was an accompanying cry of pain. Tate spun in the saddle to see what had happened. Leaning forward on his horse, Silas gripped his right leg. Guilt seared Tate's stomach at the sight. Things were deteriorating fast and it was because of him, his attempt to impersonate his brother.

"Don't slow down," he urged Silas.

A fourth shot rang out, making Tate flinch. The sheriff wasn't giving up on teaching them a lesson. But he felt no pain, proof he hadn't been hit. To his relief, there were no further cries of anguish, either. They were nearly out of shooting range. The thought brought only little comfort. It wouldn't be long before the sheriff went for his horse and pursued them. Most likely accompanied by a whole posse of men who would also be armed.

"We gotta split up," Fletcher shouted when they reached the end of the street, echoing Tate's sentiments, as well. "Meet back at camp."

Tate looked to Silas, whose face had gone pale. "Can you make it alone?"

Visibly gritting his teeth, Silas gave a silent nod.

Fletcher didn't wait to hear more. The gang leader took off at a gallop. Irritated at the man's selfishness, Tate hesitated, slowing his horse and bringing the animal alongside Silas. He hated leaving an injured man alone to fend for himself against a possible mob. And if Silas was captured and ratted them out, it would further complicate things.

But Silas waved him on. "Go. I'll be fine."

Fishing his bandanna from his pocket, he thrust it at Silas. "Use this to help stop the blood." Even as he watched, the mark on Silas's pant leg was growing larger. "I'll be praying for you." The words were out before Tate could recall them and yet he didn't regret voicing them.

Silas stared askance at him for a moment, then whispered, "Thank you."

Tate nudged his horse and raced away toward the river and the open prairie beyond. He'd head east then cut back when he felt certain he wasn't being followed.

Only when he'd left the town behind did he feel able to catch his breath. But his heart still didn't slow for another few miles as the adrenaline from the harried ordeal continued to pulse in his veins.

He was grateful for the time to think. There would be plenty of miles to figure out what he'd say to Fletcher when he asked about "Tex" attempting to rob the bank before. And the gang leader would ask. Tate felt sure of that. What could he say in response? *Sorry I failed to mention that I tried to rob this same bank a few months back?*

His thoughts returned to Silas and he silently offered a quick prayer for the man's health and recovery. This afternoon had taken a dangerous turn, and while Tate knew he wasn't responsible for Fletcher's choice to rob the bank, he still felt culpability over Silas getting hurt. Perhaps he could've tried harder to convince Fletcher not to return to Casper, though he wasn't sure if it would've changed anything.

One thing was certain. He felt even more constrained to finish this job and then the next and the next. Too many of these outlaws were harming innocent people and getting away with it. A keen sense of regret filled him at the realization that a future with Essie would never be in reach now.

After a moment Tate pushed the emotion aside. He may not ever see her again after this, but he could do one final thing to help her. He'd convince her to leave, convince her it was too dangerous for her to remain with them any longer. Sadness reared its head again, but he tempered it with the hope that even if he couldn't be with Essie, he would know she was safe.

How much longer will they be? Essie thought, stifling an audible groan as she shifted her weight on the hard ground. She felt as if she and Clem had been waiting for the others to return for days instead of hours. Their conversation had run out soon after Tate had left.

She didn't believe Clem would actually shoot her, especially after he'd put away his gun. But she didn't plan to test the theory, either. After asking him for permission to get her notebook, she'd busied herself with writing different scenes she might use in a story and detailing the landscape around them for possible future use.

This time they'd stopped on a hill with scattered trees. Below them, a narrow ravine cut through the land, which dipped and swelled in every direction. At her back were the distant bluffs they'd passed through to reach Casper.

After a time, her creative energy had run thin and she now sat staring at the elongated shadows of the trees, her thoughts circling like crows. A listless, melancholy feeling had sprouted in the pit of her stomach, but Essie had to ponder the emotion for a time before she could identify its source.

She missed Tate.

Missed talking to him, missed prompting a smile from him, missed just watching him. And she felt his absence as keenly as if she'd misplaced something precious.

Might as well get used to it, she reminded herself, even as her heart rebelled at the thought. Tate had become the closest thing she'd had to a real friend since Nils had exited this world. It was only natural to miss his presence and feel a bit sad at the reality of that friendship coming to an end. And soon.

She recalled the look on his face when Clem had pulled his gun on her—pure panic and hardened resolve. There was no doubt in her mind Tate would've leaped to protect her, though she'd sensed he was desperately trying to keep a level head in the tenseness of the moment. Would she ever find another man like him? Someone she felt completely safe with, someone she could talk openly with and who listened in return, someone who treated her as more than a silly writer who wasn't serious about life?

Sounds like more than friendship, her heart and head announced, in agreement at last. Essie jerked a glance at Clem, who was whittling, grateful he couldn't read her mind. She wasn't falling for an outlaw. Even a kind, protective, handsome one.

Drawing her legs to her chest, she rested her chin on her knees. Was it too late? Had she already fallen for him? She shut her eyes, a feeling of hopelessness washing over her. Why did she have to go and do something so foolish? How absurd for her to give away pieces of her heart to a man who wasn't free to love her back, at least not in the way she longed for.

Loneliness lodged in her throat and leaked out as tears. She hadn't felt this desolate since that first night with the group. And now she was even farther from her home and everything familiar. Traveling with a gang of outlaws, one of whom she'd irresponsibly come to care for too much.

"They'll be hankerin' for food when they get back," Clem said as he pocketed his knife. "We oughta get started on supper."

Essie sniffed, grateful for the distraction from her confused thoughts. "I can help." She stood and joined Clem at the spot he'd designated for a fire.

Soon her hands were occupied with making biscuit dough and laying out the stiff, white spheres on the heated pan, but she wished she had something more to keep her thoughts busy. They kept alighting on Tate and then darting away.

If only he would give up being an outlaw like the hero in the scenes she'd written. If Tate left Fletcher's gang and committed himself to a life of honesty, then everything would be fine. She could fully give her heart to him and him to her. But would he agree to do such a thing?

From her four interviews, including Tate's, it wasn't difficult for Essie to see what had driven these men to this sort of life and what kept them living it. And yet each of them still had a choice—whether to continue or not. Could she convince Tate to make a different choice this time?

The sound of rapid horse hooves reached her ears. "Someone's coming," she and Clem said at the same time. She leaned back on her heels, her gaze pinned to the gap in the trees the men had ridden through earlier. Her heart launched into a faster tempo as a rider appeared. But it took only a moment to realize it wasn't Tate. It was Fletcher.

Clem stood as his boss ground to a halt and leaped from the saddle. "Where are the others?" Clem asked.

Essie stayed by the fire, unsure of Fletcher's current mood. If it was as mercurial as before, she wanted to keep her distance—and be relatively silent—until she felt sure he didn't want another gun pointed at her.

Removing his hat, Fletcher glanced around the camp, his mouth pulling downward. "They're not back yet?"

Something cold and slippery slid through Essie's middle at the outlaw's words. Had something happened to Tate and Silas?

Clem grabbed the reins of Fletcher's horse. "Did you get the money?"

The leader nodded. "We did. Then we had to split up. The sheriff came after us with his gun, yellin' and shootin'." Essie covered her mouth with her hand as visions of Tate, shot and bleeding, filled her head. "Silas took a bullet in the leg, but said he could make it back here on his own."

Essie released the breath she'd been holding. Tate wasn't hurt. Her relief was followed quickly by concern and fear for Silas. These men whom she'd come to know and interview weren't supposed to get shot and hurt. That should only happen to other outlaws. The iciness in her gut increased.

Pulling a sack from his saddlebag, which Essie assumed held the bank's stolen money, Fletcher threw her a searching look and stepped closer to Clem. Clearly he had something to say that he didn't want her overhearing. Essie feigned renewed interest in her already-finished biscuits.

Fletcher kept his voice low but it still carried easily to her ears. "Apparently our friend Tex tried to rob the bank in Casper a few months back." He snarled a few curse words. "The man didn't say a thing, though, which meant we practically walked ourselves into a trap when some folks recognized him."

Tate had attempted to rob the bank before? Essie swallowed hard, feeling her hope over him changing begin to dwindle and die.

"Least we got the money." Clem's bright tone sounded forced.

Fletcher scowled. "Maybe, but I don't trust him. I didn't before and I ain't startin' now. He's hidin' something."

Essie had to agree, though she kept her opinion to herself. She'd suspected Tate of hiding something ever since they'd met four days ago. Tate had a secret, and seeing the dangerous glint in Fletcher's eyes, she had to wonder who would be hurt more by the revelation. Fletcher and his men? Or Tate?

The sounds of more riders drew her to her feet. Tate charged through the trees, leading Silas's horse behind his. One look at the prone figure draped over the saddle horn sent fear pulsing through Essie again. This wasn't one of her stories; this was reality.

"Thought we were splittin' up," Fletcher said as he untied Silas's horse, his stormy expression trained on Tate.

"We did until I found his horse wandering around a few miles back." Tate jumped to the ground and hurried to help the injured man. "He'd passed out."

Clem glanced at Silas, his face nearly as ashen as his friend's. "How bad is it?"

"It's not good," Tate said, scooping Silas off the horse.

Essie stood frozen beside the fire, unable to take her gaze off the dark stain, the size of a dinner plate, on Silas's pant leg. "Is he…?" She couldn't bear to voice the rest.

Tate carried him toward the fire. "He's still alive, but we've got to stop the bleeding and get him bandaged." With obvious care, he set Silas on the ground near Essie. "Clem, go get some water."

"Not so fast," Fletcher barked, his arm blocking Clem from walking off. "The way I see it, you might as well have pulled the trigger on him yourself."

A muscle in Tate's jaw flexed and he slowly rose. "And why is that, Fletch?"

"'Cause you tried to rob that bank before, cowboy. And yet you didn't see the need to say somethin'." He waved a hand at the limp Silas. "Silas took a bullet that was meant for you."

"We aren't going to treat him, then?" Tate asked, his words as hard-edged as steel.

Fletcher sneered. "We aren't, but you are. And if he dies, cowboy…" The threat punctured the air like the boom of a cannon. "Well, let's just say we won't be buryin' him alone if that happens."

For some reason the bitter warning snapped Essie out of her horrified trance. "I'll help." She stepped forward to stand next to Tate, half expecting Fletcher to protest. Thankfully, he didn't.

Tate threw her a grateful look. "Will you get some water?"

Nodding, Essie emptied the biscuits onto a plate, then wrapped the still-warm handle of the pan in the folds of her skirt and carted it down the hill to the ravine. Making her way into the gully proved a little tricky, but she managed to half slide, half walk to the stream below. Clem had told her during their supper preparations that the storm had caused the once-dry creek bed to fill.

Essie rinsed the pan as best she could and filled it with water. Going back up the ravine's side was even harder than coming down as she tried to keep the life-saving liquid from spilling. But she at last made it to the top. Fletcher and Clem were eating, though the outlaw cook appeared in distress. Tate had cut away Silas's pant leg and was examining the wound.

"I know a little about nursing," Essie said quietly, setting the pan of water beside him.

He glanced up and, though he didn't smile, a momentary spark flashed in his blue eyes. "From your writing, I suppose?"

A small smile tugged at her mouth. "Yes." She glanced at the wound, but it was bleeding too much to ascertain the extent of the damage. Ripping a piece of material from her underskirt, she dipped the cloth in the water and pressed it against Silas's leg. "Get something to eat," she urged Tate.

He looked from Silas to the waiting food, a look of hunger passing over his face. "Maybe just a bit."

Quiet, fraught with tension, settled over the group. In its wake Essie could hear the sounds of the men chewing and a pair of birds chirping in one of the nearby trees. She continued to apply firm pressure to Silas's wound, hoping and praying they could help him.

Please, Lord, let him live. Not just for his sake but Tate's, too.

After a few minutes she lifted the cloth away to dab at the drying blood around the wound. Tate abandoned the rest of his supper. "Is the bullet still lodged in there?"

Essie gently lifted the man's leg to examine the other side, her mind filling with information she'd gleaned from a doctor in Evanston. "I don't think so because here's the exit wound."

Tate blew out a long breath and shot her a tentative smile. "That's a blessing."

The words sounded strange coming from the mouth of an outlaw, but she let the contradiction go. Silas still needed tending. "We ought to bind the wound and then see if he'll eat anything."

"I agree."

Tearing more fabric from her skirt, Essie soaked it in the water and wrung it out, while Tate carefully washed the back of Silas's leg. The poor man let out a moan every few minutes that ripped at Essie's heart, but he mostly stayed silent, lost to pain and unconsciousness. When they'd largely stanched the bleeding, Tate tied the bandage tightly around the injured leg.

"You don't have any medicine, do you?" she asked, certain she already knew the answer.

"No." Tate shook his head. "If it becomes infected…"

Essie pressed her lips together as reality washed over her anew. They were far from any doctor or medical supplies, which greatly reduced Silas's chances. And if he died… She shuddered but refused to follow the chain of such a thought. They would do what they could and perhaps there would be something more to help him at the hideout. At least she hoped so.

"Did you eat?" Tate motioned to the leftover food.

"I will." Though supper didn't sound at all appealing. "Then let's see if he'll drink something. I can make him a little gruel, too."

Tate lifted the pan and dumped out the used water. "I'll get some fresh water."

As he headed down the hill to the ravine, she dished herself some food and tried to stomach the now-cold beans and a biscuit. Fletcher and Clem were off to the side, seeing to the horses. Like Tate, she couldn't finish her supper. But she had to do something to keep her thoughts from wandering back to what danger lay ahead for Silas and Tate.

She glanced at the dirty dishes and felt renewed purpose. She would wash them. Gathering up the soiled plates, she followed in the direction Tate had gone.

At the edge of the ravine, she paused, trying to determine if the way she'd gone down before was the best route. Below her, she could see Tate crouched on one knee beside the stream, his head hung low. The pan in front of him overflowed with water, but he didn't make a move to pick it up. Instead he remained there, eyes shut, whispering words Essie could not hear. With sudden understanding, she realized he was praying.

Confusion flooded her, but also the feeling of something light and joyful. Could this outlaw truly believe in God and prayer and faith? Hope, as sharp as it was welcome, pierced her worries. Surely if Tate was a praying man, he could be persuaded to lead a different life. A law-abiding life—with her.

Not wishing to interrupt him, Essie fell back a step to wait for him to finish. But her foot knocked a rock and sent it tumbling down the ravine. Tate jerked his head up at the noise and spun around. When he saw her standing there, he slowly rose, his gaze imploring and searching hers. An unseen but tangible current of emotion flowed between them, making Essie's heart jump and her cheeks flush.

"I…um…thought I'd wash the dishes." She hoisted the pile in her hands, unsure whether to say anything about him praying or not.

The intensity in his eyes faded as he walked toward her and held out his hand. "Let me help you down."

She placed her fingers in his, which didn't help her already-pounding heartbeat. "Thank you." At the stream, she plunged the dishes and her trembling hands into the water, grateful when the coolness helped assuage the warmness of her face and her erratic pulse. At least until she gathered courage to speak to Tate…

Crouching, he lifted the full pan of water from the stream and set it aside. "Can I help?" He nodded at the dwindling pile of dirty dishes.

"All right." She passed him a bean-stained plate, their fingers brushing as the dish passed from her hand to his.

"Did Clem keep his gun stowed while we were away?" he asked, throwing her a quick glance.

Essie dipped her chin. "He did. I don't think he really would have fired it."

"Maybe, maybe not."

"I'm sorry about Silas." She accepted the clean

plate he handed back to her and set it aside. "I'm also sorry about Fletcher. That was wrong of him to make you care for Silas by yourself and tie his possible death with your own. His being shot isn't your fault."

Tate removed his hat and stared at it, his expression taut. "It isn't?"

Gathering the clean dishes, Essie climbed to her feet. "No. All three of you had a choice whether to rob that bank or not, regardless if one of you tried to do so before. We aren't responsible for others' choices, Tate." She offered him a hopeful smile. "We're only responsible for our own."

She glanced at the pink-and-blue sky. "I'm going to make Silas some gruel before it gets dark." She started toward the side of the ravine, but Tate reached out and stilled her movement with a hand to her arm.

"Essie, wait." He put his hat back on, his gaze skirting away then back again. "There's something I need to ask you."

Her heart skipped a beat or two as she moistened her suddenly dry lips. "Actually, there's something I wish to ask you, too."

His eyebrows rose. "Do you want to go first?"

She shook her head. Perhaps his question would make hers obsolete. Perhaps he meant to ask if she would write him letters or allow him to court her once he gave up being an outlaw. Fresh hope pressed hard against her ribs. "Go ahead," she urged softly.

Lowering his hand, Tate folded his arms and shifted his weight. His entire manner breathed agitation. If only she could reassure him that she would gladly accept his offer to pursue their relationship after he left his life of crime. But she kept silent.

"I've been doing a lot of thinking today." Tate rubbed a hand over his chin.

"And what have you been thinking about?"

The trace of a smile appeared on his mouth. "You."

Essie pressed the wet dishes to her dress to still the twisting sensation in her middle. "I've thought a lot about you, too." He hadn't asked his question yet, but she couldn't wait any longer to ask hers. "In fact, I wanted to know—"

"I think you ought to leave, Essie."

Rearing back as if she'd been slapped, she blinked in surprise. "Leave?"

"Yes." His voice was edged with frustration. "You need to leave and return to Evanston."

Her thoughts swirled like cotton seeds through her mind and she desperately tried to capture one. "But… but I haven't interviewed Fletcher yet. And I can't until we reach the hideout."

"Then don't interview him." Tate stalked a few paces away then wheeled around. "But you can't stay here anymore. It's too dangerous."

Her stomach tightened with chagrin and anger. He wasn't going to ask to write her or to court her. He wanted her gone. "I think I've handled myself quite well," she declared, straightening to full height.

"No one's arguing that fact. But I can't protect you anymore. Do you understand that? Not with Fletcher clamoring for my death should something happen to Silas." He paced toward her, stopping only a few inches away. "I can't bear to see another innocent life ruined by these men…"

Essie frowned in confusion. "What are you talking about? You're not making any sense, Tate."

A look of panic crossed his face before he schooled it behind a casual demeanor. "What I'm saying is I'll help you leave tonight. But you've got to go."

Lifting her chin, she glowered at him. "No, I don't. I've been fine so far, with or without your help, and so I'm staying."

His expression clouded, turning thunderous. "This isn't some silly game, Essie. And it's not a story you can write yourself out of if things get out of hand and your life is threatened again."

A dull buzzing started inside her head and she felt as if the wind had been knocked from her lungs. The word *silly* pecked at the old wounds in her mind until they split open, leaving them raw and aching.

Tate thought she was silly, that she didn't take things seriously, just as her family had. She could hardly breathe through the pain of such a realization. He was supposed to be different, to be her one true friend. The one who saw her humanness and, even more important, saw *her*.

"I'm not leaving," she managed to say over the lump clogging her throat. "Silas needs my help until he recovers, and I won't leave without my interview with Fletcher."

Tate reached his hand toward her then let it drop back to his side. "Essie, I'm just trying to keep you safe. I don't want something to happen to you…"

The entreaty, while sweet, didn't diminish her determination to stay or to ease the pain of his earlier words. "I'll be fine."

"What was it you wanted to ask me?"

An ache clutched at her heart as she shook her head. "It's nothing." Especially now.

She turned and scrambled up the ravine, the clean dishes still pressed tightly to her chest. Moisture filled her eyes. If only she could find a secluded place to mourn the loss of something she'd been so hopeful about only minutes before. But reality often had a way of cutting down dreams.

Like the one that she and Tate were meant to be.

Sniffing, she ran the back of her hand across her wet eyes. She didn't have time to cry. There was an injured man to care for and, in another day or two, her final interview to conduct. The trick would be keeping herself mentally and physically busy in the interim. So busy that perhaps her heartache over Tate wouldn't fully touch her.

Fletcher threw her a sharp look when she approached the camp, but Essie ignored him. She wasn't going anywhere and she was helping to nurse his wounded friend. He had little to complain about. *Except for when he learns I never sent that telegram.* Another source of troublesome thoughts.

She pushed the concern aside to attend to Silas. Since Tate hadn't returned with the water for the gruel, and she wasn't going to traipse back down to the ravine, she checked on Silas's bandage instead. A bit of new blood had leaked through, but it looked as if their limited doctoring had helped stanch the flow.

Tate finally returned and set the pan of water by her. He attempted to catch her eye, but Essie busied herself with making the gruel in a cup, using the water, some flour and crushed biscuit. Silas emerged from his semiconscious state a few minutes later and asked for a drink. She let Tate assist him while she finished preparing the simple food. Once the gruel was ready,

Tate propped Silas's head against his knees and Essie spooned the mixture into the injured man's mouth.

We make a good team, she thought sadly, glancing at Tate. *Too bad it can't last.*

"No more," Silas said in a hoarse voice after half a dozen mouthfuls.

Essie frowned. "It'll keep your strength up, Silas."

He gave a slight shake of his head. "No more. Let me rest."

Tate removed his jacket and placed it beneath Silas, then lowered his head onto the bunched fabric. The simple, humane act tore at Essie. While he might be an outlaw who dismissed her as silly, Tate was still a good man, a kind man.

Not wishing to attract any nocturnal animals with the food, Essie trekked back to the stream and rinsed away the remaining gruel. She filled the cup with fresh water for Silas to drink, but she paused to stand beside the stream.

"Lord, I feel so alone," she whispered to the first stars glittering overhead. "Nothing has been quite as I expected since I left that train. But I do want to be here." And she did. Even if romance hadn't worked out with Tate, she was still grateful for his friendship and protection over the last few days. "I'm nearly done with my interviews and then I just want to go home. Bless Silas with Thy help…and Tate, too. He's a good man, Lord, even if he doesn't know it."

She ended the prayer with a murmured "Amen" and headed back to camp. The men sat near the fire, except for Silas, who appeared to be sleeping. A groan escaped his lips as Essie drew closer. She wished she had something to give him for the pain. But if he needed a drink during the night, they could at least oblige him that.

"I'll sit up with him awhile," Tate said as she set the cup of water near Silas.

She offered a silent nod and went to collect two blankets, feeling Tate's gaze follow her.

One she placed over Silas and the other she spread out nearby for herself. Exhaustion filled every one of her muscles, leaving her bone-weary and unable to think. It would be the first night since she'd come along with these men that she hadn't written in her notebook. Hadn't stayed up and enjoyed talking with Tate.

She caught sight of his tense expression right before she shut her eyes and rolled onto her side, her back to him. There was nothing more to say or to do tonight. She would try to listen for Silas and give him a drink if he needed one.

Sleep stole all consciousness from her, and it was full dark when something nudged her back to wakefulness. She opened her eyes to see no one near her. All the men had taken to their bedrolls for the night. Craning her neck, she eyed Silas in the light of the moon. He was still sleeping.

Not wishing to wake him, lest the pain return full force to his mind, she closed her eyes and attempted to return to sleep. Only then did she realize the reason for her waking in the first place. Fletcher and Clem were conversing in hushed tones on the other side of the camp.

"No lawmen…can't make it into the valley…we'd see 'em comin'…"

She half listened until the conversation wound

down, but most of the words simply floated off into the night, refusing to take root inside her sleepy mind. Should she get up and write down what she could re-call? Was any of it important? They had chosen to talk after everyone else was presumably asleep.

Opening her eyes, she slid a look at Tate to con-firm if he was also sleeping. His brows and mouth appeared relaxed with slumber but he could be pre-tending sleep while he eavesdropped, too. She hesi-tated another moment, debating what to do, then made a decision. It was late and exhaustion was once again reaching out to claim her captive.

Besides, she reasoned as she yawned, if she fished out her notebook now she would alert the other two men to her presence. And she didn't like the thought of them knowing she wasn't asleep or had overheard some of what they'd said. Clem didn't frighten her, but Fletcher was another matter.

Whatever they were discussing wasn't likely to be of any real importance, she rationalized, and morn-ing would soon be here. And with it, an injured man to care for and a handsome one to avoid.

Chapter Twelve

Light prodded at Tate's eyelids, urging him to rise. He wished he could pretend this whole mission had just been a bad dream. But he couldn't—and a good part of him didn't want to. That would mean pretending he hadn't ever met, befriended or come to care for Essie.

The couple of times he'd woken in the night, his gaze had gone first to Silas to ensure the man was still breathing and then to Essie. She'd looked so peaceful, so beautiful. Not a trace of the hurt and anger he'd seen on her face yesterday after he'd attempted to convince her to leave. He'd only been trying to protect her, or so he told himself. But sometime through the night, in between sleeping and helping Silas get a drink of water twice, he'd wondered if his motives were as pure as he'd believed.

Yes, he wanted Essie away from potential danger. But maybe he had a selfish reason, too. Because the more he got to know her, the more he'd begun fight-

ing with himself. Should he stick with what he felt
duty-bound to do or follow his heart for once?

Silas emitted a groan, prompting Tate to finally
throw off his blanket and sit up. The man was still
alive, much to Tate's relief, and yet his face now appeared more gray than white. A quick glance toward
Essie's sleeping spot sent a jolt of panic through Tate
when he found it empty.

He scrambled to his feet. Had she left, after all?
None of the horses was missing, though. Tate ran a
hand through his rumpled hair and clapped his hat
on. Where could she be?

"She went to the stream," Clem said in a low voice
without taking his eyes off the breakfast he was beginning to prepare.

So Clem suspected Tate cared for her. Did Fletcher
suspect, too? Tate looked in the leader's direction and
found him, thankfully, unaware and snoring on the
other side of the camp. The sack of bank money lay
cradled in Fletcher's arms, next to his gun.

A fresh wave of hope washed through Tate's heart
at the news Essie hadn't left. *But you want her to
leave, don't you?* his head protested. He didn't know
anymore. And the uncertainty gnawed at him more
than hunger this morning.

Unsure if Essie would welcome his company at
the stream, he stayed in camp and checked on Silas
instead. The bandage was soiled, but Tate didn't see
any new blood, which he took as a good sign. Still, he
worried what further injury traveling would inflict on
the outlaw today. He offered the man another drink,
then helped Silas lie back. There was no reason to
move him any sooner than they had to.

Essie returned from the stream, a pan of water in her hands. Her gaze interlocked with Tate's before she tucked her chin down. He recognized the gesture for what it was—he still wasn't forgiven. Was she angry about him insisting she leave or was it something else?

"There's no new blood," he said as she came and knelt beside Silas.

She nodded. "I noticed that, too." With steady hands, she untied the cloth from around Silas's leg, then rinsed it in the water.

Tate watched her fingers with fascination as she re-dressed the man's wound. Over the past few days he'd watched those same hands write, cook, nurse and comfort. But his favorite thing about her hands was holding them. Would he ever have that chance again?

Silas asked for water and Tate hurried to help him. After draining the last bit from the cup, the outlaw lay back, breathing heavily.

"I don't think he ought to travel today," Essie whispered, throwing a look at Fletcher over her shoulder.

The man had finally risen and was starting in on some of Clem's breakfast without even checking on the injured man, as if he didn't care one whit about Silas. Anger sparked inside Tate, but he directed his scowl at the ground. "I agree, but I don't think staying put is an option."

She finished tying the wet cloth around Silas's leg and rose. "I'm going to say something." Her eyes had darkened to green with determination.

"Essie, wait." Tate stood, as well, placing his hand on her arm. She flinched and looked away. Remorse cut sharply through him. Only yesterday they'd taken shelter from the storm together, his arm around her and her head on his shoulder. Now his touch elicited discomfort. He dropped his hand to his side. "I don't think that's a good idea."

"Nonsense." She marched over to Fletcher, while Tate clenched his fists. He'd be ready to jump into the fray if needed. "Mr. Fletcher," Essie commanded in a firm tone. The man set down his breakfast and glanced up, his eyebrows raised in annoyance.

"What it is, Miss Vanderfair?"

"It's important that we let Silas rest. He shouldn't be moved yet."

Fletcher cut a look at the injured man. "That isn't going to work. Especially if that sheriff is still on our trail." He picked up his plate again. "We'll be to the hideout the day after tomorrow. He can rest there."

Essie glared down at the man. "If he makes it that far…"

"Well, that's Tex's problem. Not mine." His eyes narrowed. "Or yours."

Concerned at the growing tension between the two, Tate stepped forward, gripped Essie by the elbow and steered her back toward Silas. "We'll do what we can for him," he said in a low voice. "But confronting Fletcher is like trying to tame a beehive with a stick."

Her mouth turned down into a frown, but she didn't shake him off. "All right. But I'm worried, Tate. He needs medical attention."

"I know. Maybe the hideout has some supplies."

She threw him a sharp glance at the same moment he realized his mistake. "You've never been there?"

He didn't want to keep another truth from her, so he feigned interest in breakfast and ignored the question. "We'd better eat, then see if Silas wants something. It's nearly time to ride."

Feeling her intense gaze on him, he filled two plates with food and handed one to her. Essie thanked him, though she still didn't appear happy. Tate wasn't sure if her frustration was aimed at him for not answering her or at Fletcher for refusing to let Silas rest. Maybe both. They ate in silence, reminding him of the night before when she'd gone straight to bed without writing. He'd realized in that moment how much he'd come to look forward to their time together in the evenings when she'd write and they'd talk. He couldn't help wondering if they would ever have that again.

After he'd finished eating, Tate fed Silas the gruel Essie had prepared. The outlaw managed a few more spoonfuls than he had the night before, but he was still visibly weak. The ride today would be difficult for him.

Tate offered another prayer for Silas as he saddled the horses. Once Clem and Essie had breakfast cleaned up, it was time to go. With as much care as he could, Tate lifted Silas onto one of the horses.

"Tie me on," the man whispered, his face twisted with agony before he hunched over the saddle horn.

After locating some rope, Tate obeyed Silas's request. He helped Essie mount next and then climbed onto his own horse. Clem and Fletcher took the front two positions for the group, which served Tate fine. He wanted to keep pace with Silas in case the man needed help.

He half expected Essie to ride ahead, seeing that she was still frustrated with him. But she matched her horse's pace to his slower one, keeping Silas be-

tween them. Before long, Clem and Fletcher were
far ahead, though with every rise Tate would catch a
glimpse of them.

The day proved especially warm, making yesterday's storm feel like a distant memory. Tate was grateful for his hat, but Essie had nothing. "Do you want
to use my hat?"

She seemed to shake herself back to the present.
What had she been thinking about? he wondered.
"No, but thank you." Her face and tone had lost some
of its edge and yet Tate still suspected all wasn't forgiven.

The three of them rode in silence, broken only by
the sound of the horses and the occasional grunt of
pain from Silas. To his credit, the outlaw didn't complain and he stayed relatively upright on his horse.
After a while, though, the quiet—something Tate used
to crave—began grating on his nerves. He wanted to
talk to Essie, to discover what she was thinking, to
hear her tell another story. Anything to break up the
monotony of the landscape and the lingering tension
between them.

Dropping back, he guided his horse around Silas's
and drew alongside Essie's right side. "You doing all
right?"

She looked up and nodded. "I'm worried about
Silas." Twisting in the saddle, she peered at the injured man who'd shut his eyes some time ago.

"I am, too," he admitted. He tried to swallow his
next words but they wouldn't quit pushing against his
tongue. "I'm praying for him."

Turning to face him, Essie frowned, her brow
bunched in confusion. "I know. I saw you last night."

Should he reveal any more? "I…um…" He wet his dry lips. "Despite what you might think, Essie, I am religious."

"Then why keep doing this?" She waved a hand at the rocky hills and sagebrush plain, clearly meaning a life on the run.

"Because I have to," he said, low enough that he wasn't even sure if she heard him. He wasn't pretending to answer as Tex right then. He was answering for himself, about his decision to be a Pinkerton detective.

A pained look filled Essie's eyes before she faced forward. The nagging silence returned, but Tate no longer had the energy or words to fill it. Letting himself fall back once more, he circled to Silas's left side. But his gaze kept skittering to Essie. He'd never seen her so despondent; her normal spark and smile were noticeably absent. If things could only go back to the way they'd been… Tate thought about the other night when they'd talked at the ranch and again during the storm. Controlling her good opinion of him might be as impossible as controlling the wind, and yet he hated to think his decisions and words had permanently cost him her friendship.

Tell her the truth.

The realization came to him as unexpectedly as a slap to his face. The only way to fix things between them was to be honest with her. But could he do it? Tate tightened his grip on the reins, shaking his head slightly. If he told her, he risked ruining his entire mission.

More firmly and insistent, the thought filled his mind a second time: *Tell her the truth.*

Tate frowned and tugged his hat lower. *Is that what You want, Lord? Do You want me to tell her who I really am?*

A sense of peace and certainty filled him, overpowering his fear. He'd wanted to tell her, for some time now. But would it make a difference? Would he still be able to complete this mission if he did?

"Trust in the Lord with all thine heart and lean not unto thine own understanding..." How many times had his mother read him and Tex that Bible verse from Proverbs? Tate had always liked it, but he wasn't much for trusting—not his brother, not others and, more often than he cared to admit, not God.

But he could change that—starting today, starting right now—by trusting Essie with everything. All he needed was an optimal opportunity, out of earshot of Fletcher and his men. *I'll do it, Lord. Just please make a way.*

By the time the group stopped to eat lunch, Tate had attempted to prop Silas up half a dozen times. The poor man needed rest. It was evident in his slumped shoulders, his pinched face and the way he winced whenever the horse had picked up its gait.

"Let's get you some shade," Tate said as he carefully untied Silas from the saddle and helped him to the ground. There were no trees in sight, though a nearby trickle of water offered some reprieve from the long, hot ride.

Essie dismounted on her own and approached them. "How is he?" Concern drew lines on her brow and around her mouth. "I thought for sure he'd fall off, even with the rope and your help."

Tate glanced around at the landscape. A rise in

the land created a patch of shadow, but Fletcher and
Clem had already staked it as theirs. Fresh annoyance warmed him. Why did these men still choose
to follow Fletcher when he clearly had no real regard
for them?

Because they feel they have to, he thought, answering his own question. Wasn't that what Essie had discovered through her interviews?

"See if you can find me some sticks." Tate removed
his jacket. "I'm going to make him some shade."

He caught a flash of admiration in her eyes before
she turned away. "I'll see what I can find."

"We're going to get you out of the sun if we can,"
Tate said, kneeling beside Silas. The outlaw gave a
small nod of his head. "Something to eat, too. Are
you hungry?"

"No." The word sounded like it had been scraped
from the bottom of a dry barrel. "Just water."

Nodding, Tate stood and went to collect a cup from
Clem. Fletcher's hard gaze bored into his back as
he crouched beside the tiny creek and filled the cup
with water. He helped Silas drink until the man had
drained the cup twice.

Essie came back, a sagebrush in each hand. "I
couldn't find any large sticks, so I figured these would
have to do."

"How did you pull them out?"

"I managed." She set the brush on either side of
Silas, and Tate placed his jacket over the top, shading
the injured outlaw beneath.

Only then did he get a look at Essie's hands. They
were lined with pricks of red from wrestling the sagebrush. This sign of her determination and compas-

sion pierced him straight through the heart. Surely he'd never find another woman he admired as much as he did her.

Clem interrupted the poignant moment with a call for lunch. Cold beans and jerky were all they had. They ate without speaking. Even Essie didn't attempt her usual dialogue about the ride or anecdotes about life. When he'd finished, Tate crossed back to where they'd left Silas. They needed to check his bandage, but the man's chest rose and fell with sleep.

"Time to go," Fletcher announced even before the lunch dishes had been cleaned.

Tate stood and walked back over to join the others. "It's too soon, Fletcher." He pointed over his shoulder at Silas. "He nearly fell off his horse before we stopped. He needs rest."

"It's true," Essie added, squaring her shoulders as though preparing for a fight. Which there very well might be.

"I said he could rest at the hideout." Fletcher took a step toward Tate and stopped, his stance full of challenge. "If he doesn't make it there, that's on you, cowboy."

Tate fisted his hands. He wanted nothing more than to plant one of them in Fletcher's face. But no good would come of it—not for him, or Silas, or Essie.

Clearing his throat, Clem rose, wedging himself between Fletcher and Tate. "Fletch, we can take an hour to rest the horses. Even get a quick nap."

Fletcher's face registered the same surprise that Tate felt. He couldn't recall ever seeing Clem stand up to Fletcher before. Perhaps the man was tired of being ill-treated or perhaps it was out of concern for

Silas. Or perhaps Someone else had softened the outlaw's heart.

Whatever the reason, Fletcher finally acquiesced. "All right. One hour. Not a minute more."

Tate fought a grin, certain Fletcher would change his mind if he caught sight of it. Walking back to Silas, he made certain the outlaw was alive and sleeping. Tate studied what he could see of the bandage beneath Silas's pant leg. It had collected dirt and dust throughout their ride, and several spots of fresh blood penetrated the cloth. He figured that was probably normal given all the jostling. When they woke Silas in a bit, he'd see if Essie would help him re-dress the outlaw's wound.

A glance in her direction revealed she was setting out the newly rinsed lunch dishes to dry in the sun. Clem and Fletcher had already stretched out in the shade, their hats covering their faces.

It's now or never, Tate thought. His heart banged wildly in his chest. He might not have another chance to talk to her without being overheard. But would she hear him out, especially after last night's disastrous conversation?

She straightened and looked around as if unsure what to do next. *Please help her listen, Lord.* Catching her eye, he motioned for her to join him. Her mouth pursed in hesitation, and then, after visibly releasing a sigh, she walked toward him. "Does Silas need anything?" she asked without sitting.

"His bandage needs re-dressing, but he's asleep right now. It can wait. Why don't you sit a spell?" He patted the ground beside him.

Her obvious reluctance pinched at his hope for rec-

onciliation, but she finally took a seat. "That was…
kind of you to rig up some shade for him." She peered
at the stream instead of at him and yet he sensed her
sincerity. Essie was always authentic.

"So was yanking out the sagebrush." As if on its
own accord, his hand reached for one of hers and
turned it over. His thumb traced the pattern of scratches
across her palm.

She stiffened, her eyes darting to his. "Tate, please…"

"Essie." Squeezing her fingers, he exhaled slowly
as he prepared to voice the words he'd both feared and
hoped to say to her. "I'm not an outlaw."

Her face furrowed with confusion. "What are you
talking about?"

He threw a glance at the others and saw they were
still sleeping. "It's true," he said, lowering his voice
anyway. "I'm not an outlaw. I'm a Pinkerton detective agent, working in disguise."

"But…" She shook her head in disbelief, seeming
to forget all about him holding her hand. Tate wasn't
complaining—he wanted to cradle her soft fingers a
little longer. "But you look exactly like the Texas Titan.
Same eye color, same hair color, same build. Everything the same as listed on those Wanted posters. Well,
except for that scar behind your ear."

Tate leaned forward, bringing his eyes to the same
level as hers. "And that is the biggest difference between me and my twin brother."

"Twin?" she repeated, her expression stunned.

He nodded. "My twin brother, Tex Beckett, is the
real Texas Titan."

"You have a twin?" Her voice had risen in volume.

Tate released her hand to clap his over her mouth. If she woke the others before he could finish...

Above his fingers, her green eyes stared in shock at him. "The others don't know," he murmured. Her gaze flicked to Silas and she dipped her head in a nod. He lowered his hand and continued his explanation. "My brother disappeared a few months back and I saw it as an opportunity to infiltrate Fletcher's gang by pretending to be Tex."

"So you really haven't ever been to the Paiges' ranch. That's what you meant when you said I had to trust you." Essie swiveled to face him. "You weren't the one who tried to rob the bank in Casper, either."

He couldn't help smiling at her skills of memory and deduction. "Right on both accounts. I didn't know Tex had been to the ranch or even to that bank. Which made both situations pretty tricky to navigate while I was pretending to be him."

Instead of joining in his merriment, though, she glanced at her lap. "Why didn't you tell me sooner?"

The smile dropped from his face. Taking her shoulders gently in hand, he waited for her to lift her chin before he continued. "I wanted to, Essie. Soon after getting to know you. But I didn't think I could risk it. There was—still is—the possibility of harm coming to me and to you if Fletcher finds out."

"Then why tell me now?"

He rubbed her sleeves with his thumbs, a longing to hold her close, to kiss that drooping mouth, filling him to distraction. "Because," he said, clearing his throat, "I feel like you ought to know." Tate released her and fiddled with the brim of his hat. Emotions pushed against his logic and won out.

"I wanted you to know," he added in a half whisper, "because I want you to know the real me."

The smile he'd been missing for hours finally bloomed on her lips. "Even if I thought you were an outlaw, Tate, I've known the real you for several days now."

Her words struck with force inside his heart and mind. Had his seemingly irrational hunch been correct all along? Had God intended for him to meet Essie?

"I have a question, then," she said, pulling him from his thoughts.

"Just one?" He prompted another smile from her with his teasing.

"Whose story were you telling the other night by the corral?"

Tate shifted on the hard ground. "I told it from Tex's perspective, but I was sharing my story, too. Everything happened just as I said. I was so angry that night, for a lot of reasons. Something inside me just snapped when I saw Tex meant to sell our mother's cherished earrings." He lifted his hand and absently rubbed at the scar behind his ear. "When I came to after he hit me with the lantern, I wasn't able to find him. He'd disappeared completely. Eventually I sold the farm and joined the Pinkerton agency."

Reaching out, Essie touched his ear. "So that's why you have that scar. I wondered why the newspapers or Wanted posters hadn't mentioned it."

"Telling you that story from my brother's viewpoint caused me to see things I didn't at the time."

"Such as?"

"I was too hard on him, Essie. Always goading him about responsibility and working for what you get. In a lot of ways he reminded me of our pa and I couldn't watch him turn out like that. Even if I was older by only a few minutes." He lowered his head, the burden pressing down anew. "In the end, I drove him to a life that was much worse."

Her hand settled on his arm. "Tate?" she said quietly. He didn't want to lift his head, didn't want to see the accusation he knew he'd find in her innocent gaze. But when he finally dragged his eyes upward, the compassion emanating from those green-brown eyes surprised him. "You didn't drive him to do anything."

"But—"

She shook her head, silencing his protest. "Tex's choices are his. Just as your choices—to sell the farm, to become a detective, to come on this mission—those are yours and no one else's."

He couldn't help eyeing her with skepticism. "But I was too hard on him. He was hurting just as much as I was after our ma died, but he showed it differently. I didn't understand that at the time. And I was jealous of him and Ravena. They were the only family I had left and they wanted to leave me behind."

The honesty and bitterness of his own words caked his mouth with acid. He hated admitting them, but he wanted Essie to understand everything. "I've done my best to make things right. I've hunted down outlaw after outlaw to keep people like Tex from hurting the innocent. But there's always another job, another robbery to investigate."

"Is that why you became a Pinkerton agent?" Her eyebrows rose in question. "For your brother?"

Hearing her voice his motive out loud made him shrink inwardly. "I was trying to balance things, to bring justice to a world Tex is determined to undermine."

To his annoyance, Essie regarded him with sorrowful empathy rather than admiration. "You have to stop paying penance for your brother's mistakes. They aren't yours."

He scowled at the stream, his mind whirling like a jetty. Did he truly think bringing justice to the world would make up for Tex's wrongdoings? Or was he really trying to atone for his own?

The poignant question smacked him in the forehead, bringing sudden clarity. He'd been running from reality just as surely as Tex had. By not owning his part in their argument that night. By thinking he could control his brother or make different choices for Tex—or even atone in his place. By putting all of his energies into a job he didn't truly love.

All these years he'd lived under the shame of having an outlaw twin brother, thinking he had to do something about it. But Essie was right. He wasn't responsible for Tex's choices, just as Tex wasn't responsible for his.

A peace he hadn't known since boyhood filled him head to toe. No wonder his prayers about continuing to do his duty had gone unanswered.

That's what You've been trying to tell me all along, Lord. That I was only responsible for my part, not his.

"It's not too late to make things right with your brother, Tate." Essie's imploring glance drew him back to the conversation. "But that isn't going to happen by rounding up every criminal you can find. It'll happen when you tell him you're sorry for the things you said and did, and how those affected him. Hopefully he'll say the same, but even if he doesn't, you'll be able to move forward."

Tate studied his hands—they were so similar to his brother's. Were Tex's as lined and weathered with growing age as his were? "I have to find him first."

Linking her fingers through his, Essie offered him a smile. "I believe you will." Hope as warm and comforting as a hot meal filled him as he studied her pretty face.

"I think he might be hurt," he said, drawing strength from Essie's touch. "The sheriff in Casper was yelling about shooting me—or rather, him—again."

"Then we can pray for him. Right now."

He'd done the right thing in telling her. A physical weight had dropped from his shoulders now that he wasn't carrying the burden of truth alone anymore. Tate cast a glance at the sleeping outlaws. "All right."

Lowering his head, he murmured the words that filled his heart. He wasn't sure if Essie could hear him, but he welcomed the chance to pray openly in her presence. "Father, thank You for Essie's wisdom. Thank You for using her to show me my own stubborn blindness. Bless Tex. Keep him safe." A lump crowded his throat and prompted a cough. Essie squeezed his hand, encouraging him to finish. "He's my brother and always will be. And I want to find him and make things right between us. In the name of Thy Son. Amen."

He opened his eyes to find Essie peering openly back at him. Her gentle smile, and the fact that she still held his hand, encouraged a scene to form inside his mind. He and Essie were riding astride matching horses, silhouetted by a frame house in the distance with plenty of farm acreage surrounding it. No outlaws, no covert jobs, no more running ragged trying to redeem the past. The image stirred dreams he'd thought he had long ago buried—dreams of working a farm again, of having a family, of being at peace.

"Thank you for telling me the truth, Tate."

Her soft voice disrupted his imaginings, but a feeling of liberation remained within him. Somehow everything would work out, especially now that he was committed to truly trusting the Lord. Even though Silas was still injured and Tate still had to see this mission through to the finish, he no longer felt alone. "It's nice not to have to keep that secret from you."

Instead of responding with mutual happiness, Essie slid her hand from his and fiddled with the hem of her borrowed dress. Her bright expression had grown cloudy again, reminding him of earlier.

"What is it?" he asked.

She released a sigh as she clasped and unclasped her hands. "There's something I ought to tell you… now that I know you're not an outlaw." Tate waited, his relief at voicing the truth evaporating at her reluctance. "It's about…"

A noise from Silas drew their attention; he was stirring. But it could wait a moment. "Essie, what is it?"

Standing, she shook her head. "I can tell you later. We need to re-dress Silas's bandage before Fletcher demands it's time to go."

Tate consulted his watch. They had less than ten minutes of their rest hour left. Though he didn't like the idea of putting off their conversation, Silas did need their help if he was going to make it through another long ride. "All right. But will you tell me when we stop tonight?"

She hesitated then dipped her chin in a quick nod. Concern and uncertainty still reflected in her gaze. They returned to Silas's side and Essie removed the soiled bandage. Working quickly, she soon had the cloth rinsed and tied once more around the injured leg.

After waking Clem and Fletcher, Tate helped Silas back into the saddle. The man's face had a little more color, but he still insisted on being tied onto his horse. They started out again, Tate feeling less burdened than he had in years. One look at Essie, though, told him something was still bothering her. She threw him a smile but it didn't fill her eyes or light up her face. What could be bothering her? She knew the whole truth about him now.

Or did she?

He hadn't confided everything. There was something he'd kept back. He hadn't shared how much he'd come to admire her or how she figured prominently into his new dream for the future. Tonight he'd tell her. Then she could choose if she felt the same or not.

One way or the other, he hoped revealing more of his heart would help put the sunshine permanently back into her demeanor. Because whatever his future held over the next few days or weeks or years, he hoped Essie would be a part of it.

Chapter Thirteen

Tate's not an outlaw. Tate's not an outlaw. The re-
frain ran through Essie's mind like a music box someone kept winding up to play over and over again. She
was hardly conscious of anything else.

She hadn't come to care for a man who wasn't free
to care for her in return. Because Tate wasn't an outlaw; he was a Pinkerton detective. That truth had
greatly soothed her battered spirits, though she still
wondered if he thought her silly. Perhaps the kindness of his touch and the happiness in his blue eyes as
they'd spoken by the stream were only evidences of
his relief and nothing more.

Then there was the matter about the ransom. He'd
told her his secret and she needed to tell him hers. But
would he be angry with her when he found out there
was no money coming? Or worse, would Tate see her
deception in destroying the telegram as further proof
that she didn't take life seriously?

Essie grasped the reins more tightly and then winced
as the leather scraped the cuts on her palms. Perhaps

Tate wouldn't be upset with her. After all, he'd concealed important information, as well. Though, if she were truly honest with herself, she knew he had greater reason for doing so. Keeping his true identity to himself was critical to saving his life and fulfilling his mission.

And what of your mission? her head persuasively argued. *You wouldn't have been allowed to come along if they'd known about the ransom that first day.*

This was also the truth. But now that Tate had shared his secret, Essie felt compelled to do the same. No matter how upset he might get or how silly he accused her of being. He needed to know, long before Fletcher ever did, that the money wasn't coming.

Resolved, she tried to smile each time Tate looked her way, but her stomach wouldn't cease its churning. She'd inadvertently and carelessly plunged herself into the middle of a dangerous situation. A detective in disguise, an injured outlaw and a man desperate for her money didn't make for the most safe or ideal companions, especially when there was likely a bunch of lawmen on their trail. The circumstances looked dire, even to someone as imaginative as herself. What had seemed like the perfect solution to her worries over her writing career now felt more like a nightmare, a trap.

Except for meeting Tate. Essie twisted to look at him, but she hurried to face forward when he turned in her direction. Was it possible they could have a future together? Neither of them had voiced any real feelings, though Essie had felt them growing the more time she spent in his company. And yet would being a detective's sweetheart or wife be much different than an outlaw's? While on the right side of the law, the job was still dangerous, still allowing for long periods of time without seeing one another. Then there was her own career to consider. Did she wish to give up writing dime novels to be a wife and mother? She loved her life as an authoress...didn't she?

Regret pressed hard against her ribs at the question. Of course there were moments of exultation when she was writing and creating, when she was caught up in a world of her own making. But what of building a fulfilling life for herself in the real world instead of retreating into her imagination? Since leaving home, she hadn't put much effort into really cultivating friendships or relationships outside her made-up characters. She'd convinced herself, especially after Harrison's rejection, that her fictional world and a life on her own were enough to satisfy her. And yet over the last five days she'd begun to see that wasn't true. Befriending Tate had thrown harsh light onto her solitary existence in Evanston.

Since Nils's death, she'd thought she was so brave to finally move away from the ranch and pursue her bold career. But perhaps she'd only been running from her past, like Tate had from his. Every decision driven by the hurt that she wasn't accepted by her own family. Tears pricked Essie's eyes at the raw feelings such realizations drew from deep within her.

Was she writing for the love of it or as a way to escape? Was her career an excuse for avoiding real life? She sniffed hard and rubbed at her eyes, the ache in her chest expanding. Perhaps what she really feared was not being enough. With her naturally cheerful personality and carefree, adventurous outlook, would she even make a suitable wife or mother?

She had no answers to such painful questions and

their chorus snuffed out any spark of desire to create scenes inside her head today. In the absence of her usual creative distraction, the ride felt longer and hotter, their final destination farther and farther away.

The dust stirred into the air by the horses scratched at her eyes and collar. She slowed her mount to match the plodding pace of Silas's animal. The outlaw appeared to be sleeping, slumped forward in the saddle. *Probably better for him*, Essie thought with concern.

She guided her horse into a canter up a slight incline behind Silas. Suddenly the outlaw slipped from the saddle. The rope around his waist prevented him from tumbling to the ground, but he'd clearly lost consciousness.

"Silas needs help," she screamed, urging her horse forward toward the outlaw. Up ahead, Tate echoed the cry to Clem and Fletcher, then jerked his horse around.

Essie managed to snag the reins of Silas's mount to stop it. She could see the man was still breathing, but he seemed oblivious to having stopped or fallen from the saddle.

"What happened?" Tate asked, dismounting.

"I don't know." She shook her head as she slipped from the saddle, worry renewing the twisting in her stomach. "I thought he was sleeping and then all of a sudden he dropped over to the side."

Fletcher and Clem rode up as Tate propped up Silas and instructed Essie to untie the rope. "What's going on?" The outlaw leader scowled at them from atop his horse.

Essie hurried to untie the knots to free Silas. "We have to stop. Silas is unconscious. And look at his leg." She gestured to his tattered pant leg where fresh blood had begun seeping through.

Mumbling a curse, Fletcher surveyed the grassy plain, squat trees and rocky buttes surrounding them. "There's a ravine about half a mile north of here," he barked, pointing his finger in that direction. "Get him there and we'll camp for the night."

"He can't ride anymore," Tate said, hoisting the unconscious outlaw.

"Guess you'll have to carry him, then, cowboy." With that, Fletcher grabbed the reins of Silas's horse and started forward again. "We'll see you in a bit."

Clem cast a pinched look over his shoulder, but he followed after Fletcher.

Too tired and worried for Silas to be angry, Essie took the reins of her horse and Tate's in hand. She would walk, too. "Can you carry him?"

Tate's face tightened with determination. "Half a mile's not that far." He set Silas down and then propped his shoulder underneath the man, before slowly rising again. Silas's hat dropped in the process and Essie hurried to pick it up. "All right. Let's go."

Silas hung limp and ashen-faced over Tate's shoulder. The sight made Essie want to weep. She followed alongside them with the horses. The muscles in Tate's neck and back visibly tensed under the strain of his load, but he didn't complain.

They walked in comparative silence for a minute or two before Essie voiced the thought foremost in her mind. "He isn't going to make it to the hideout, is he?"

"Not at the speed Fletcher wants. And maybe not slowly, either."

It was what she'd feared. Silas needed rest and

medical attention to recover—not another few days of trying to stay on his horse. She thought back over what she'd heard about the outlaws' hideout. Clem had said they ate better there and cabins provided shelter. But if Silas wasn't well enough to make it that far...

A recollection niggled at Essie's conscience. "Clem and Fletcher were discussing the hideout last night."

Tate turned to look at her. "What did they say?"

She searched her memory, but it was like riffling through drawers without remembering what she was looking for. "I can't recall," she said, shaking her head. "I didn't think it was important and I didn't want to get up and write it down."

Stopping, Tate shifted Silas's weight, his expression anxious. "Can you remember anything? You've been able to recite your interviews word for word to me these past few days."

"Because I wrote them down within hours of hearing them. Too much time has passed since last night."

She half expected him to get frustrated, but he simply blew out a breath and plodded forward again. "Maybe it'll come back to you."

"Maybe," she echoed, but with little hope. The overheard conversation had occurred at least twelve hours ago and she'd been half awake, not fully listening.

Was there any part of it she could remember? She focused her mind on last night. "They said something about lawmen and the hideout."

Tate whipped around, sending Silas's upper body swinging. "Anything else?"

Words floated through her head, but they remained just out of reach. "I'm sorry, Tate. I can't think of anything more."

"It's all right, Essie." He threw her a tight smile.

Still, she could sense his disappointment, could feel its sharp jab inside her. What if the information she couldn't remember was lifesaving? "I'll keep trying."

He nodded. "I know you will. I'll be praying for you, too."

His words eased some of her frustration. "Good idea." She tugged the horses' reins to get the animals moving again and offered her own silent petition. *Please, Lord, if it's important for Tate to know what Clem and Fletcher were saying, help me remember. And, please, continue to bless Silas and protect Tate.*

She felt a little better, though her worries were far from gone. The sun felt hotter now that she was off her horse and walking slowly. She wished she had some water for her and Tate. Several times he stopped and shifted Silas's weight. He would carry the injured man in his arms like a child, then switch to holding him over his shoulder like a sack of flour. The outlaw made no noise and didn't regain consciousness, but each time they stopped, Essie was grateful to see his chest still rising and falling in spite of his seemingly lifeless state.

At last they reached a wide ravine, guarded by buttes to the north. Essie guided the horses down the gradual slope to the ground below, Tate following behind with Silas. Clem and Fletcher were waiting in the shade. Shivers ran up Essie's arms at the change in temperature as she stopped in the shadow of the ravine's walls.

Tate carefully lowered Silas to the ground, though Essie could see from his fatigued face and hunched shoulders how exhausted he was. Dropping down beside the injured outlaw, Tate sprawled on his back, his breathing heavy.

"Is he all right?" Clem asked as he approached his friend.

Essie released the two horses to join the others and went to stand beside Silas. "He's still alive." *Thanks to Tate and the Lord*, she thought as she peered down at the unconscious outlaw. "But his wound needs cleaning and re-bandaging. And, of course, he needs water to drink." They all did, including the horses. But no stream ran along the bottom of this gully.

"There's a stream west of here," Fletcher said, rising. "We'll camp there."

Tate sat up, but Essie could see it cost him to move. "You said we could camp here, Fletcher. Silas isn't going to make it any farther." And neither would Tate if he had to keep carrying him.

Lifting his hands in a pacifying gesture, Clem walked toward Fletcher. "You and me can take the horses to the stream to water them." He pointed a thumb back at Silas. "Let 'im rest, Fletch. None of them are goin' nowhere. Not with us havin' the horses. They can hike to the water when we get back."

The outlaw leader scowled at Clem then tossed his arms in the air. "Bunch of whimperin' children. Fine. Get the horses, Clem. We'll water them and come back."

"I'll try'n bring water back for Silas," Clem said quietly to Essie. "So he can drink sooner."

The two outlaws climbed onto their horses and led the other two down the ravine, heading west. When they disappeared around a bend, Essie walked to Tate's side. "Are you all right?"

He'd slumped back to the ground. Without opening his eyes, he nodded. "Just catching my breath. How's Silas?"

"Still not awake."

"Here." Tate rose to a sitting position just long enough to remove his jacket, then handed it to her. "He can use this as a pillow."

Carefully lifting Silas's head, Essie tucked the jacket beneath him. Hopefully it would help him be more comfortable. "I feel as if this is all my fault, Tate." She collapsed next to him, no longer able to stand herself. The worry and fear she'd felt the last twenty-four hours had depleted her strength to nothing.

"How is any of this your fault?" Tate asked, his eyes still shut. His hat had been knocked askew, which gave Essie an unobstructed view of his handsome face.

She twisted her mouth in indecision. There was still the real possibility of him getting angry when she voiced the truth. And yet she'd resolved to share it—to be as honest with him as he'd been with her. "It's my fault because…well, because there is no ransom coming."

His eyes flew open and locked with hers as he slowly sat up. "What do you mean there's no ransom coming?" His voice held a note of tension.

Glancing down at her hands, Essie forced her next words from her lips. "It's true that I am Henry Vanderfair's great-granddaughter." She picked at a broken fingernail. "What I didn't share is that my grandmother chose to marry a poor man and so her father cut her off, completely. I've never even met my great-grandfather, nor is he likely to even be aware of my father's existence. Let alone my own."

"Essie…" He spoke her name with a note of cautionary warning.

"I know, I know." She looked away, unwilling to see the disappointment in his blue eyes. "I was desperate to interview all of you and so I allowed Fletcher to believe what he would about my connection to my great-grandfather."

Tate scrubbed his hands down his face and bristled chin. "There's still the slim chance Henry Vanderfair will take pity on you once he sees the telegram."

She shook her head. "No, there isn't."

"Why is that?" he asked, his voice rising in volume with obvious alarm.

"Because…" She glanced at the comatose Silas before spilling the truth in one great rush. "Because I didn't send the telegram. When Fletcher had me go back inside the telegraph office alone to change the message, I realized I could prevent the telegram from being sent at all. That way I wouldn't be around when they got a message that either denied my existence and relation to Henry Vanderfair or curtly declined sending any funds to ensure my well-being."

Tate climbed to his feet and began pacing in front of her with agitated steps. "Fletcher is counting on that money, Essie." He paused long enough to pierce her with a stern look. "He may very well kill to get his hands on it."

"I know," she repeated in a whisper. She felt as though her heart had dropped into her stomach. "It seemed the only logical thing to do at the time, but now…"

"You have to leave." He whirled to face her. "Right now. It's not safe for you to stay here anymore."

She stood, as well, her hands held out in a helpless gesture. "I can't leave. I don't have a horse. And where am I to go?"

"Back home," he barked, but his expression had lost some of its edge. "You can leave tonight, then."

"Fine." She turned her back on him as she faced the ravine wall, her eyes filling with tears. His anger was reasonable, but she'd hoped he might try to understand her motive a little more. "I'll head back to Evanston tonight."

What a ninny she'd been to think there was a future between them. Tate cared for her, yes, but surely it was more out of duty than anything else. Even if there had been times when she thought she'd read something more in his gaze and actions.

She startled when his large hands gently gripped her upper arms, but she didn't turn around.

"Essie, I don't know that I can protect you if you stay." The anguish in his tone melted her frustration like sunrays on a frozen pond. "And I can't bear the thought..." She heard him swallow hard. "Of anything happening to you. Ever."

She nodded, not daring to speak for fear of revealing the irrational hope that rose sharply inside her at his words.

"You're courageous and strong and beautiful and smart. And you're also human." He gently turned her around to face him. "Even you aren't immune to getting hurt. But I understand the desperation that made you ignore such a fact."

Her heart thudded faster at the tenderness in his

blue eyes, and the apprehension she felt at erasing it with her next question, but she plunged ahead. "Do you find me incredibly silly and naive for what I did? With the ransom and the telegram?"

He released one of her arms to trail his thumb down her jawline. "Naive, maybe. Bold, definitely. But never silly."

Never silly. Gratitude and warmth seeped through her. Tate didn't find her silly. Others, like her family, might, but he didn't.

Essie parted her lips to thank him for understanding—but the words stilled in her throat when she realized his gaze had dropped to her mouth. She didn't have to be a novelist to know he wished very much to kiss her. And she couldn't deny how much she, too, wished for that kiss. His eyes rose to hers, questioning, then softening when she offered him a small smile of encouragement.

Tilting her chin upward, Tate bent toward her. It was a moment she'd written about in fiction numerous times, but today she would get to experience this kiss as the heroine of her own story. This time she, and not one of her fictional female characters, was about to be kissed by a man she deeply cared for.

Tate's lips pressed to hers, filling Essie from head to toe with wonder and joy. Shutting her eyes, she kissed him back. And for the span of several moments nothing else existed but them—not Silas's injury or the lack of her ransom or the possible danger they faced. It was only her and Tate and the marvel of her first real kiss.

A mumbled request for "water" from Silas pulled them apart and ended the kiss, to Essie's disappointment. She blew out a calming breath as Tate turned toward the wounded outlaw. But not before he threw a keen look at her over his shoulder. He didn't speak, but he didn't need to. Essie read his emotions in his blue eyes—hope, regret, protection. And possibly love?

She wasn't sure, but she knew what she wanted now. The interview with Fletcher no longer mattered. Her next book no longer mattered. She would put all of her energy at present in keeping herself—and Tate—safe. For that was the only way a future together might change from fictional dream to possible reality.

Chapter Fourteen

Keeping Essie's hand firmly grasped in his, Tate led her along the bottom of the gully in the direction of the stream. They each held a cup to fill with water. Thankfully, Clem and Fletcher had arrived not long after Silas had stirred, so the man was able to get his much-needed drink. A little color had returned to his cheeks then, but he was still weak and in pain. If only there was more they could do for him...

Tate shot a glance at Essie and couldn't help smiling, in spite of their situation. How long had he wanted to kiss her? If he was honest with himself, probably ever since he'd found her doggedly trying to follow Fletcher's gang after the rainstorm that first day. But the actual moment had proved much sweeter than he'd anticipated.

Now he just had to get her out of harm's way so there might be more such moments. That was, if she returned his growing affection for her. Everything in him said she did, but there were still his own feelings to sort out about his job and the completion of this mission to focus on first.

As if reading his thoughts, Essie drew alongside him and asked, "What is your plan once you and the others reach the hideout?"

Tate squinted up at the sun, guessing it was nearing four o'clock. Plenty of time to figure out how to spirit Essie away tonight before Fletcher could learn her ransom wasn't coming. "I didn't have the best plan," he admitted. "Once I saw where the hideout was located, I was going to sneak away to the nearest town and convince the sheriff to follow me back."

"What if Fletcher and the others hid somewhere else once they discovered you were gone?"

He'd had the same thought a number of times. "That was a risk I knew I was taking doing this mission on my own. But I didn't see any other way around it. No other lawman has been able to ingratiate himself into Fletcher's gang until now, let alone discover his hideout."

Essie suddenly jerked to a stop, her eyes widening in surprise. Had something spooked her? Tate searched the ground for a snake but saw nothing except dirt and yellowing grass. "What's the mat—"

"That's it, Tate."

"What are you talking about?" he asked.

Her full smile radiated relief. "I just recalled what Clem and Fletcher were discussing last night. What you said about the lawmen helped me remember."

Thank You, Lord, he silently prayed as he waited for her to share. He'd been disappointed earlier when she couldn't remember the late-night conversation, though he didn't fault Essie. She could recollect far more than he ever could. But a niggling thought at the back of his mind had him fearing this information might be crucial to his finishing this mission.

"They were talking about the hideout and how no lawman has ever made it inside."

Trepidation began roiling within his stomach. Was this undertaking already doomed to fail? "Did they say why?"

She nodded. "The hideout can be defended with little trouble. Anyone who attempts to access it, friend or foe, is easily spotted. That's why no lawman can reach it."

"Because they'll be seen before they make it inside," he finished in a flat voice.

"I'm sorry, Tate." Her expression conveyed her sincerity and dismay.

He shook his head and drew her to him for an embrace. "It's not your fault, Essie. I'm proud of you for remembering all of that, especially so long after hearing it."

Lifting her head, she regarded him with those expressive green-brown eyes. "I'm grateful that I did. I've been praying to remember since this morning."

"Me, too." He brushed a strand of blond hair from her forehead.

"What are you going to do?"

A mirthless chuckle escaped his mouth. "I don't know. I can't stay there all winter with them, in hopes of apprehending them next spring during a robbery. But I can't lead the lawmen into an ambush."

She rested her cheek against his chest, giving him a moment of comfort and clarity. There had to be another solution. Another way to arrest Fletcher and his men without getting shot up trying to reach the hideout. But what?

"Too bad you can't get word to the sheriff in Casper," Essie said, her hand lying directly over his heart, "for him to meet you here. Then you wouldn't have to venture all the way to this impenetrable hideout."

"Yes," he murmured, "it is too bad."

He stroked her hair, his mind running circles as it searched for a solution. *What am I missing, Lord?* Essie's idea of having the sheriff meet up with him before they reached the hideout wasn't a bad one; it was just a matter of how to reach the man and get back before Fletcher bolted, injured Silas or not. If someone could go in Tate's place, though...

"Essie, you can go." He eased back to peer into her face, his hope for a successful mission no longer destroyed. It was the perfect solution.

"Me?"

Tate nodded as the idea began to take full shape inside his head. "You're leaving tonight anyway, right?"

She frowned. "I was considering it, yes."

"So you can ride to the sheriff in Casper and tell him to return here. It's only forty miles. You can do that in half a day."

"Tate." She shook her head, her expression anxious. "How am I going to convince the sheriff that a gang of outlaws and one Pinkerton detective are really half a day's ride away?" Folding her arms, her cup clutched to her middle, she gave him a pleading look. "And what if Fletcher decides to up and flee after I've disappeared and the sheriff can't find you?"

"It'll work," he said, softening his voice. "I know it.

Somehow I'll keep Fletcher here. All you have to do is convince the sheriff and then you can head home."

Essie glared at him. If the situation hadn't been so dire, he might have laughed at her petulance. "*If* I ride all that way, I'm not going to abandon you by heading home to Evanston. I'll return with the sheriff."

Frustration began chipping away at his hopeful plans. "It's too dangerous. You've got to stay far away from Fletcher once you leave here."

"I'm not a pampered child, Tate. And I refuse to ride away and not know for days or weeks if Fletcher shot you in my absence." She straightened to her full height, her arms held tense at her sides. "I can take care of myself. Besides, I'll be with armed men."

He wanted to insist she stay away from any possible harm. But he couldn't. He hadn't been able to do that with Tex and he certainly wasn't going to be able to do that with Essie. He could only pray and hope and do his part.

"It's your choice," he said softly, cupping her cheek. "Just promise me you'll be careful."

She leaned into his touch as some of the agitation drained from her face. "I promise."

Taking her hand in his again, he headed once more toward the stream. He heard the trickling of the water before he saw it. The small brook offered them clear, cold water, and he and Essie both drank before filling their cups.

"Ready to head back?" he asked. They could iron out the details of their plan on the walk back to the camp.

Instead of nodding, though, Essie sat back, her full cup forgotten beside her. "What if I can't do it,

Tate? What if I can't convince the sheriff to come back with me?"

He set down his cup and threaded his fingers with hers. "I have every faith in you, Essie. Look how you tracked us that first day. How you thought on your feet when those lawmen came. How you've nursed Silas with limited supplies."

A few tears leaked down her smooth cheeks, drawing his attention. Reaching out, Tate brushed them away, glad for another excuse to touch her lovely face. "It isn't about being capable or not," she said, sniffing.

"What is it, then?" He wanted to help her, to ease her troubles and cares.

"I'm afraid."

He bit back a chuckle. "I don't think I've seen you afraid once. And we've faced a lot in the last five days."

She plucked up a stiff piece of grass and twisted it around her fingers. "It isn't outlaws or storms or injuries that frighten me."

He waited through her pause, not wanting to interrupt her.

"I fear what's in here." She touched her heart. "No one but you and Nils have ever seen me as strong. I was the overly cheerful, flighty child growing up. 'Never takes anything seriously,' my older siblings and parents would say."

Sorrow for Essie spilled over into a scowl that he leveled at the water. Why couldn't others see her natural abilities to cheer and comfort, not to mention the strength and resolve she carried underneath her optimism? "I'm sorry they said that, Essie. But it isn't true."

"Isn't it?" she countered, but there was no real fight in it. "I left home to pursue my dream as a dime novelist, but even that hasn't panned out as I thought. This new story, whatever it is, might not be enough to sustain a career. And then what?" She glanced down and shrugged. "Do I go home, tail between my legs, and admit that I've failed? That maybe I'm not serious enough about anything to be successful?"

"Whoa, whoa. Hold up right there." He tugged her toward him and looped his arm around her shoulders. "How many people have dreams they never go after? But you went for them. And whether your next book is a huge success or not, you didn't fail. You've worked at this, tirelessly, and grown because of it. That is not the definition of *defeat*."

She pressed her cheek to his shirt, reminding Tate how natural it felt to hold her. "Maybe."

"Have you ever told your family how you feel?" He thought of Tex and all the things that needed saying between them.

"No," she said, shaking her head.

"Then it sounds like we both have people we need to talk to."

"Do you think they'll listen?"

Tate considered the question for a long moment. "I hope so. But maybe the talking isn't as much for them as it is for us. Because whether they listen or not doesn't change who we are."

"When did you get to be so wise?" He sensed her smile in her voice.

"Sometime after this pretty dime novelist ran into me on the train."

She laughed lightly and the sound made him want

to grin. "I did run right smack into you, didn't I? Although I think the Lord might have pushed us together."

Tipping her face up toward him, Tate had to swallow before he could speak. "I think He did, too, Essie. And no matter what anyone else thinks, you matter to Him. He's given you some amazing gifts, like your ability to bring laughter and sunshine and hope to people. Even hardened outlaws." He prayed she could feel his earnestness as she quietly watched him. "So no matter what happens with your family or your books, you are enough exactly as you are, right now. To God...and to me."

Her smile started at the corners of her mouth and finally bowed in the middle. "Thank you," she said softly. "There's just one last concern."

"Just one?" he teased.

She nodded, her demeanor growing solemn again. "What if Fletcher finds out who you really are before I get back with the sheriff?" A shudder ran through her and he could easily imagine what scenarios she was envisioning.

"I can't say that won't happen, but I have hope that things will end up all right." He rested his chin on her hair, wishing he could guarantee their safety. "I suppose we just have to do our part and trust the Lord with the rest."

"Trust the Lord," she repeated. "He's seen us through so far, hasn't He? Even if it doesn't always look that way."

He tightened his clasp around her shoulders, feeling gratitude again for her timely entrance into his life. "Yes, He has."

With her brow crunched in thought, Essie sat up. "Rather than me just sneaking away, what if we give Fletcher a believable reason for my going? Then maybe he wouldn't try to hurt you or come after me in retaliation."

Tate rubbed a hand over his chin—he hadn't thought about Fletcher attempting to retrieve Essie. "You'd still need to leave at night, after they're asleep. Fletcher isn't just going to let you go on your own, whatever the reason."

"I agree. But if he believed it was for something other than running away…" She glanced around as if the answer might be sitting nearby. Perhaps for Essie it was. "Is there anything we need?"

"Food, medical supplies, a closer source of water."

She rose to her knees and grinned at Tate. "That's it. Medical supplies. I can say I've gone to get Silas some medical supplies."

The more he considered the idea, the more it made sense. And it just might keep Essie safe, too. "I think that could work. But to really make it believable, we may need to do some acting."

Smiling, she tossed her hair over one shoulder. "You just happen to be looking at the author of *The Actor's Atonement*. I spent some time observing a local theater troupe for that book."

"Why am I not surprised?" he said, laughing as much with admiration as mirth. "All right, then. Why don't we stage a bit of an argument about Silas's care?"

"Yes." Essie clapped her hands with enthusiasm. "Then I'll leave a note saying I've gone to get the supplies. What do you think?"

"It just might work." And everything in him hoped

it would. Standing, he pulled Essie up onto her feet. "You're sure about going? If you don't want to do this, we'll come up with some other way for me to finish this job."

There was no hesitation in her gaze as she said, "Yes. We can do this."

He'd been hoping to instill greater confidence in her and, in return, she'd bolstered his. "Then we've got an argument to act out." Tate picked up his cup of water.

"Probably not our first or our last." A teasing smile lit her pretty face as she hefted her cup.

As they walked back to the camp, Tate couldn't help smiling at the hinted promise behind her words. Once they'd made it through the next twenty-four hours—alive and well, he hoped—he would make it a priority to analyze his heart. It was past time for him to figure out what he really wanted out of life. And even more important, he thought, glancing at Essie, who he wanted to spend it with.

Essie rinsed the supper dishes in the stream, grateful Fletcher had decided to move their camp the quarter mile westward after all. On her and Tate's return, they'd found Silas partially revived, but more water was required to properly care for his wound. Fletcher had, thankfully, announced they move camp, though he wasn't pleased about doing so. Silas had endured the short ride well enough and Essie had access to all the water she needed from the brook to re-dress his leg bandage.

It was a good thing she planned to get supplies along with the sheriff. Silas's leg had stopped bleeding, but it looked infected to Essie. Out of earshot of Silas, Tate had concurred that it wasn't healing as it should.

Before she could get supplies, though, she and Tate had to stage their argument. She pulled in a cleansing breath to calm her rapidly thudding heart and straightened. It was one thing to discuss or write about bravery; it was another matter entirely to live the principle in real life.

I can do this, she reminded herself. *With Thy help, Lord.* Tate's words from earlier filled her mind and heart with peace as she carried the dishes back to Clem. She was enough to God, exactly as she was right now, and she needed to trust that, to trust Him.

Now that supper was over, Essie returned to Silas's makeshift bed. "How are you feeling?" He'd managed to down some biscuit earlier.

"Been better," he answered with a grimace as he tried to move his injured leg into a different position. "Think it'll heal, Miss Vanderfair?"

She sought Tate's gaze from across the campfire and caught the slight nod of his head. It was time for their little show. "No, Silas, I don't." She straightened and her heart broke a little at the expression of dismay that crossed his already-haggard face. But she was speaking the truth. "Not without the proper supplies," she added, letting her voice rise in volume. "Your leg needs attention from a proper doctor."

Wheeling around, hands on her hips, she glowered at Fletcher seated near Tate and Clem. "He can't continue on, Mr. Fletcher. His wound is likely to become even more infected. And that means he could lose his leg."

"It can't be that bad—" Silas started before Fletcher interrupted.

"I'm not the one that shot him," the outlaw jeered at her. "If he can make it to the hideout, he'll be fine. Won't you, Silas?"

The man nodded, but Essie wasn't convinced he believed it.

She feigned a huff of indignation. "This is ridiculous. Casper isn't that far away. We can ride back for supplies and then continue on to the hideout."

"We are not goin' back for supplies." Fletcher's voice dripped with vehemence, causing Essie to inwardly cringe. "Get that through your head, woman. We are ridin' out tomorrow. Got it?"

"But a man's life—"

Tate threw her a rather convincing scowl. "Essie, let it go. For once I'm in agreement with Fletcher. We were almost arrested last time we were in Casper. Someone would be sure to recognize us if we returned. *We* can't go back for supplies, not now. Silas will be fine."

If she hadn't known he was acting, she would have fully believed his tone of finality. "Does no one understand the seriousness of this?" she persisted as she waved a hand at the prone Silas. "This man needs help. More than you or I can give him out here in the desert. He needs real medical attention."

"Enough," Fletcher hollered, drawing his gun. From the corner of her eye, she saw Tate tense, but he held still. "Sit down, Miss Vanderfair." He waved at the campfire with the gun. "And I don't want to hear another word out of you. Not about medicine or Silas or anything. Understood?"

Nodding, Essie took a seat. A glance at Tate rewarded her with his brief smile. He approved of her performance. The conversation around the fire picked up again, but it felt stilted. Silas asked for a drink and Essie silently obliged. She'd pushed Fletcher far enough; she would comply with his demand for silence—at least while he was awake.

When Silas had drained the cup, she put it with the other dishes and fished out her notebook. She busied herself with writing a note to the men, declaring her intentions to ride back to Casper for supplies. With that complete, she tried thinking up new possible scenes for her book, but the longer the shadows grew, the more nervous she felt at what lay ahead.

Finally, Fletcher insisted Clem bank the fire. Essie exchanged a look with Tate, then got up to get a drink at the stream. The cold water helped calm her as did the approaching steps of Tate from behind. He crouched by the water as she handed him the cup to drink from.

"I'll wake you when it's time to go," he said in a whisper, his lips barely moving. He lifted his hand, as if to touch her face, but he lowered his arm back to his side instead. Essie felt a quiver of disappointment, though she understood the importance of maintaining needed distance in front of the others.

Her heart resumed its fast pattering as she stood. Surely no one watching them would think anything suspicious. She went and prepared her bed. With that done, she tore out the note she'd written to the outlaws and tucked it inside her notebook.

Tonight reminded Essie of her first one on this journey. The earth bit into her side, making it impossible to get comfortable, and her blanket barely kept the night breeze at bay. Her thoughts were as snarled now as they'd been then. This time, though, she had the added measure of uncertainty and adrenaline racing through her to keep her awake.

She feared she might never sleep, but the next thing she knew, someone was gently shaking her shoulder. "Essie," she heard Tate whisper near her ear. "Time to go."

Her eyes flew open, though the rest of her took longer to awaken. She sat up slowly, the blanket still gripped in her hand, and glanced at the other three bedrolls. From the light of the bright moon, she could see that each of the outlaws appeared to be lost in slumber.

"Do you have the note?" Tate asked in a low voice.

Nodding, she located her notebook and pulled out the folded slip of paper. Tate placed it near the cold ashes of the fire, beneath a fist-size rock.

Essie clasped her valise and got to her feet. Shivers tripped down her back and arms, as much from the cool air as from her apprehension. "What time is it?" She kept her voice soft and quiet.

"Two o'clock." Tate motioned for her to follow him.

Stepping as lightly as she could, she trailed him to where the horses had been tied up. Tate undid the reins of her horse, but instead of helping her into the saddle, he pantomimed that she should follow him farther away from the camp first.

The stream's cheerful gurgle grew fainter as they moved away from the sleeping outlaws. The ravine's shadows stretched like ghoulish fingers toward them, renewing Essie's shivering. The nighttime hour fueled her active imagination, conjuring up all sorts of villains hiding in the patches of brush.

Tate didn't stop until they were about a quarter of a mile from the camp. "You know the way back to Casper, right?"

"Yes," Essie said with another nod. "Just head south. I'll run into the city eventually."

Tate rubbed the nose of the horse. "Rest him as often as you think he needs it, but maintain a steady pace. You'll pass by a couple of streams where you can both drink." Reaching into his jacket pocket, he produced a half-crumbled biscuit and some jerky. "It's not much, but it'll tide you over until you reach Casper."

Tears blurred her vision for a moment at the care behind his action. "Thank you. I'll be back by sundown, with the sheriff and his men." And not a minute later, if she could help it. "Will you be all right?"

"Yes." His confident tone eased some of her concern at leaving him. "Don't you worry about Fletcher. Just get yourself safe and sound to Casper and back."

"I will."

He locked his fingers with hers and drew her a step closer. "Can we pray together before you leave?"

She smiled. "I would like that."

Resting his forehead against hers in a comforting gesture, Tate quietly intoned a prayer for their safety and well-being. He thanked the Lord for her friendship and then closed with a final entreaty for their plan to work. Essie opened her eyes to find him peering at her from beneath his hat.

"When this is all over, Essie…"

"Yes?" she prompted when he paused.

Instead of finishing his thought, though, he cupped her face with his other hand and captured her lips in a kiss. A kiss full of hope and fear and something greater than friendship.

All too soon Tate stepped back, but Essie understood they couldn't linger. It was time to go.

He helped her climb onto the horse. "God be with you," he said.

"And with you." The tears were back and this time they dripped freely from her lashes. "Keep yourself safe, Tate."

"You, too, Essie. Until tonight."

"Until tonight." She hesitated, torn between staying and going. What would happen to him in a few hours? Would he still be here waiting, alive and whole, when she and the sheriff arrived?

Her indecision ended when Tate slapped the rump of the horse and the beast leaped forward. Clutching the reins, Essie led the animal up and out of the ravine. At the top, she stopped and spun around to look back at Tate. In the moonlight, she saw him lift a hand in parting.

Swallowing back a sob, Essie squared her shoulders and waved back. Then, pointing the horse south, she spurred him into a gallop. She had a sheriff to find and bring back and only one day to do it.

Chapter Fifteen

Tate was in the middle of a dream—one in which Essie had lost her horse and was trying to make it to Casper on foot—when he found himself jerked from his blanket and onto his feet.

"Where is she, cowboy?" Fletcher snarled into his face, his breath rank. "Where did she go?"

He blinked in the bright light, trying to understand Fletcher's words. Over the outlaw's shoulder, Tate saw Clem and Silas watching them with concerned expressions.

The sight of a white paper in Fletcher's fist brought sudden remembrance to his tired brain. "Essie's gone?" Tate said, playing innocent.

Fletcher tightened his grip on Tate's shirtfront. "Yes, she's gone. Took a horse, too. But not before writing us a pretty little note." He shoved the page under Tate's nose.

"What does it say?"

Anger flashed in Fletcher's eyes right before he shoved Tate backward. He stumbled but managed to stay upright. "She says she's gone for supplies, but I don't buy it. She's split, I know it." Wadding up the paper, he tossed it onto the ground near Tate's feet.

He stooped to pick it up and unwrinkled the paper to read Essie's words. He hadn't bothered to read them earlier.

Dear Gentlemen,
I cannot abide to see Silas suffer any longer or lose his leg because of negligence. Therefore, I have taken it upon myself to ride back to Casper and procure the needed medical supplies. I will return with them by sundown.
Your companion in travel,
Essie Vanderfair

Fighting a smile at the pluck and formality of her words, Tate folded the note and pocketed it. "She says she'll be back by sundown."

"And you believe her?" Fletcher stalked the edge of the camp, his tension palpable. "For all I know, you helped her, cowboy."

Tate kept his face impassive. "Guess we'll just have to wait and see."

Fletcher ground to a halt. "Wait and see? Wait and see?" His face had grown red with fury. "We ain't waitin' or seein'."

For a brief moment Tate thought of Winnifred Paige. Had she been given a real glimpse at this man she pined for? He hoped so; he hated the idea of her stepping blindly into the choice of aligning her life with any outlaw and Fletcher in particular.

"Clem." Fletcher whirled on the man who winced

in response. "Saddle up your horse. You're goin' after the girl."

"Now, Fletcher," Tate said, keeping his voice calm and soothing. "She said she'll be back. We don't need to go traipsing—"

The gun was drawn and pointed at him before Tate could finish. Belatedly he realized it was his revolver. Fletcher must have relieved him of his weapons prior to waking him. "You aren't traipsin' anywhere, cowboy. You're stayin' here where I can keep an eye on you. But Clem..." Fletcher waved the gun at the other outlaw. "He's gonna see if he can apprehend Miss Vanderfair. Got it?"

Tate knew when to keep silent. Now would be one of those times. Dipping his head in a nod, he remained in place, even as Fletcher moved backward to join Clem by the horses. The man never broke eye contact with him.

Once Clem had ridden off, Fletcher marched back to the ashen campfire and motioned to it with the gun. "You get to make breakfast, since Clem and the girl won't be doin' it this morning."

Though he wouldn't admit it to Fletcher, Tate was grateful for the task, for something else to occupy his thoughts. He felt mostly confident Clem wouldn't reach Essie, not with her four-and-a-half-hour lead. But what if her journey had been impeded by a thrown horseshoe or an encounter with Indians or simple fatigue?

He closed his mind to the possibilities as he set about starting the fire and heating some beans. Biscuits weren't his specialty, but he did his best.

Fletcher remained in a dark mood as he ate, and

neither Tate nor Silas said much through the meal. When they'd finished eating, Tate asked if he could attend to Silas's leg. Despite a vicious glare from Fletcher, the man gestured with the gun for Tate to go ahead.

After removing the bandage, Tate rinsed the cloth in the stream. He didn't like the coloration on the fabric—Silas really did need those supplies. He wrung the bandage out and carried it, dripping, back to Silas.

"She's not going for supplies," Silas whispered in a hoarse voice, his keen eyes on Fletcher.

Alarm robbed Tate's mouth of moisture and stilled his hands as he tried not to gape at the injured outlaw. The man was supposed to have been comatose yesterday when they'd discussed the absence of Essie's ransom and her leaving.

"You're wrong," Tate replied in an equally low voice, bending over the man's injured leg and doing his best to keep his expression impassive. "She *is* going for supplies." At least he suspected Essie would get them in addition to convincing the sheriff to come back with her.

Silas gave a thoughtful nod, then added, "But that ain't all she's going for, is it?"

For a man of few words, Silas knew how to say the ones that inspired the most fear. Would he speak to Fletcher? Did he know Tate's true identity? He kept silent as he finished wrapping the man's leg and tied the ends of the cloth.

"I ain't telling." Silas held Tate's gaze long enough that he could see the sincerity there. "After this," the outlaw said, gripping his leg, "I'm out. He don't care about us. Not anymore. Maybe not ever."

Fletcher lumbered to his feet. "What're you two yappin' about over there?"

Without hesitation, Silas said, "Just jawing about the past and our hopes for the future."

"Well, quit it." Waving the gun at a spot near the dying campfire, he growled, "You sit over here, cowboy."

Knowing he needed to comply, at least until Essie and the sheriff showed up, Tate obeyed the order.

The next two hours passed slowly. Fletcher alternated between sitting and pacing the camp in agitation. Silas mostly slept.

Tate attempted to nap, as well, certain he'd need all his wits about him later on. But it was hard to snatch more than a few minutes of sleep when he wasn't certain if Fletcher would get fed up and plant a bullet in him, after all. No one spoke. The only sounds were the restless noises of the horses and the distant trill of birds. The sun rose higher. Tate welcomed the warmth.

Another thirty minutes passed, according to his watch. He tried figuring out where Fletcher had stowed his rifle, but without being allowed to move around the camp, he couldn't be sure where to look. He was debating if the gun was by the horses or tucked inside Fletcher's bedroll when the man went suddenly still.

"Someone's comin'." Fletcher lifted the revolver, pointing it down the ravine. The plodding sound of a single horse carried on the morning air.

Tate tensed. It couldn't be the sheriff, not yet. Which

meant it had to be Clem returning. Did the outlaw have Essie with him?

Several anxious minutes ticked by before Tate spotted the horse and rider. It was Clem, all right, but he was alone. Tate exhaled with relief.

"Where is she?" Fletcher hollered, his face creased with wrathful lines.

Clem stopped the horse. "I didn't find hide or hair of her, Fletch. She musta been long gone by the time we got up." He dismounted and led the horse over to the others. "Guess we'll just have to up and wait like her note said."

Wheeling around, Fletcher shot Tate a hateful look. "I know you're behind this, cowboy. So here's what we're gonna do." He barked over his shoulder at Clem, "Tie him up, Clem—good and tight. I don't want him takin' off like the girl did."

Tate wanted to leap up and have it out with the outlaw leader now. But he couldn't risk acting irrational and botching up bringing these men to justice. Fighting the instinct to run or defend himself, he allowed Clem to approach and tie his hands in front. Then removing Tate's boots, Clem tied his feet together at the ankles.

"Sorry, Tex," the man apologized in a low voice. But that didn't deter him from doing a thorough job. The ropes dug into Tate's wrists and through his socks from Clem's secure tying.

Tate nodded, wanting Clem to know he understood— they were both just doing their jobs. There was goodness in these outlaws, after all. Just like there was goodness, he still believed, in his brother. At least he'd seen it in Silas and Clem. He wasn't so sure about Fletcher.

"Get nice and comfortable," Fletcher mocked as he finally holstered the gun. "You're gonna be there all day, cowboy. Until Miss Vanderfair decides to show up. And if she doesn't…" He let the warning float there before continuing. "I already told you at the beginning that her life and yours are tied together. It don't matter no more if Silas makes it or not. Come sundown, if the girl ain't back, you won't live to see sunrise."

Full sunlight lit the prairie by the time Essie reached Casper. She'd managed to limit her rests to a handful, stopping only when she found a stream. While she'd grown used to riding nearly that far in a day, she felt exhausted in mind and body. Her fears over Tate's safety had drained her of energy. She'd only been able to stomach a few bites of the biscuit and jerky.

She nudged the horse to pick up its pace as they headed down the street toward the sheriff's office. There was no time to dawdle. If there had been, she would've liked to stop off at the hotel and freshen up in one of the rooms. But her appearance, or the lack thereof, was a low priority this morning.

When she reached the office, Essie dismounted and tied the horse's reins to the hitching post. She hastily ran her fingers through her windblown hair and flicked a mite of dirt from her dress. Then she marched to the door. Twisting the handle didn't produce the desired effect. Locked. Was the man not in yet? Panic throbbed in her chest as she tried peering through the curtained window. A flicker of movement from within confirmed someone was inside.

Essie lifted a fist and pounded as hard and loud

as she could against the door. She didn't let up until the door flew open and an older man with graying hair stood there, scowling at her. A napkin had been tucked into the collar of his shirt.

"What are you causing such a ruckus for at this hour of the morning?"

Standing at full height, Essie gave him a patient smile and swept past him into the office. "Sheriff, I'm here to collect you and a posse of your best men to ride after some outlaws."

The sheriff looked taken aback, but she wasn't sure if it was from her words or from her barging into his office uninvited. "Come again?"

"A runaway outlaw gang is a time-sensitive matter, sir, so I ask you to pay careful attention to what I'm going to tell you." She took a seat in the chair opposite his desk where a breakfast tray sat. "Please, sit down, Sheriff."

Frowning still, he shut the door and plunked down into his chair. "You're interrupting my breakfast, miss."

"And for that I do apologize," she said, bending forward to show her earnestness. "But a man's life is in danger if we don't act fast."

He blew out a sigh as he picked up his toast and began buttering it. "What seems to be the trouble?"

"A few days ago, three men robbed your bank." Essie fought a satisfied smile when the man dropped his toast. "Two of those men are outlaws, but the third isn't. He's really a Pinkerton detective posing as his outlaw brother. Now they're camped about forty—"

"Hold up a minute." The sheriff leaned back in his chair, eyeing her suspiciously. "I happen to know for a fact that the Texas Titan was with those two men. I saw him with my own eyes. And that ain't the first time, either. I shot that man several months back— actually thought I'd taken him out for good."

Essie demurely clasped her hands together. "And it did not strike you as odd that he made such a complete recovery only a few months after being almost fatally wounded—and that he'd be addle-brained enough to come back and rob the same bank *again*?"

At that, the sheriff's confidence faltered a little. "Well, he must have," the man blustered. "I'm telling you I saw him."

"You are mistaken, sir. The man you saw two days ago is not the Texas Titan. It was his identical twin brother."

The man laughed and picked up his toast again. "Now you're just joshing me. I never heard anything about the Texas Titan having a brother, let alone a twin."

"They look exactly alike," she said, fighting her growing irritation. She hadn't expected this meeting to be easy, but the man seemed dead set on not believing her. "The biggest difference is a scar the detective has behind his right ear. I've done plenty of reading up on this particular outlaw, and there's never been a single mention of such a scar in any of the newspapers or on the Wanted posters."

The sheriff lifted his shoulders in a shrug as he took a bite from his toast. "Don't mean he doesn't have it." He swallowed and patted his mouth with his napkin. "What did you say your name was?"

Essie forced another cordial smile. "I didn't. I am Essie Vanderfair."

"Like the millionaire Vanderfair?" he asked, his eyebrows rising.

"Distantly related. Now, we still need to discuss your plans for riding back—"

He held up his hand to stop her. "How do you know anything about these men?"

It was a fair question, though she didn't relish answering it. What would he think of her actions? "I am a dime novelist." She sat straighter and kept her chin lifted in confidence. "While returning to Evanston after a visit to my publisher, six days ago, my train was beset by a gang of outlaws."

"I heard the train was robbed by five men," the man said around another bite of breakfast, "down Medicine Bow way."

"Yes, and the outlaws included a man who I mistook to be the Texas Titan, not knowing he was really a Pinkerton agent posing as his outlaw brother."

When the sheriff made no further comment, she continued. "Being at a crossroads in my writing career, I seized what seemed to be a fortuitous opportunity to ride with these men and interview them. This way I could collect, in person, valuable research."

His eyebrows shot upward again. "Let me see if I have this right, Miss Vanderfair." She nodded for him to go on. "You are a woman writer of dime novels who knowingly went with a group of wanted men. And now, for some reason that you still haven't told me, you're asking for me and my men to ride off with you to meet up with these five outlaws."

She tried not to grimace at his incredulous tone. "Three outlaws, actually. One of them ran off with the money from the train robbery during the storm a few days back—that's why the leader decided to rob your bank."

"That still leaves four," the sheriff replied.

Essie shook her head. "Remember, one of them is a detective."

The sheriff shot her a placating smile. "Forgive me. One is supposedly a detective who no one has ever heard of, posing as his outlaw twin brother."

"Put like that, sir…"

"I'm just stating the facts, Miss Vanderfair." He bent over the desk, his napkin dragging through his eggs. "And where exactly am I gonna find these men?"

Was he warming to her? Essie couldn't tell, but she plunged on, anyway. "They are camped forty miles north of here. One of them, the man you shot two days ago, is seriously injured. The other two, along with the detective, were in good health when I left them this morning."

"You rode forty miles to Casper this morning?"

"Well, I did leave at two o'clock."

Instead of looking suitably impressed or concerned, the sheriff hooted with laughter. "I can't tell where the fiction begins and ends with you, Miss Vanderfair."

"I assure you, sir," she declared, not bothering to hide her frustration any longer, "that none of what I'm telling you is fiction. This detective, Tate Beckett, needs the law's help to apprehend these men before they reach their hideout for the winter. He charged me to ride and fetch you."

"Fetch me, huh?" He sniffed and folded his arms

over his napkin-clad chest. "How do I know you aren't leading me into a trap?" His gaze narrowed on her.

Essie matched his penetrating look. "I am not making this up. The lives of two men depend on my errand this morning."

He pushed up from his chair, jerking the napkin from under his chin as he did so. Tossing it on the breakfast tray, he loomed over her. "I need proof, Miss Vanderfair."

"Proof," she echoed, dismayed. "I'm afraid I don't have any other proof besides my word."

"Then I'm afraid I can't help you."

"But—"

He spread his hands in a helpless gesture. "Not without sending a telegram to the Pinkertons, verifying your story about this Beckett fellow."

Essie glowered at him. "I don't have time to send a telegram, sir." Her voice hitched when she spoke of Tate. "The detective, who is a brave and kind man, is in very real danger if Fletcher discovers who he is before I can get back there with help."

"Fletcher?" He looked suitably surprised. "As in the Fletcher gang? That's who you tagged along with?"

She nodded, feeling the first flicker of hope since their conversation had begun. But it was dashed a few moments later when the sheriff rubbed his jaw and pushed out a defeated sigh.

"I wish I could help you, Miss Vanderfair." He shook his head. "I really do. But I can't gather up my men and ride into who knows what, solely based on the word of one person."

She'd failed to convince him. Standing, Essie felt

suddenly light-headed. She gripped the edge of the desk to stay on her feet. "I…" She closed her lips, not even sure what more to say. She'd told him the truth. But it hadn't worked.

Head high, she walked to the door. Not until she'd turned the handle and stepped through did she find her words once more. "Just remember, Sheriff, if the Fletcher gang goes free once again and one of the Pinkerton agents ends up dead, you will be culpable for disregarding the information I've given you."

He puffed out his chest and scowled at her. "I can't just ride off every time I get wind of some tall tale of criminal behavior. Good day, Miss Vanderfair."

Without bothering to return the sentiment, she exited the building. The door shut firmly behind her. *Now what, Lord?* she thought, turning in a slow circle. *I'm trying to trust You, though I'm not sure what to do next.* Would Tate be angrier at her if she gave up or if she returned without the law?

A longing to lay her head on a pillow somewhere and weep for hours filled her to near distraction, but she reminded herself that wasn't an option. On weary legs, she moved to the edge of the sidewalk and sat to think.

Even if she hadn't been able to convince the sheriff to come with her, she could still get the medical supplies Silas needed. She also needed to see with her own eyes that Tate hadn't been harmed in her absence. Of course, riding back alone would be dangerous, especially if Fletcher had somehow guessed the truth about her ransom. But she couldn't give up. Not when she loved Tate.

Loved? Essie lifted her chin and stared unseeing

at the passersby. Did she really and truly love Tate? The answer came swift and sure—*yes*.

"Then we are not quitting," she told her horse as she shot to her feet.

Fresh energy pulsed through her. Climbing back into the saddle, she got directions from a gentleman to the doctor's office. Unfortunately, she found his door locked, as well.

"Is no one else up and about this morning?" she grumbled. Time wasn't something she had in abundance right now.

At least thirty minutes ticked by, most of which she spent pacing the sidewalk and imagining what Tate might be doing. Just when she'd determined to seek out the doctor's residence, a man with a black bag approached the office.

Essie got right to the point as the doctor let her inside. She told him about Silas being shot in the leg, and that while the bullet had gone clean through, the wound wasn't healing properly. The doctor insisted on having the injured party brought in to the office to be examined until Essie informed him "the patient" was forty miles away. That was enough to convince him of the critical nature of her visit. He readily agreed to let her purchase the needed supplies.

With relief, she paid him for the medicine and bandages, and stowed everything inside her valise. The doctor walked her outside, instructing her on how to care for the wound. After thanking him, Essie climbed onto her horse once more.

Armed with supplies, she decided her final piece of business would be to procure a new horse. She needed a fresh mount that could get her back to Tate as quickly as possible. Her funds were rather limited, but she hoped there might be a decent animal she could afford. She located the livery on her own and led her horse inside.

Unlike the other two establishments she'd visited so far, this one teemed with commotion and noise. A group of men were selecting horses and saddling up. Essie stopped at the edge of the fray, knowing they would have to finish before she could commandeer the livery owner's attention.

"Miss Vanderfair!"

She turned to see the sheriff hurrying toward her, leading a horse. "Sheriff?" She gawked at the man.

"We thought you'd left. Been looking for you." He grinned. "Now that you're here, though, this'll be your horse for the ride."

Essie blinked in confusion. "The ride?"

"Yes, to apprehend the Fletcher gang."

Crossing her arms, she gave the sheriff a hard stare. She wouldn't be going anywhere with him until he explained himself. The man she'd left in the sheriff's office had been rude and unwilling to listen. The man standing in front of her now seemed to be in a frightful hurry to do the very thing she'd begged him to do. "I don't understand."

"After you left, I decided to wire the Pinkertons myself. Turns out you were right." He had the decency to look embarrassed. "They confirmed their detective Tate Beckett was indeed posing as his outlaw twin brother and that we were to assist him in bringing in the Fletcher gang—posthaste."

"Really?" A smile pushed through her disbelief. "You're going to help me?"

With a nod, the sheriff handed over the reins to the other horse. "Not only are we going to help you, but we're going to reunite you with your fella."

"My fella?" Her cheeks warmed as she situated her valise on the new horse. He couldn't know the revelation of her heart outside his office. "I'm not sure I know what you mean."

She caught the way his eyes twinkled with amusement. "Just a hunch, Miss Vanderfair. But most girls wouldn't ride eighty miles in a day just for the fun of it or to see justice served, as decent as that may be. I figured this detective has more to do with it than you're letting on."

Essie offered him a full smile as he assisted her into the saddle. "That would make a rather fascinating story, now wouldn't it?"

"Indeed it would. You ready to ride back?"

"More than ready." They were setting out much later than she'd originally hoped, but at least she wasn't riding back alone now.

He collected a horse for himself and climbed onto its back. "Let's go," he called, waving the other men forward.

Outside the livery, Essie couldn't help peering up at the blue sky and offering a silent prayer of gratitude, thankful that she had the lawmen and the Lord on her side.

Her greatest wish now was to reach the camp in time.

Because the sheriff was more right than he knew. Tate Beckett, a detective in disguise and a twin brother to an outlaw, was the "fella" of her heart, through and through. And she hoped to have the chance to tell him exactly that.

Chapter Sixteen

If the morning had crawled by, the afternoon passed twice as sluggishly. Tate attempted to move with the changing of the sun's direction into whatever patch of shade appeared. Under Fletcher's orders, Clem had taken over Silas's care, which meant getting the injured outlaw food and water and maneuvering him into the shadows and away from the warm sun.

Tate passed the time with dozing or thinking. He imagined what he wanted to say to Tex once he finally found him, realizing how much he wanted to seek and give forgiveness. Not just with his brother, but somehow with his father, too. Then there were the things he hoped to say to Essie if and when she returned. About how he didn't want to envision a future without her, how he was ready to give up detective work.

He thought about having a farm of his own again. Palming a handful of dirt from a newly turned field... listening to the wind whisper through the shade trees... tasting fresh berries from the vine. He'd missed these things and hadn't even realized it. But now his heart filled with new aspirations that had nothing to do with tracking down outlaws or putting on a disguise.

When Fletcher barked at Clem to start preparing supper, Tate's stomach twisted with anxiety and his heart spiked to a double-time rhythm inside his chest. Had Essie made it to Casper? Was she all right? Had she convinced the sheriff to come back with her?

He offered another prayer—surely his hundredth since waving goodbye to Essie in the middle of the night. He prayed again for her safety and for his—and for the chance to share with her just how precious she'd become to him.

Supper was a quiet, tense affair. Tate managed to get a burned biscuit into his mouth, in spite of his bound hands, but his hunger ran out before the food did. Fletcher wasted no time on talking. Silas was sleeping again and even Clem kept mostly silent.

"That girl better show up," Fletcher grumbled in a dark tone after Clem went to rinse the dishes in the stream.

Tate studied the man seated before him. Hard lines had worn ruts into the outlaw's face, though Fletcher couldn't be that much older than Tate. A perpetual scowl had pulled his mouth downward, so even when he smiled, it looked like a grimace.

"How'd you end up here?" he asked without really thinking. Essie might not get her desired interview with the outlaw, now that they wouldn't be reaching the hideout, but perhaps he could find out something to share with her.

Fletcher glared at him, the revolver still resting across his knees. "What do you mean?"

"Why did you choose this life?" Tate attempted to gesture around them with his tied hands.

Approaching them, dripping dishes in tow, Clem remarked, "It was his stepfather."

"Shut up, Clem." The gang leader's jaw visibly tightened.

"What about your stepfather?" Tate prodded. The sun had dipped lower in the sky, which meant sundown wasn't far off. If he could keep Fletcher talking until Essie showed up…

Fletcher pushed his hat up then yanked it back down. "He was a rotten, lazy no-account."

Tate refrained from saying anything more and the wait paid off.

"I don't remember my real pa," Fletcher said, a bitter edge to his voice. "My ma married Franklin when I was six and the man turned out to be nothin' but a liar and a drunk. Roughed us up more when he was sober, though."

Something akin to compassion sprang up inside Tate. He knew what it was like to have a father who betrayed trust and caused pain with his choices. "When did you leave home?"

"At fourteen." Fletcher sat straighter. "Struck out completely on my own and never went back." A pained look momentarily crossed his hardened features, and Tate wondered if he was thinking of the family members he'd left behind. "It didn't take long to prove my stepfather wrong. I wasn't a lazy no-account like him. I was the best pickpocket you ever did see. Never got caught for it.

"Eventually I tired of that, so I got work on a number of ranches. But the foremen were always brutes, workin' you to the bone while they made the better money. I stole a horse at eighteen and went to prison for a year."

Tate kept his expression neutral, not only to hide his shock at Fletcher's story but also his apprehension at the time that was passing. The sky in the west had turned the color of a blushing lady. It was almost time. He listened intently for the sound of horse hooves but heard nothing.

"I worked another ranch after I left prison, but it was more of the same." Fletcher tapped his thumb against his knee, his gaze haunted. "I got tired of not bein' my own man, not bein' able to do what I wanted. I'd lived under another man's thumb for too long. So I went back to horse rustlin'. But that didn't pay up front like train or bank robberies. Eventually I upped and formed my own gang." He smiled smugly. "Things have been goin' my way ever since."

And, hopefully, that was about to end. Tate shot a glance up the ravine. Was Essie coming? He couldn't quite allow himself to believe she might not, that something might have prevented her return. Flexing his fingers, which only succeeded in tightening the rope at his wrists, he tried to focus on Fletcher's words again.

The gang leader looked downright proud of his accomplishments. "I don't answer to anyone out here and there's no measly pay for my hard work," Fletcher concluded.

"You didn't tell the part about your stepfather comin' to see you in prison," Clem added.

The man's arrogance vanished in a moment, replaced by barely concealed rage. "That ain't part of the story, Clem."

The other outlaw looked a bit cowed but not entirely. "You're always sayin' it's the most important part of the story."

Ignoring the pink-and-azure sky above, Tate feigned continued interest in Fletcher's story. "Your stepfather sought you out in prison?"

Fletcher no longer drummed his knee; now he gripped the gun tightly between his hands. "Sure did. Came to see me and wanted an apology for shamin' my family with my evil ways. But I spat in his face and told him I'd never say sorry. If anyone ought to apologize, it was him."

The man went still, his voice quiet but deadly. "He told me my ma had died from a broken heart, over me." He lifted hate-filled eyes to Tate's. "It wasn't until years later that I found out she'd been killed in an accident. An accident involvin' my stepfather."

A charged silence followed his gut-wrenching admission. Then Clem cleared his throat. "Good thing the man was gone and buried by then, right, Fletch?"

Fletcher jumped to his feet. "I'm sick to death," he hissed at Tate, "of pious folks like you, Franklin."

Tate exchanged a glance with Clem, who blanched. "He ain't Franklin, Fletch. That's Tex sittin' there."

The burning hatred didn't dim as Fletcher wheeled on Clem. "Don't you think I know that? But it's like I always said—you can't trust anyone." He pointed the revolver at Tate, his gaze wild. "Not even your own partners."

"What're you gonna do?" Clem asked. On the other side of the camp, Silas slowly sat up, his expression taut as he watched Fletcher.

To Tate's remorse, the outlaw finally focused his

attention on the sky above. The sun had already set, leaving the world cloaked in twilight. A sinking feeling tethered Tate to the ground.

"She's not comin', is she, cowboy?" A cruel smile spread across Fletcher's mouth. "Like I said, you can't trust anyone..."

Essie was too late. The realization brought no anger, only deep sorrow and concern. Tate feared something had happened to her and he grieved his lost chance to tell her how he really felt about her.

The sound of the gun being cocked set his heart slamming into his chest. He shut his eyes and braced himself for the inevitable blast.

"So long, cowboy."

"Nooooo!" The feminine cry pierced the air. Tate jerked his eyes open and glanced toward the sound. A flash of movement and blond hair on the ridge above caught his eye. Essie had made it! But was she alone?

Fletcher recovered quickly from the surprise of Essie's scream and fired a shot toward the edge of the ravine.

"Essie, watch out," Tate yelled in warning. Fletcher fired again, his demeanor seething.

Taking advantage of the man's distraction, Tate rolled forward and knocked the outlaw off his feet. The revolver went flying and, from the corner of his eye, Tate saw Clem scramble to grab it.

"You lyin', no-account—"

Tate didn't care to hear the rest of Fletcher's insults. Lifting his bound hands, he drove them hard into Fletcher's side. The gang leader groaned and instinctively curled into himself. If Tate could just hold him in place until Essie—and, hopefully, the rest of her party—reached them, they might all get out of this without any further injuries.

"Leave him be, Tex." Clem's tone held a panicked edge Tate had never heard before.

"Why? So he can treat you rotten again?" He dodged a wild blow from Fletcher by scooting backward. But his advantage had disappeared. "You don't want that anymore, do you, Clem?" He glanced at Silas, who sat so still that he appeared to be made of stone instead of flesh. "Look at how he treated Silas."

The outlaw cook's expression hardened. "That was your doin', too. Fletch's all the family we done got. And we don't turn our back on family."

Holding a hand to his side, Fletcher climbed slowly to his feet until he loomed over Tate. "Nice try, cowboy. You still lose." He reached out for the gun and Clem handed it back. "I'm only tryin' to figure out if you and the lady have been plannin' this all along."

"Leave Essie out of this," Tate snarled. Movement behind the two outlaws drew his attention. Essie and the sheriff were charging up the ravine, leading a group of seven men. Tate darted a look at Silas, who'd also seen them. Would the other outlaw alert Clem and Fletcher to what was coming? But the injured man's mouth remained shut.

"I'll leave her be until I get my hands on that money of hers." Fletcher aimed the revolver a second time at Tate. "And there's nothin' you can do about it once you're dead, cowboy. Because, face it, you're outnumbered."

"No, he's not," the sheriff shouted from behind. "We got eight guns to your one, Fletcher."

Fletcher's face went white and his eyes widened in

shock. Without turning around, he glanced at Clem, who now faced the posse. Clem visibly gulped and nodded the truth to Fletcher.

Tate blew out his breath. Thankfully he was already seated or the intense relief coursing through him would have driven him to the ground. "This is the end of the road for you, Fletcher."

"Put your hands in the air and turn around," the sheriff directed.

Raising the gun above his head, Fletcher slowly spun to face the group. "You!" he cried out bitterly when he saw Essie. "You lied, woman. Said you were goin' to get supplies."

"I did get supplies," Essie countered, her voice calm, her chin high, as she hoisted her valise in the air. "But I decided to pick up a few extra...*things*... while I was there."

He's going to shoot her. The thought leaped into Tate's mind right before he saw Fletcher's arms begin to drop. He reacted at once, propelling himself forward and ramming his body into Fletcher's. The gun fired as the outlaw toppled to the ground. An accompanying scream shot straight through Tate's heart. Was Essie hurt? He hurried to climb to his knees to see.

The sight of her ducked down next to the sheriff, the man's hand protectively over her head, made Tate want to weep with joy. She wasn't harmed. Four men rushed forward, grabbing Fletcher and Clem. Lying back on the ground, Tate drank in several gulps of the evening air. His mission was completed. "Thank You," he breathed out in a prayer.

"Tate." Essie appeared above him, her expression

full of fear. "Are you all right? He didn't shoot you, did he?"

"No. I'm all right." He felt exhausted in mind and body but also liberated. "You did it, Essie," he said as the sheriff came forward and freed him from his bindings. Tate rubbed at his sore wrists. "You made it."

She knelt beside him once the sheriff stepped back. "It took some softening from the Lord—" she cast a meaningful look over her shoulder at the sheriff "—but it all worked out." She took over the job of rubbing his wrists with her cool fingers, and Tate momentarily shut his eyes at the gentleness of her touch. "Did they find out who you really are?"

"What is she talkin' about?" Fletcher groused as the lawmen finished tying him up. "Who is he?"

Essie turned to face the outlaw leader, an amused smile on her lips. "You are looking at the identical twin brother of the Texas Titan, Mr. Fletcher. May I introduce you to Tate Beckett?"

Tate caught Fletcher's eye. "My real occupation is working as a Pinkerton detective, tracking down outlaws like you."

Fletcher's face went dark red and he began spewing incoherent phrases. "Looks like you need a little time to cool off," one of the lawmen barked. He yanked Fletcher to his feet and half dragged him up the ravine, away from the rest of the group.

Clem gawked at Tate, looking almost hurt, then turned to Essie. "You in on this the whole time, too?"

"No, Clem," she said kindly as she shook her head. "I only found out the truth about Tate yesterday. My true aim in joining all of you really was to conduct my interviews and that was all."

His expression bordered on skepticism for a long moment before Clem finally nodded, his demeanor softening. "And we ain't never had a more agreeable traveling companion than you, ma'am."

"Hear, hear," Silas rasped, bringing another smile to Essie's mouth.

"I've got everything we need to fix you up until the doctor can look at you, Silas." She started to rise, but Tate detained her by taking her hand and tugging her back down. "What is it?" she protested, but she was laughing.

Tate regarded her lovely face framed by her unbound hair. "I just want to look at you. Reassure myself you're really well and safe."

Her green-brown eyes sparkled. "I am well and safe. And grateful we made it here on time." She frowned, the mirth fleeing her gaze as she placed her palm alongside his jaw. "He might have killed you, Tate."

"But he didn't." He leaned into her hand, wondering how he'd ever thought he could say goodbye to her. "There is a part of me that's hurting, though." He maintained a deadpan countenance.

Her brow furrowed in concern as she studied him. "What is it?"

Tate brought her hand to his heart. "It sort of hurts right here," he said, keeping his voice low to avoid being overheard. "'Cause I've realized there's this girl I fear is going to ride out of my life tomorrow."

Essie's mouth turned up at the corners. "Ah, I see. And what can I do to help ease this pain?"

He twisted his face in feigned concentration. "Consider sharing your future with me?"

Her eyes went wide. "Are...are you serious, Tate?"

Gently pulling her closer, he nodded, setting all levity aside. "Yes, Essie. I know it's only been six days, but I want to be your husband, your protector, your provider and your greatest champion."

"What about your career?" A small frown pinched her forehead. "I love you, Tate. But I don't think I can be a detective's wife."

She loved him! Tate wanted to shout with joy. Instead he lifted her hand to his mouth and kissed the back of it. "Good thing I decided earlier today that I want to go back to farming. Once I figured out I don't need to apprehend every criminal out there, I realized how much I miss working the land. It's in my blood—being a detective isn't."

"You really mean that?"

"Absolutely," he said, grinning. "And I want you to keep writing."

Essie lowered her gaze. "I'm not sure I want to."

Tate tipped her chin upward. "Is this about failing?"

"No." A blush spread over her cheeks, enhancing their loveliness. "I never thought I'd have a chance at a regular life, as a wife and mother, so I gave up those dreams for other ones."

"And now?"

Tears glittered in her eyes. "Now I think I'd like to write one more book and then see about going after those other dreams I gave up on."

A lump lodged in his throat as he thought back over the last six days. Maybe asking her to marry him would seem too soon to some. But Tate knew his own heart now, and there was nothing else in the world he wanted more than to wed this beautiful, wonderful dime novelist kneeling beside him.

"I love you, Essie Vanderfair. And I'm wondering if you'd do me the honor of marrying me." A sniffle pulled his attention to Clem, who sat tied up nearby, watching them and wiping at his eyes with the back of his hand. Silas appeared to be sleeping, but the grin on his face told a different story.

Essie followed Tate's gaze and smiled. "Yes," she said more loudly, "I will marry you, Tate Beckett."

Not caring that they had an audience of outlaws and lawmen, Tate sealed her answer with a long kiss. Nothing felt more right to him than kissing Essie and thinking of their future together. It wouldn't be any less challenging than this mission had been for both of them, but they'd both proved they could do all things with the Lord on their side.

"By the way," he said, easing back. A flicker of disappointment filled her eyes, and Tate grinned. "I have a pre-wedding gift for you."

"You do, do you?" She laughed lightly. "And what is it?"

He bent forward and whispered, "I got Fletcher's story. About how he became an outlaw."

Her eyebrows shot upward right before she pressed another kiss to his lips. "Thank you, Tate."

"Once you finish bandaging Silas, I'll tell it to you."

When she smiled fully at him, Tate felt as if the sun had sunk from the horizon to lodge inside his chest. "I can't wait to write it down."

"Do you know what your next book will be about?" he asked as he rose and helped her stand beside him.

"I have a pretty good idea." Her impish look made him laugh. "And it starts with a dashing outlaw and his secret."

Epilogue

Ten months later

Essie added the last page of her completed manuscript to the stack on the desk in front of her and aligned them neatly. Tomorrow she would mail her next, and final, dime novel to her publisher. He'd loved the idea she'd presented to him in her letter last October. She might have had the whole thing written sooner, but there'd been a wedding to plan, her family to reconcile with and a farm to buy.

Running her fingers over the title—*A Detective in Disguise*—she couldn't help smiling. She'd long believed fiction to be more adventurous and interesting than real life. But this time she'd taken her story idea from her own experiences, and that had made for a far more gripping novel. When the heroine pleaded to go along with the train robbers, Essie had known exactly how she'd felt. And when she and the hero, who was posing as an outlaw, kissed for the first time, she knew the wonder and happiness of that moment.

Her smile deepened. She no longer harbored a desire to beat Victor Daley. She only wanted to deliver the best story she could, and she felt deep satisfaction that she had.

Leaning forward in her chair, she picked up the framed photograph on her desk. It was of her and Tate, dressed in their wedding best.

The wedding had taken place on a beautiful autumn day, at the church she'd attended as a girl. All of her family had been in attendance. She'd gone to see them several weeks before to introduce Tate and to finally share her true feelings with her parents and siblings. They'd listened attentively then reassured Essie that they did appreciate her unique gifts and talents. All of them admitted to missing her sunny personality and she promised to visit more often.

"There will be another reason to do so, too," she whispered to the photograph. Her free hand came to rest against her stomach. She'd suspected weeks earlier what she now knew for certain—she and Tate were going to be parents.

The sound of the front door opening pulled her from her reverie. "Tate? Is that you?" she called, pushing back her chair and standing.

Her husband rushed into the room. He clutched a letter in his hand, but she couldn't decipher from his expression the nature of what was written there. "I have news," he said calmly.

"I do, too." She wanted to tell him about the baby, now that she was sure. But she couldn't resist teasing him a little by sharing something else first. "I finished copying down my book. It's ready to mail tomorrow."

"Excellent," he murmured, but his gaze was on the letter.

Essie stepped forward and placed her hand on his forearm where his sleeves had been rolled back. "And…we're going to have a baby, Tate."

Her words had the desired effect. He jerked his chin up and stared at her in shock. Then his blue eyes softened with tenderness before he tugged her to him and kissed her fully. "A baby," he repeated when he eased back some minutes later, grinning foolishly. "I'm going to be a father."

"Yes. And a wonderful one at that."

He kissed her nose. "Congratulations on your book." She laughed when he waggled his eyebrows and added, "And even more so about our baby."

She wrapped her arms around his waist and placed her head against his chest. Here, in his arms, she felt such gratitude for her new life. "What is your news?"

Tate hugged her back but didn't speak.

"Aren't you going to tell me?" She lifted her chin to look at him. That was when she saw the glitter of tears in his eyes. "Is it bad?"

"Not at all." He cleared his throat. "The private investigator we hired has tracked down Tex."

It was Essie's turn to gape in astonishment. They'd been trying for months to find Tate's brother. "Where is he?"

"In Idaho, apparently," he said, lifting the letter for her to see. "Near our old farm."

"Oh, Tate, that's incredible news." She embraced him again, her heart overflowing with joy. "We should go to him at once."

Nudging her to look at him, he searched her face. "Are you sure? You won't be too tired? It's a long trip."

She smiled lovingly up at him. "I'll be fine. Besides, I had my chance to reconcile with my family, and now it's yours."

He pressed another lingering kiss to her mouth. "How did I ever convince a beautiful, talented, independent dime novelist such as yourself to settle down with an average farmer?"

"Because that average farmer was really in disguise." She let her impish smile break through as she circled her arms around his neck.

Grinning, he nestled her closer. "Disguised as what, I might ask? Not as a detective."

"No, not as a detective," she said softly as she gazed into his face, the face of the man she loved with all of her heart. "As my real-life hero."

* * * * *

Don't miss these other Western adventures from Stacy Henrie:

LADY OUTLAW
THE EXPRESS RIDER'S LADY

Find other great reads at www.LoveInspired.com.

Dear Reader,

I find the stories of Old West outlaws fascinating, including that of my state's most famous bandit, Butch Cassidy. He and his gang were known to have used the valley at Hole-in-the-Wall in Johnson County, Wyoming, as one of their hideouts. This hideout was easy to defend because the outlaws could spot anyone trying to enter the valley. Legend has it that no lawmen were ever able to infiltrate the hideout. And while these outlaws appeared to have lived adventurous, carefree lives, they nearly all experienced tragedies in their pasts.

The Grand Central Hotel in Casper, Wyoming, appears to have been in existence by at least 1893. For the sake of the story, though, I have it existing the year before. There were also likely two banks operating in Casper in the year 1892, but for the purposes of this story, I didn't distinguish which bank the men rob.

The Occidental Hotel in Buffalo, Wyoming, is another actual building, founded in 1880, and is still in operation today. Butch Cassidy and the Sundance Kid reportedly stayed at this hotel.

I've very much enjoyed introducing readers to the Beckett brothers in this book, and I'm thrilled to share the story of Tex, Tate's identical twin brother, later this year. It was also lots of fun to give Essie, this optimistic and fearless dime novelist, her own story and share some of the melodrama of these bygone novels through her.

My hope with this book is that readers will identify with what Tate and Essie come to learn: the importance of being ourselves, our unchangeable and infinite worth in the eyes of God, and the reality that we are only stewards of our own choices. I also hope readers will enjoy the fun adventure of this outlaw-in-disguise story!

I love hearing from readers. You can contact me through my website at www.stacyhenrie.com.

All the best,
Stacy

REQUEST YOUR FREE BOOKS!

2 FREE INSPIRATIONAL NOVELS
PLUS 2 FREE MYSTERY GIFTS

Love Inspired HISTORICAL

"I'm your mail-order bride."

"What?" Philip wished he could cover the shock in his voice, but he couldn't.

"I answered your advertisement for a mail-order bride." Bella's cheeks flushed and her gaze darted to the little boys on the couch.

Philip didn't know what to think. She didn't appear to be lying, but he hadn't placed an ad for marriage in any newspaper. "I have no idea what you are talking about. I didn't place a mail-order-bride ad in any newspaper."

She frowned and stood. "Hold on a moment." Bella dug in her bag and handed him a small piece of newspaper.

His gaze fell upon the writing.

November 1860

Wanted: Wife as soon as possible. Must be willing to live at a pony express relay station. Must be between the ages of eighteen to twenty-five. Looks are not important. Write to: Philip Young, Dove Creek, Wyoming, Pony Express Relay Station.

Philip looked up at her. He hadn't placed the ad, but he had a sinking feeling he knew who did. "Did you send a letter to this address?"

Bella shook her head. "No, I didn't have the extra money to spare for postage. I just hoped I'd make it to Dove Creek before another woman. I did, didn't I?"

"Well, since this is the first I've heard of the advertisement—" he shook the paper in his hand "—I'd say your chances of being first are good. But this is dated back in November and it is now January so I'm curious as to what took you so long to get here."

"Well, I didn't actually see the advertisement until a few weeks ago. My sister and her husband had recently passed and I was going through their belongings when I stumbled upon the paper. Your ad leaped out at me as if it was from God." Once more she looked to the two boys playing on the couch.

Philip's gaze moved to the boys, too. "Are they your boys?"

"They are now."

Sadness flooded her eyes. Since she'd just mentioned her sister's death, Philip didn't think it was too much of a stretch to assume that the boys had belonged to Bella's sister. "They are your nephews?"

"Yes. I'm all the family they have left. The oldest boy is Caleb and the younger Mark." Her soulful eyes met his. "And you are our last hope to stay together."

Don't miss
PONY EXPRESS MAIL-ORDER BRIDE
by Rhonda Gibson, available March 2017 wherever
Love Inspired® Historical books
and ebooks are sold.

www.LoveInspired.com